Park Life

by

Katharine D'Souza

ISBN-13 978-1478354796
ISBN-10 1478354798

PARK LIFE

CHAPTER ONE

CRAIG

That went well. I had an answer for every question. Firm handshakes, smiles all round – this job will be mine. I am the business.

I was last into the room. I know I made a good impression. So why haven't they offered me the job yet? I've been here, putting in the hours despite the stress of the day, but no call has come to ask me back to the boardroom, the boss hasn't dropped by my desk to have a word. What could possibly delay their decision?

'Not going home today?' asks Gav. He shrugs into his jacket, pats a couple of pockets to locate his phone and keys. 'Thought you might fancy a beer on the way out.'

'Got to see it through, haven't I? Besides, Amisha's still here.'

Gav looks over his shoulder. 'Nope, she's gone.'

I jump up, knocking papers from my desk to check if he's right. He can't produce an accurate report on a balance sheet, let alone identify a colleague at fifty paces. He's right though. The far side of the open plan office is deserted. As I watch, the motion sensor controlled lighting dims meaning no-one's moved there for the last ten minutes. Ten minutes in which Amisha either went home or was welcomed into the boardroom.

I can't have lost to a girl.

She must have gone home. Must have. I want this promotion so much I will win it by pure stamina and I'll throttle Gav if he suggests that's not the case.

'Hmm,' he says. 'She never leaves before us, does she?'

~

SUSAN

I used to be a nice person: someone who never had a bad word to say about anyone and always looked on the bright side. Of course, it was often an act and everything changes. These days I'm all new, but perhaps not improved. Although, now I'm in my forties, it may be too late to realise that life's a game and, if anyone knew the rules, nobody's playing by them. It seems that everyone cheats, moves the goalposts, tells you it's a marathon when it turns out to be a sprint.

I mean, 'til death do us part' was supposed to last forever. I dreamt it would.

Dreams are one thing though, reality quite another. So, now I'm breaking the rules, and why shouldn't I? I do wonder one thing though: does everyone else feel this guilty?

It's taken me less than twenty four hours to unpack. I'm alone in this strange space. The front door opens straight into the main room where the kitchenette squeezes into a corner. The bedroom is too small for the double bed crammed into it;

although what do I need a double for anyway? I have a bathroom. Well, shower-cubicle room doesn't sound right even if it is more accurate. It's a bijou apartment crammed into what used to be a storage depot – a large space securing items of value within its red brick walls now converted to a tiny space to hold me.

The flat isn't that bad. It's just not what I've been used to. The first time I sat on the economically thin foam cushions of the grey sofa, trying not to identify the stains left by the previous tenant, I cried so hard it felt like a scream.

~

CRAIG

Right now all I want is to be at home. Not on a bus stuck in traffic with some other bugger crammed in my personal space. This entire day has been total shit. I deserved that job; proved myself, worked hard for it. Not enough though, is it? Because I'm not a woman and that's who they wanted: a pretty face to tick the diversity box. Not a white man. Not me. Even though I've been there longer, pulled more clients in, made more dosh.

They claimed she interviewed better than me. Huh, that's a joke. Like her timid, squeaky voice sounds like a Marketing Exec. Yeah, she's a looker, but interview better than me? No way. I ace that stuff and I've more experience. But Amisha gets the promotion, and me? I just get to carry on.

There must be some kind of rule about how many people the driver's supposed to let on the bus. But here he goes, picking up more passengers and holding up the traffic. It's standing room only and no-one's going to give up their seat to this grandad shuffling

3

down the aisle. Not the fat woman with her head stuck in a magazine, not the shaved head jerk plugged in to his iPod. Guess it's down to me then. At least the old guy says 'Thank you,' as he takes my seat. Like that'll make up for having to let smelly people squeeze past me to get off. Doesn't anyone wash their clothes?

I need a beer. And to take off these fucking uncomfortable shoes. I don't have pointy feet. What made me think pointy shoes were a good idea? Can't even go out and get pissed tonight. No, because I've got a meeting with the boss tomorrow morning. Even though they reckon I'm not as good as Amisha, he wants my input.

Guess I'll stay in. There's beer in the fridge. I'll roll myself a joint, order a pizza and slam some sounds on. Hope the new woman next door isn't going to be the noise police. Still can't believe Davo left. OK, he wasn't the perfect neighbour, but he was pretty damn close. Always plenty of booze and weed and girls loved him. Always got lucky on a night out with him. But now the flukey shit's in London 'cos his firm thought he was promising enough to transfer. Tell that to my lot. If Davo's promising, I'm the fucking Messiah.

This driver is doing my head in. It's like he doesn't want to get there. They're all the same. Fucking Formula One when you're early; tortoise speed when you just want to get home after the day from hell. Like he'd know anything about pressure at work – sat there in his perspex box, pretending he can't speak English when anyone tries to ask something. If this guy's setting the standard, you don't even need to be able to drive to get the job.

The price of parking in this city is a sick joke. Forcing me to put up with this bastard bus every day. Twice a day. And it's always full, always got a random empty Lucozade bottle rolling around the floor, and today some wanker's playing bhangra on his mobile.

No one else wants to listen to crap music on the bus. Not at eight am. Not at six pm. Not as amplified by Nokia. Not ever.

But I can't say anything. Oh, no. He'd take me for a racist. So I can't say, 'Look mate, it's nothing to do with the colour of your fucking skin, or what mosque or temple you go to. This is a public space and it's already hell on earth without you giving me some soundtrack that makes it a horror film as interpreted by fucking Bollywood.'

No. I can't say that. I don't want to get stabbed.

Almost there now; nearly at the flat. First thing I'll do is get that beer out the fridge. Feel the shape of the bottle snug in my hand, condensation running clear tracks down frosted glass. Hear the fizz as I flip the lid off. Then drink. Drink deep. Gulp after gulp of that sharp, cold, sanity-saving nectar. I'll crash in my chair, kick off these damn shoes and stick on the PlayStation.

They should give you a double decker as one of the rides on Gran Turismo. I'd thrash it round the circuit, show this bastard driver how it's done. Knowing my luck they'd give it the fucking Bhangra soundtrack.

I'll stick to Pro Ev Soccer tonight. A couple of beers. Pizza. Or maybe a kebab from across the road. Then, I suppose, I'll have to ring mum and tell her I didn't get the job.

~

SUSAN

I smiled at the young man from next door as we crossed on the stairs this morning. He said 'Hello' but frowned and dashed off. This place seems so cold and anonymous. Late into last night there were thumps and sounds of dragging across the floor coming from upstairs.

My first task today was to arrange my possessions. I brought several boxes with me, all taped and labelled: kitchen, bathroom, living room. Even though I left home in a storm of resentment, the carefully laid plan saw me through with a minimum of fuss.

Now there's a good summary of my life so far: a minimum of fuss. Until recently, anyway.

One box gave me a problem, the only one I hadn't labelled with a destination. You could pin labels on the contents: sentimental, nostalgia, keepsakes. But where do they belong? Hidden at the back of a cupboard? Tucked under the bed? Out on show and gathering dust? I'm not sure reminders of the past belong in my new life, but I couldn't throw them away. Not yet.

I've heard of people who write diaries every day. What do they find to say in them? Some days are so dull, so dreary and full of humdrum pointlessness. I never wrote a diary but do like to record things. Well, I did. When things happened. In recent years there hasn't been much worth noting; until now.

I put the box on top of the wardrobe, but took out the book. It's an old school exercise book probably intended for a much more important purpose. It may have been issued to me for the noting of chemical formulae, or to record the dates of important historical happenings.

I ambushed it, press-ganged it into recording events of staggeringly minor significance, details only of relevance to me. It's pale blue, A4 size with thin card covers. Feint ruled. Blue biro is the ink of choice throughout with occasional forays into black or pencil. I was too shy to write the title on the cover and even left the first page blank to deter any casual, uninvited readers.

It looks so insignificant. This is the record of my formative events between the ages of thirteen and twenty. I wish I'd splashed out on fancy stationery rather than using stolen school supplies.

In my mind it's called 'The Book of Experience', and I'm going to read it to see if I can spot where I went wrong; what I should have done differently. And I'll write in it. Because I'm changing and one day I might want to work out how.

~

It didn't seem as though we'd talked in weeks. Well, of course we'd talked:

'What's for dinner?'

'Have you put the bins out?'

'What time's that programme on TV?'

We hadn't talked about anything important and, now I've no one to talk to, I wonder if there is anything important anymore and, if there isn't, when did it go quiet?

'Susan!' he shouted as I walked away.

Well he would: it is my name, I was refusing to look at him and Pete has always been prone to aggression. He called it assertiveness of course and told me I could use more of it. I told him he could use a more pleasant tone of voice when he talks to people.

OK, so I didn't. I'm not assertive enough.

But I did leave. After making my plans, I packed while he was at golf, the man finished loading the van as Pete got back, and I walked away down the block paved drive while he stood his ground in the uPVC porch. How could I?

My marriage would have been described as happy if you only talked about the first few years. He was wonderful, my Pete. Tall, not ugly even if not quite handsome, popular, gainfully employed. What more could a woman want?

It was more a case of 'what more could a girl want?' of course. At only eighteen, and a young eighteen at that, I was naïve and dazzled by the confident, fifteen years older, Pete. I worked in the pub he drank in where I washed glasses as well as wearing them and felt a thrill whenever this charismatic leader of the pack tossed a comment my way.

It was my only proper job; I've looked it up in 'The Book'. A typical entry I think:

My first job - 1986

Started my first job today and can't believe how grown up I feel. Was so nervous, wanted it to go well, didn't know what to say, hoped people would be nice to me, didn't know what to wear. It was all OK though. I started at six and it was pretty quiet so they showed me what's where and how to work the till, then at six twenty I pulled my first pint. Messed it up with a huge head frothing over the side and people laughed, but I've got the hang of it now. Wednesday night, so not too busy. Shattered though, need a lie in tomorrow.

Not exactly a thrilling read, and that's me recording something important.

Reading it revived the memory. The pub was an ancient building, all fireplaces and stone lintels, wooden floors and brass beer pumps. My job began in the summer holidays and they kept me on at weekends when college started. So I always treated it as a casual thing, a pocket-money job. Now I'm shocked it's the only job I've had, the only work I ever earned a wage for. My contribution to the economy didn't exactly make waves. Well, Pete came along and said wasn't it great, that I didn't need to work now he looked after me? Weren't we the lucky ones, able to afford for me to stay home?

I don't think I was fortunate in the end. I never finished that college course; it's not easy when you're pregnant. Then, through the nineties I devoured magazine articles about women who were stressed out trying to have it all: the home, the career, the babies. It felt as if I'd made the right choice because I had the best bit: the beautiful home, the adorable baby. Now though, the adorable baby is eighteen (and not naïve like his mother at that age, worldly wise, self assured, with no need of his mum anymore) and the beautiful home felt more like a prison with each day I worked in it. I could have done more. Now I want to do more.

Pete wouldn't listen when I said I wanted a job ('But we don't need the money') or go back to college ('What would you need a qualification for? Waste of time'). Pete always thought he knew best. Bit like my friend, Jo, in that respect. But now I do need the money. It's time to join the ranks of the employed.

Of course, there aren't all that many jobs around and I'm qualified for nothing. Well, I'm good at telling people what they want to hear. I can cook and clean. I can devise a secret plan and carry it out. So, my options are what? Housekeeper or undercover agent?

I have, at least, made a start with my escape to here but the rest of the world has already arrived. I went to the parade of little shops across the road last night; they all stay open late. With the light from neon signs, illuminated adverts and blazing windows, the cluttered street is as brightly lit as in daylight. The general store sells food from Poland or Pakistan. The DVD rental place supplies films from Hollywood or Bollywood. The chip shop seems to be Chinese, but sells Turkish kebabs. The windows of the mobile phone shop are plastered with signs bearing phrases I don't recognise as English.

The items available confused me so I bought tea bags, cereal and milk and came home. Home is what I'll have to call it I suppose. Bye-bye sleepy, country town; hello inner city Birmingham.

I don't know this city and it scares me. It's so big, so crowded, so capable of swallowing me without a trace. Which is why I came here. Which now fills me with terror.

Double decker buses plastered with adverts rumble along the road every few minutes. I'll be a little bit brave and catch one towards the suburbs; that might be less daunting than the city centre. I'll travel to the next place that looks interesting and see if I can find an opportunity. It's spring – the time for new beginnings. Turning the clock back is not an option.

CHAPTER TWO

CRAIG

Crap, it's Steve from work. Just what I need after yet another shitty day at the coalface. I only came to the gym for a quick workout to burn off the bad mood. Get the heart going, get the blood pumping – feel like I'm actually alive. Not like I've got anything better to do tonight. Was only going to run a couple of miles, lift a couple of weights and leave the rest to the soft porn that passes for the music vids they show in here.

Now though, the games are on. Don't think he's seen me so I can make the first move: free weights I think.

'Hey, Stevo.' I wander past the mat he's doing his warm up stretches on. Pause long enough for him to clock the 20kg dumbbell I'm carrying. I look over his head and check my reflection as I bicep curl it to the beat of the pumping music. Not bad, impressive bulge in the muscle. Couldn't do many reps at that weight though.

He's frowning already – nice one. I wouldn't kick a man when he's down, but intimidation while he

11

stretches his hamstrings is a legal move as far as I'm concerned. He meets my eye in the mirror and stands up. 'Craig. Been here long? You look whacked.'

Fuck him. I do not look whacked.

'Not too long. Don't think the air con's on high enough.'

I stroll back to the weights rack. The mirrors show me he's still stretching. Trust that arse to behave like he's some kind of athlete.

Next round, rowing. I clip my feet into the footrests and flick the dial up to the highest setting. Forget the quick workout, time to go for the burn.

I'm well into rhythm by the time he sits down at the machine next to me. Pull, release, forward, then back. Love the swish as the chain recoils; almost like oars through water. Almost. Just need to stay in the zone. I can keep this up for ages.

Steve picks up his hand grip and says, 'City are going down then.'

Bastard! Talking about football is a sneaky move and the chain stutters as I lose my rhythm. I force a smile.

'Yeah, it's pretty much over for this season.' But I'm not going to let him win that round. Time to start messing with him. 'Villa have had a good run.'

I don't even say it grudgingly. It's out there, all sweetness and light. He looks up, his face all "Wot, no put down?" I smile and look up at Kylie wiggling her tiny bum at me from the screen over our heads. Release forward, then pull back. Oh, I could keep this up as long as you want it, darling.

'Yeah,' says Steve. 'They're playing well.'

We carry on rowing in silence, both fixed on the succession of girls in bikinis on the screens. Dammit, he's going faster than me. Mustn't get distracted. I go for a sprint finish, dropping the grips as the digits on the timer hit dead on ten minutes. Accuracy is just as important as speed.

Steve catches my eye as I bend to lift my towel off the sticky lino. He's hardly sweating. I think that round's a draw.

Now to the weights machines. Wouldn't look out of place in a torture chamber these. I slide onto the firm padding of the abs cruncher seat, pull the bars that bring the weights down onto my chest and begin to lift. I tense my gut, visualising the six pack. It's good, it's easy, it's on the girly setting. Now, where's Steve?

The mirrors reflect back angles of the room to me – women in baggy tracksuits climbing the steppers, girls in tight shorts jogging on treadmills, macho men in vests spotting each other on the weights benches and here comes Steve. Shorts slightly too, well, short; as if his mum bought them for school and he never got new ones. He's casually wiping his forehead with a stripy towel that's definitely his mum's.

Quick as I can, I move the pin up to a higher weight setting and just about manage a couple more crunches so I can stand up as he arrives.

'Here, do you want this?'

I make a show of wiping the seat down for him and step away, checking the mirror for evidence of him trying to lift, failing and having to adjust the weight back down.

So it's cheating, winning by deception, whatever. Sometimes it works, sometimes it fails when some girl manages to get between us and undoes the plan. Can't win 'em all, but today: today I'm on top. I stretch briefly and hit the showers.

It's not even that Steve's a bad bloke. Same sort of age as me, doing all right in the audit department. It's a combination of little things that annoy me about him, like wearing dodgy shoes, drinking his coffee out a Villa mug, being promoted recently.

'Sorry to hear they gave Amisha that job.'

I look round the door of my locker to see Steve twisting his padlock along the row. This is the problem with using the gym near work: can't get away from the stuff.

'Yeah,' I say, 'but she is good.' Well, I'm not sure what his connections are, best to be professional.

'You've done a lot for the company though,' Steve goes on, 'they should reward you.'

'I think they call it my salary. But, next time, that job is mine.'

He smiles. Maybe he's not such a bad bloke. I'm definitely fitter though, absolutely no muscle definition on his chest.

'D'you play cricket?' he asks.

'Not since school.'

'Oh, well, if you ever fancy a match, my team are sometimes short, that's all.'

'I don't have any kit.'

'Could lend you some. Shall I let you know if there's a place?'

'Er, OK.'

How did that happen? Are we mates now, am I following the nerd herd? Shit, I think he just won.

~

SUSAN
From what I saw of how busy these suburbs are, I

14

feel certain there'll be something here for me. They must have once been village centres, all these High Streets now merged into one city, shining bright like dyed beads on a necklace strung by terraced houses. As centres they make no sense anymore, they're placed as arbitrarily as the bus stops. The first place the bus drove through was Moseley, then on to Kings Heath, but I'm not sure where the one became the other.

The High Streets, the shopping centres, are certain at least. They're different, even if the shops are much the same. I stayed on the bus through Moseley – just taking it in. I looked and wondered, trying to work out where I could fit. Lots of people got off and others got on as we stopped outside Sainsbury's.

The people were varied; they wore different clothes and I heard several languages, but most of them carried orange plastic bags. They trooped past me in leggings or low-slung jeans while I hunched down in my buttoned up mac.

Kings Heath seemed bigger with more going on. I decided it would be easier to lose myself there and, when clusters of the orange carrier bags appeared again, I got off the bus. As I walked back along the High Street I tried to hold my head high. Tried to avoid the track-suited women who steered buggies into my ankles, the shuffling men who blocked the way, the school kids swinging bags at each other. It was a battlefield and survival of the fittest didn't look likely to include me.

The oasis of a side street drew me in and the pang of my stomach identified a café. As I scanned the menu in the window for the cheapest item, a pleasant-looking man behind the counter gave me a hopeful smile. He clearly wanted to encourage me in; a quick glance beyond him showed that the only customer was an elderly man, reading the newspaper over an empty plate pushed to one side.

The door stuck as I opened it, wedged on a rut in the sanded floorboards. The waiter leapt forward to help, overenthusiastic as he tried to hold the door and greet me at the same time.

'Here, let me, lovely weather, please come in.'

I smiled, not thinking any of that needed a reply. He seemed younger than me, and even more nervous.

'Please, sit anywhere. A menu, here's a menu. I'll just…'

I kept my silence and he shut up and returned to hover by the counter, pretenting to polish the already gleaming chrome of the coffee machine . He pounced as soon as I laid the menu down, a pen quivering over his pad for my order.

'Two slices of toast and a pot of tea, please.'

His face fell, my meagre order obviously not quite what he'd hoped for. The menu did describe some more interesting dishes – strong flavours, bold prices. I'd chosen from the other extreme.

'Of course,' he said and forced a smile. 'Um, English Breakfast, or Earl Grey, or …?'

'Just normal, thanks,' I interrupted, pleased with myself for being assertive but guilty, oh so guilty, for disappointing him.

I tried to make it up when he delivered the drink. 'Bit quiet today.'

'Yes,' he said, his face regretful as he pushed an overgrown fringe away from his eyes with the back of his wrist. 'And we were so busy on Saturday we sort of didn't cope. Still, it's early for lunch yet, the crowds may come. Oh, not that there's anything wrong with…, I didn't mean to suggest that… Of course you should eat whenever you're ready.'

He blushed and left me to wonder if he ever finished a sentence he started or if he always stitched them together like that – a patchwork of words – serviceable sentences, their pattern uniquely his own. I smiled again, I liked the place with its air of freshly painted hopefulness, and I liked him. His anxiety made me feel confident.

He delivered my order without a word, turning away as the crunch of the door sticking signalled the arrival of more promising customers. Once I'd eaten and tidied my tea things back onto the tray he'd left behind, I went back to the High Street to investigate what the crowds of people were doing.

~

Now I have to try and join them. Perhaps in the past I was too proud. Too proud to admit to anyone that things weren't perfect. Too proud to say, 'Please, won't you listen?' to my son. But not too proud to make a big decision. I couldn't convince my husband we had a problem; I could walk away from it.

The thing about pride is how much it costs: not only financially – emotionally, physically too. Then along with pride comes this silence, and guilt.

It's not as though I had a close circle of friends. I was sociable, I mixed with other women; not men so much, Pete didn't like it if other men spoke to me, but I was never even that close to my female friends.

This is how it things used to be: Jo, who knew me from school, would ring and say, 'Come over for coffee. Tomorrow. Ten thirty.' It was an order, not an invitation. We'd gather to admire her new curtains, praise her home baking, let her lecture us on how we should handle what she perceived as the problems of our lives.

I didn't fit in for so many reasons. Jo herself (she liked us to call her Jo, thought it sounded more fun than Joanna, although she's a true Joanna through and through: all rounded, middle England vowels – a voice you know is the owner of a Labrador), she intimidated me. Felicity (Jo's mother and charmingly dotty) was from a generation too far removed from my own. Adrienne (French, and there for the challenge between her and Jo of who could be most patronising) barely acknowledged me despite living two doors away. I simpered in the corner, not much to say and always offering to do the washing up.

It wasn't a gaggle of girls sharing gossip and providing support. It wasn't female friendship as seen on TV. I haven't had a friendship like that since school – junior school – but it looked OK from the outside, which is what mattered to Pete. It seemed normal enough; it allowed him to be condescending or to make critical comparisons between me and them. It gave me nothing at all.

As groups of friends go, they were useless. I didn't bother to say goodbye. I'm wondering now though. What would Jo's advice have been if she'd known my plans? Would Adrienne have been impressed by my previously undemonstrated bravery? Has Felicity even noticed I've gone?

Now that I'm really alone, I miss them. But that's looking back, possibly even with regret. Much better to remember why I'm here and what my intentions are.

This is all about remembering how to be me.

~

CRAIG

I'm in the home straights. Seconds from the sofa. Got my keys to hand and it's one final sprint up the steps to the landing, where I find my new neighbour looking out the window.

'Hello,' I say, a little embarrased about the fact I deliberately blanked her when I was in a rush yesterday. Seeing how I'm now pals with the office geek, I might as well do my help the aged bit too.

'Oh,' she says.

I guess she hadn't heard me climbing the stairs because she did that comedy flinch people do when they're surprised: over exaggerated jump followed by embarrassed blush. To top it off she drops a pile of papers.

'I'm Craig, by the way,' I say as I pick them up off the floor for her and gesture towards my front door. 'Number Eight.'

'Susan,' she replies, holding out a hand to shake.

I can't because I'm holding her stuff. Not that I'm nosy, but I notice they're application forms: Sainsbury's, Boots, WHSmith.

'Looking for a job, Susan?'

'Needs must,' she says with one of those half-smile, half-sigh things.

'Right. Not a bad view from here is it? Although, your flat faces the main road. Probably tactless of me to say I like this one.'

Why is talking to her unnerving me? It's not like I fancy her, she looks nearly old enough to be my mum. Although, actually, she is more MILF than minger. It's probably that she looks nervous; it's rubbing off on me.

'I think I prefer looking towards the road,' she says, frowning at the view of the city skyline. 'I find this a bit menacing.'

Well, it's the same as the view from my living room so I'm instantly defensive. I mean, menacing? I look again, trying to see what she's seeing. Our building's on high ground and the cluster of tightly-packed, high rise buildings a mile or so away glows in the dusk. The lights promise excitement, saying 'this is where life is'. The height and density of the buildings say 'this is where the money is'. How can that be menacing? I can't think of a reply.

'I'm from the country,' she says by way of explanation.

'Oh, right. Guess you didn't follow the draw of the bright lights?'

'No.'

OK, don't elaborate then. I jingle my keys and am about to say 'see you' when she says, 'Actually, Craig, could you help me?'

CHAPTER THREE

SUSAN

Unable to believe I'd been so bold, I double locked my front door and shivered as I sat down. What possessed me? Poor Craig had only met me two minutes earlier and was not prepared to be burdened with my problems. But after my day of investigations in the suburbs, the enormity of my situation hit me while I stood in the chill of the concrete floored stairwell and looked at that view. The bulk of the dense hub of city centre buildings, imposingly framed and illuminated, really rammed it home how vulnerable I am.

Until today, it's almost felt like an adventure or planning a holiday. I decided where to come, found somewhere to stay, chose what to pack. Even my actual departure felt like a scene from a soap opera.

Now that I'm here though, now it's all real, well, the reality is huge. Birmingham is a big city and I'm one tiny immigrant from the Warwickshire countryside. Just one more refugee. I realised I need to get my papers in order.

I need to get a divorce.

But I know nothing. This isn't the day every girl dreams of. I haven't picked out dress styles or flowers; I haven't designed cakes. Not once did I imagine the day of my divorce. I was a wedding junkie, 'The Book' proves it:

My first wedding 1982

It was my cousin Jane's wedding yesterday and it was absolutely wonderful. She looked so beautiful in her ivory dress with its huge puffball skirt and lace trimmed top. She wore a long veil and her sisters wore peach dresses with ruffled sleeves and carried bouquets of carnations. I so wish I could have been a bridesmaid too, then I wouldn't have to have worn the hideous, green, dropped-waist thing Mum chose for me. They looked like princesses; I looked like a fat, spotty pea pod.

The groom and his best man had on really slim fitting suits and skinny thin ties. It was obvious Auntie Lizzie wasn't impressed. She kept saying it wasn't traditional. But I think that's the point. A wedding doesn't have to be traditional, it has to be right for the couple; and Jane and Steve looked so happy and so in love.

After the church, they had a reception in the rugby club function room with a buffet, a three-tiered cake and a disco. Steve and his friends were dancing to the ska music and Steve even asked me to dance once.

Weddings are great. I can't wait for my own.

As it turned out, I didn't wait long. Not nearly long enough. Pete was my first and only boyfriend and I gasped 'Yes' the second he said 'Will you…?' Good job I'd guessed right about the end of the sentence really. Although, what else could he have been doing down on one knee?

So from Jane's wedding day, I had seven years of dreaming until my own. I wish I'd done seven years thinking about what comes after instead. Then maybe

I wouldn't find myself realising I need a divorce but with no idea how to get one.

~

'Could you help me?' I said to Craig. He looked panicked of course, wondering who the loony next door was no doubt.

'Um, how?'

I smiled at him with what I hope looked like reassurance. I liked that he was well brought up enough not to say no or ignore me. 'I think I need a solicitor. I don't even know where to start looking so I wondered if you knew anyone, or anything?'

With my nerves about asking him, and feeling desperate enough to reach out to a virtual stranger, I handled it badly of course. I'd managed to give the impression I might be a criminal. Craig tried really hard not to look shocked but he's so young, bless him, he sort of stuttered, 'Ah, well, I …'

'For a divorce. Not anything more sinister,' I clarified, amused by his relief.

'Oh, I see. Well, I'm not sure. The only solicitor I've ever used did the conveyancing when I bought the flat. I don't know if they…'

'Gosh, you own your flat? I thought they were all rented.'

'No, it's mine. Well, part mine, part the building society's – you know.'

'Of course, I just thought you seemed young to own your own place.'

'I'm twenty five. Not really so young and it seemed like a good idea, getting a foot on the property ladder.'

When I looked at him properly I could tell he wasn't as young as I'd first assumed. The trendy haircut and youthful speed in his movement and gestures had tricked me into thinking he was closer to twenty, closer to the age of my own son.

'It's very sensible,' I said. 'I'm impressed. Reading the newspapers you'd think no first-time buyers could afford to buy anything.'

'Yeah, well my mum always persuaded me to save money not spend it all.' He shrugged as if the wisdom of the advice was still in doubt. 'So anyway, I can give you their phone number, the solicitors, but you should probably ring round and talk to some others. Make sure you get someone you're happy with.'

'Of course. The phone number would be a great start.'

He promised to look it out and pop it through my letterbox, then disappeared into the security of his owner-occupied flat with a view. I returned to the low-rent, not so des res I'm calling home.

I spent a long time thinking about my James – whether he'll be doing as well as Craig when he's twenty five, whether he'll have a job, or a flat. Have I've managed to instill the kind of life skills in him that Craig demonstrated, or will he be unable to fend for himself independently?

Now I've pulled the safety net of the family home out from under him, I'll have to hope so. Because it will be sold I suppose, when Pete and I divorce. I might never have contributed directly to the mortgage payments, but my name's there next to Pete's on the title deeds.

I know it's one of the things he's going to argue about, and arguments there will be. I could have worked. I could have earned money, if only he'd let me.

The detailed and problematic practicalities of my new life have only now become clear. My little windfall, the surprise in the post – the cheque with enough digits to fund my escape – allowed me to get this far. But from here, I'll need a bigger number. One with enough digits to mean freedom. Divorce lawyers are bound to charge big fees for a start. My first thought as I read the letter accompanying the cheque had been to invest the unexpected money for James, my second was to realise that I needed it more. And now I definitely need a job.

~

CRAIG

This evening gets weirder and weirder. First the fact that Steve and I are now mates. Second, the new neighbour is not normal. Third, there's a message from Julia on the answerphone.

Julia: whose voice still hits on something in my mind, making me listen more intently to what she's got to say. Julia: whose message makes me freeze in the act of trying to kick my shoes off without undoing the laces. Julia: the bitch I haven't heard from in two years.

Her message is concise, ambiguous, impossible to ignore.

Not like the other message, which is from Mum and goes, 'Oh, Craig, you're not there.' (Leaves five second gap for me to reply 'No, Mum, I'm not back from work yet.') 'Just wanted to remind you about Aunt Jean's birthday.' (Another gap for me to say 'What would I do without you, Mum?' Holding back on the sarcasm of course.) 'Will you send her a card or shall I put your name on mine?' (Pause long enough for me to reassure her that I am no longer a fucking baby and will sign and send my own card.) 'OK, well, I'll speak to you then.'

That is a perfect example of what a message should be, even if it was delivered in Mum's unique style. I know what I have to do as a result: send card, call Mum back so she doesn't go off on one about ingratitude.

Julia's message though, that is a different matter. I have no idea what I have to do. I hit the button to play it again. Get Mum's by mistake. Swear and hit delete. Experience cold panic that I deleted the wrong one. Hit Play, Stop, Play, Stop. Take deep breath. Hit Play and her voice sounds again.

'Craig. Look, I know it's been a long time. I need to talk to you. I have some news.'

Nope, no more clues the second time. The tone of voice is neutral; not apologetic, not friendly. There is no hint whether the news is good or bad. There are no instructions about whether I should call her back or wait for her to call me. I have not been informed whether the ban on me ringing her has been lifted.

I may be guilty of overdoing that in the past. Specifically when we split up. I may have rung her once or twice. Late at night. Under the influence. It's possible I wasn't entirely a joy to speak to on those occasions.

There was provocation of course. I'd like to meet the man who could stay cool when his girlfriend gives him the old 'It's not you; it's me' and turns out two weeks later to be fucking his ex-best friend. So it really wasn't me. It was him.

Now here's her voice echoing round my flat again. I bang on some sounds to get it out my ears. I mean: fuck her. What, I'm supposed to drop everything and listen to her because she has 'news'?

Well, I've got news, babe. You don't get preferential treatment round here any more. I'm a busy man. Things to do.

I go across the road to buy a birthday card and a take away. It's great that the random shop does such a wide selection of cards to suit old dears. The ultra-flowery, lilac lettering type. Sometimes it seems that shop is stocked to suit me. Any item I discover a need for, I find on their shelves. I can't guess what their stock selection policy is, but they've solved more of my problems than the management consultancy I work for could.

In need of a late night tin opener 'cos yours just broke in your hands? Khan's General Store will see you right. Same for batteries, milk, shoe polish, brown sauce, plasters, tonic water or condoms. Whatever time of day, if I need something, they're there. They could write the book on supplier reliability. Not always best on price of course, but on anticipating the consumer's needs, they're world class.

I write the card. Dig the address out my diary. Scribble the solicitor's number on a scrap of paper for Susan and pop out again. Didn't need to go to the gym, amount of stair climbing I'm doing tonight.

I shove the number through Susan's letterbox and take the card to the post box, stopping at Khan's again 'cos I forgot to get stamps. The bloke behind the counter grins at me. Not the first time I've made repeat visits within the hour.

As I'm opening my front door, Susan reappears.

'Oh Craig, I thought that'd be you. Thank you so much for the phone number. I just wanted to say sorry again, for if I made you uncomfortable before. I really do appreciate your help.'

'No probs,' I say and shut the door behind me.

Older women are so straightforward and easy to please. I wish one of them would teach Julia that trick. So much for a nice, relaxing evening. My peace of mind is well and truly fucked.

~

SUSAN

The sun shone as I left the flat this morning with my partially completed application forms in a carrier bag. I didn't button my mac and lifted my face to the light as I walked to the bus stop. I almost allowed myself to feel optimistic.

As I took a deep breath to fortify me, I got a gulp of exhaust fumes and began to cough. Petite ladies shrouded head to foot in black turned to look and gathered small children to them as I spluttered. Surely they weren't afraid of me? But, as I looked around, it was obvious I was the one who looked out of place. No one stopped to ask if I was OK. I dropped my head and hurried to the stop. While I waited, I was careful not to look into the broken windows of the abandoned industrial building behind me. I'm sure the only movement behind the jagged edges of the glass was pigeons enjoying a well-appointed roost. I just didn't want to look too closely.

All the confidence I'd dredged up was lost. As the bus carried me into Kings Heath I realised that my plan to drop off the forms and explain in person why I have no referees to give, no past experience to commend me, was certain to fail. I am unemployable because I've never been employed.

I abandoned the bus and walked instead, trying to think up options or alternatives. I shouldn't have noticed this: the paving slabs don't match. They're broken, angled, scarred with bird poo and chewing gum, daubed with flourescent paint where a council worker meant to return. Hanging my head showed me a vista of the unloved streets where I have to make my home.

'Big Issue, my love?'

I wasn't sure the voice was talking to me so I hesitated and looked up. I made eye contact with the kind of man of whom I used to be scared. He had dread locked hair, a pierced lip, pierced eyebrow and clothes which put me in mind of the Himalayas.

He held my eye contact and spoke more hopefully. 'This week's Big Issue?'

I promised myself I wouldn't be scared in my new life so I forced myself to smile. 'No, thank you.'

'OK, love. You have a good day,' he replied and loped across to try his luck with the next passer-by.

There was nothing to fear after all. I didn't lose anything; not even the price of the magazine. Actually, I don't know how much it costs. One pound? Two? Perhaps you pay what you choose. Perhaps that's why he asks so politely; to convince you the transaction has a higher value. Manners cost him nothing and the exchange improved my mood no end.

Except, then I felt indebted. He'd made me feel good but I didn't even buy his magazine. That made me feel bad.

I walked on wondering if homelessness was even the 'big issue' anymore? There don't seem to be as many homeless people as I expected. I know one is too many but – the 'big issue'? Perhaps not. The news gives the impression that it's debt which is everyone's big problem these days. But, if that's right, why aren't more people homeless? I knew I would be unless I found work.

I couldn't face going to deliver my pathetic applications straight away, so I went to my café instead. It's funny how quickly I've started thinking of things as 'mine'. My flat (rented); my neighbour (poor lad, not through choice); my number 50 bus (well, I've ridden it several times now) and my café (as if one tea and toast gave me any claim).

I didn't have the place to myself this time. It was quite crowded so I slotted myself into a table squeezed next to the counter and looked around at the other customers. A group of students were counting out their change as they split the bill. A couple of builders turned away from the till with take away cups of tea and the door slammed behind them. The same old man looked as if he'd taken up residence behind his newspaper.

When he'd finished checking the students' stack of change, the waiter came over. He recognised me but his face was anxious as he said 'Hello, again' in that jokey way as if to imply you've hardly gone but you're back again. 'Your usual?' he added. Very funny.

'Just the tea this time, thanks.'

He went out to the kitchen from where I could hear a second voice, an unhappy voice, telling him bad news. 'She says she won't be coming back,' the disembodied voice said. 'After the holiday, she won't come back. I mean, how does she think that leaves us?'

'She doesn't think,' my comedian replied and returned to my table with a clink from the crockery on the tray he carried.

I thanked him and busied myself arranging the cup and saucer, the milk jug, the pot. Good pourers those. Not your usual café rubbish that dribble milk and tea over the table. Green and white striped tablecloths as well; it's a very nice atmosphere.

He went to lean on the counter with his chin on his hand and the weight of the world on his shoulders. It seemed I wasn't the only one whose day wasn't going to plan. The motor of the glass fronted fridge began to whirr, causing the tightly packed bottles inside to rattle against one another. The sudden noise roused him to set to work wiping smears from the illuminated window which showcased the drinks, and reminded me to stop staring.

The owner of the second voice came in to the main room and exhaled a dramatic sigh. He flounced across to the counter, removed his apron and flung it at the comedian. 'Women!' he said. 'You can't trust them.'

Funny Guy started to fold the apron, raised his eyebrows and tilted his head to let drama queen know I was within earshot.

'Oh, sorry, darling. Not you of course. The customer is always right.'

I waved a hand to indicate I wasn't offended and gave him one of those little, tight lipped smiles which could mean anything but usually mean 'Oh, don't worry about little old me'.

The two men returned to their conversation, at a lower volume. I lifted my tea cup and challenged yet another of my opinions. I have nothing against gay men. Why would I? I just haven't met many and wouldn't have guessed that Funny Guy was gay.

Leading Man clearly is though, no woman his age could pull off the histrionics he'd performed and he was standing lover-close to Funny Guy, leaning on his shoulder. They must be partners – in business and pleasure. Of course it really doesn't matter. It's only my small town mindset getting another stretch.

I was flicking through my Sainsbury's application form when Funny Guy came over to clear the table.

'Sorry about Mark,' he said. 'Tends to over-react I'm afraid.'

'It doesn't matter,' I said. 'We're all entitled to react when things go wrong.'

'Yeah, he just doesn't always get the whole front of house professionalism bit right though. That's why I keep him in the kitchen. That, and the fact he's the one with the catering qualification.'

He smiled again. It was a nice smile and I liked his humour in the face of adversity attitude. I could do with more of that myself. So I smiled back.

'Is this your business then, the two of you?'

'Yeah. We started a couple of months ago. It's going fairly well. Weekends are busy. Mornings sometimes – we get a crowd of stay-home mums who come here to socialise.'

I nodded, recognising an echo of my old crowd round at Jo's. He seemed less anxious as he talked about his business. His knowledge of the topic gave him confidence.

'I wish we were busier at lunchtimes,' he went on. 'It's hard to compete against the fast food guys on the High Street.'

'I suppose so.'

'A few more regular customers like you would be good.'

'Somehow I doubt there's much profit margin on a pot of tea.'

'You'd be surprised,' he said as he lifted the tray. 'Oops, now look who's being unprofessional.'

'I won't tell, don't worry.' I started to put the forms away again.

'Are you something in retail?' he asked.

'Me? Gosh, no. I'm nothing in anything. I'm just wondering how to persuade one of this lot to give me a job,' I replied, fanning the pages so that the logos of national retailers passed before my eyes like cherries on the wheels of a fruit machine. Rather fitting for the likelihood of my getting a job with one of them.

'You're applying for jobs?'

'Yes, afraid so.'

'Don't be afraid,' he said with excitement in his voice. 'We have a job. I mean, a vacancy. That's our problem. Well, the biggest of today's problems. We had a girl but she went off on holiday yesterday without telling us. Mark just got her on the phone and now she says she won't come back either. Don't apply to those guys, apply to me. I mean us, apply to us!'

Well, that threw me. One minute I had despaired of getting a job, the next I was being offered one without preamble. I couldn't think what to say.

'I know it's only waitressing and maybe you wanted something entirely different, but, please, would you consider it?'

I opened my mouth, but faltered. His sudden eloquence and certainty confused me.

'Let me get Mark. He'll persuade you.' He hurried back to the kitchen, put the tray down with a rattle and crash, and returned with Mark in tow. 'Talk about lucky timing,' he said. 'She's looking for a job, we

33

have a job going. It couldn't be any more perfect.'

Mark looked uncertain. 'Could you really be the answer to our prayers?'

'Well,' I said, still having trouble engaging the gears in my brain. 'I am looking for a job, but I don't have any waitressing experience. Not unless you count years of ferrying meals from kitchen to table at home, I suppose.'

'That doesn't matter,' Mark said. 'Full training could be provided for the right applicant.' He raised an eyebrow as he looked to his partner. 'Isn't that right, Andy?'

'Yeah, look, we're really stuck here. Do you think you'd be interested?' Andy said.

'Well, yes. I don't see why not. But aren't you going to ask me to apply properly?'

'No need.' Mark pulled out the chair facing me with a scrape of its legs against the floorboards, slung the green checked tea towel he'd dried his hands on over his shoulder and sat down. 'We'll use these – what's good enough for Sainsbury's is good enough for us.'

He took the application form and began to read. Andy looked at me uncertainly as if worried I might complain. I didn't so he brought a chair from the neighbouring table and sat down. The old man who seemed to be a permanent fixture looked over but wasn't interested enough to put down his newspaper. Everyone else was too engrossed in their own conversations or food to notice what was happening to me.

'Susan Clarke,' Mark read out as he flipped through the form. 'You live not too far away, you have a collection of exam results, you worked in a pub, but since then…?'

I blushed. At least it was better to be humiliated there rather than in a large shop. 'Since then I've been a housewife I suppose.'

'Which is the perfect experience for working here,' Mark said. He grinned and tossed the pages back on the table. 'How soon can you start: tomorrow, next week?'

'Well, maybe next week would be OK…'

Mark and Andy exchanged looks.

'Then we really wish you would,' Andy said. 'We could maybe have a trial period, a week or so. See how we get on? And we can only offer you minimum wage, to start with anyway.'

'That sounds ideal,' I said, not quite able to believe getting a job had been so easy. My immediate future was secure and my new life had begun. A celebration was in order.

CHAPTER FOUR

CRAIG

It was a mistake to meet her in my lunch break. Huge mistake. I should've insisted it had to be the evening. Why the fuck did I just go along with what she said?

Because it's always been like that with Julia, that's why. Always was and it always fucking will be. She says 'Jump', I say 'Long or High?'

We used to be good together. Lots of laughs. Great sex. Life was sweet. What was once sweet, must now be sour. It couldn't go any other way.

I walk into the foyer of my office building. Plains of polished marble floor stretch before me. Every footstep I take is an effort, using more energy than I have, bringing me no closer to the safety of the lift, my floor, my desk where I can slink behind the screens surrounding me and hide.

Out here I'm exposed. Vulnerable. I need privacy. I need to think about what just happened.

'Hi, Craig.'

Amisha. Worst of all possible scenarios. Her stiletto heeled steps tap towards me.

'Hey,' I mumble.

'Great weather, isn't it?'

'Guh.' I can't control what's coming out of my mouth.

'You OK, Craig?'

'I, er, yeah. Yeah, fine.'

'I see. It's just, you don't look fine.'

She touches my arm and I'm forced to meet her eye. She looks concerned, sincere. She's wearing a great outfit. Sheer, long-sleeved blouse, tight fitting pullover, wide-legged trousers snug around the hips. Modestly dressed to all traditional definitions. Barely any flesh on show. The absolute image of a nice girl. Effortlessly, unintentionally sexy.

I haven't managed to speak. My mind's lost control of the functions that control polite behaviour. I'm processing some serious shit here, but my mind's off on a tangent about Amisha looking hot. Conniving, arse licking, career-thief Amisha? Got to get a fucking grip.

'C'mon,' she says, and steers me to the lift. 'I'll get you a drink.'

~

It must be because Julia looked so different when I saw her a few minutes ago. Gone was the sleek blonde hair – replaced by a ponytail with dark roots. Gone was the short skirt, high heels combination – replaced by jeans and trainers. Gone was the designer handbag – replaced by a nappy bag. No longer was she toting the tiny, Gucci bag only containing mobile, keys, fags and lippy.

She hadn't looked like the Julia I know. Knew. I don't know her and it seems I never did because the girl I knew couldn't have done this.

'Craig,' she'd said, face grim.

37

'Julia,' I said and gave her my best grin, the one she used to say made her feel frisky. Well, I figured I'd let the girl see what she'd been missing in the two years since she'd dumped me. Not that she'd made any effort to dress up. 'And this is…?'

'Wolfgang.'

'Pleased to meet you,' I said to the little guy, proud of myself for not adding, 'You poor bugger, the playground will be a place of terror for you.'

'My son,' Julia added. 'Wolfie, look – why don't you go and play with those toys?'

So that's why she hadn't wanted to meet in a bar. Department store cafés are obviously designed with the needs of parents in mind. This one certainly hadn't been designed for anything else. It was a maze of prams, high chairs and cutesy little furniture around a table of nailed down toys.

'So, a son. You've been busy,' I said.

'Yes. Don't you want to know how old he is?'

What? Why would she think I'd care? Unless… Oh, fuck. Unless.

'Nearly eighteen months.'

She said it with the kind of look that means 'I want you to know something, but I don't want to tell you.' I was good at maths at school, and biology. That meant, that meant this child could conceivably be conceived by me. Fuck.

'How's Trev?' I asked. At least pretending I cared about the scumbag who double crossed me was buying me thinking time.

'We split up last week,' she said. 'He insisted on a paternity test and found Wolfie's not his. It gave him the excuse he needed to throw me out.'

'Right. Which means…?'

38

'Which probably means you're the daddy.'

'Right. Um, probably or certainly? I think the exact word might be important.'

'Certainly. I'm not a complete slag.'

'No, well. I suppose it's a relief to know you were only shagging two of us, not more.'

'Craig, I'm sorry. And I'm sorry you had to find out about Wolfie like this. I really did think he was Trev's.'

'Did you know you were pregnant when you left me then?'

'No.'

'Right.'

'You keep saying that.'

Well, what did she want from me? World class oration? I was struggling to think of any sentences that didn't include the words 'fuck', 'shitting hell', 'you bitch' and 'I'm screwed'.

Following my principle that if you can't say anything nice, you should say something stupid, I said, 'Fucking hell, Julia. You're really screwing with my head here.'

'I know,' she said. 'I didn't know how to tell you.'

'So, what?' I said, as I peeled my shirtsleeves off the sticky table top. 'What do you want from me?'

'Well, you need to decide what you want. Whether you want to be involved.' She folded her arms and stared at me. 'I think you should be, but it's your choice. Obviously, financially...'

She let that one hang. Shit, all those news stories I'd never paid attention to – child support payments, Fathers for Justice. I'd become a statistic and my pay packet was going to be made to, well, pay.

~

I can't tell Amisha any of this. She led the way to the kitchen and is making me a drink. I'm slumped in a seat and staring at the handbag she's left on the table in front of me. It's petite, shiny, new. It has pink leather flowers all over it.

'Radley,' I say, when she puts the drinks down.

'Yes. I like the little doggie.' She swings the leather, dog-shaped tag hanging from the bag with one finger and pushes my drink towards me.

'Tea,' she says. 'Two sugars.'

'Thanks. How did you know?'

She does a convincing impression of Gav's Black Country accent, 'Kipper Tie, Craig?' and my response 'Milk and two if you're going, Gav.'

'Oh, are we loud? Sorry.'

'It's not so much the volume as the repetition. Six or seven times, every day.'

'Right,' I say, realising I probably should stop saying that. 'New bag?'

'A treat to myself, for getting the job. Sorry, by the way.'

'Oh, no problems. Best man won and all that.' I realise this is probably highly offensive and try to sound sincere as I add, 'Congratulations. My ex had a bag fetish.' Perhaps that didn't work.

'Many women do. So, I guess it's not the job you're upset about?'

'No, um, bad news, that's all.'

Guilt smacks me in the guts. I just described my son as bad news. The nausea rises. I just used the phrase 'my son' to myself. I put the mug down before I spill my tea.

'Anything I can do?' Amisha asks.

'No, I, er...'

40

Truth is I don't know what the fuck to tell her. I don't know what to think, or say, or do.

'Perhaps you should go home,' she suggests.

'I have some contract documents to check and send out.' Can't believe I'm still worried about work when my world's collapsing.

'Pass the files to me. I'll sort it out and cover for you. You really don't look like you should be here.'

What? Is this some new ploy, an attack when my defences are down? Was it not enough to steal a fucking promotion from me, is she going to undermine me in other ways too?

'Err,' I say, brain unable to formulate any kind of defence.

'It's OK. I'll handle it. You can owe me one.'

I have no choice. Everything has changed. Enemies are now friends. I am now a father.

~

SUSAN

I treated myself to a session of window shopping before I returned to the flat. The café stands on Poplar Road; perhaps why they've called it Tall Trees. The other businesses are an interesting, independent mix ranging from the niche market of Caribbean delicacies to the practicality of a launderette. A steady stream of cars and pedestrians flowed to and from the High Street and back.

I like the road. Something about the atmosphere has elements of the familiar small town scale, but then there are the hints of spice, undercurrents of exoticism: the contemporary, cosmopolitan attitude I want for myself. I know I'll only be a waitress here, a role which won't be too challenging, but it's a start, and a good one.

41

Once the road meets the High Street everything changes. The shops are mainstream and the traffic is heavy. As I walked, music pumped out from doorways to pummel one ear, the rumble of engines and squeal of brakes assaulted the other. It was a relief to step into the protection of the bus shelter; although the drunk already occupying it didn't smell pleasant.

The bus limped along the High Street, then picked up speed as soon as the road was troubled by fewer interruptions. From my brave front seat on the top deck I looked out across more greenery than I'd previously registered. The end of the High Street is marked by the entrance to a park which offers a glimpse down into an open space filled with budding leaves.

More trees line the road, the houses well set back behind wide grass verges. On into Moseley the bus slowed again but I didn't see the traffic control, I saw the trees: mature, imposing, drawing my eyes up to admire the detailed brickwork and tiled patterns above the bland shop fronts.

On again and the verges and front gardens disappeared, the housing more tightly packed as the bus got closer to my stop. Even the fact that here the trees sprout from concrete beds couldn't depress me. They thrive in this hard paved landscape – growing tall, surviving – and so will I. I'd decided to cook myself a celebratory meal and popped into the general store where I found Craig gazing at the display of chilled food.

'Got an afternoon off?' I asked.

'Um, not feeling so good. Thought I should come home.'

He wasn't looking very well actually: pale and distracted. A rush of maternal sympathy made me touch his arm. The muscles were firm under the crisp poplin of his shirt, which made the despair in his eyes even more heart breaking.

'Are you ill, Craig? Is there anything I can do?'

'No. I'm not sick. Just, um, shocked, I suppose.'

'OK, well I was going to cook myself something nice for dinner. Why don't I cook for you too?'

His expression told me that selfless acts of generosity weren't normal between neighbours here.

'Nothing fancy,' I assured him. 'Call it a flat warming for me. You'll be doing me a favour. Now, what sort of thing do you like?'

The mother hen routine broke the spell he was under and he started to respond. I coaxed out of him the fact that his favourite meal was chilli con carne, instructed him to carry some items for me and bustled him back to the flats.

'Come over in a couple of hours,' I said as I unlocked my front door.

He nodded and turned towards his own flat, leaving me wondering whether he was acting ten years younger than he is or if I was acting ten years older. As I unloaded the shopping into my fridge and cupboards I realised a flat warming was just what I needed. My first few days here I've behaved as if I wasn't staying – buying ingredients only for one meal, not planning ahead.

Now my position here is assured, for the immediate future at least, and the cupboards are no longer bare. I have to provide for someone else too. That was always something which made me feel good.

Cooking my first roast dinner – 1983

Mrs Watson from Home Economics set us a task to prepare the Sunday roast this weekend and I was dreading it. Mum sort of smirked when I told her and Dad started joking about how the family'll be going hungry.

I showed them though. Mum set a budget and I went shopping. I'd made a plan, like Mrs Watson told us, and I had all my timings worked out. I got the meat in, prepared the veg – two types of potatoes:roast and new; carrots; beans and a cauliflower, and made my own gravy from scratch. Not granules like Mum uses.

Their faces when I called them to the table were priceless. It really did look good – crispy skin on the chicken, butter melting on the carrots and the smell of gravy wafting round the room. They didn't know what to say because I'd shown them. I hadn't messed it up like they expected. I hadn't burnt it or spoiled the food. It was all ready at the right time. There was nothing to criticise. I'd even cleaned the kitchen.

~

Cooking was my one talent. When I didn't achieve anything anywhere else, I could always go into a kitchen and feed people. I took over Sunday dinners after that first time. It was as if Mum couldn't be bothered to compete. She just said, 'Well, as you enjoy doing it so much…'

I suppose it was embarrassing for her, that her useless daughter was actually better at something than she was. With hindsight, I didn't handle it well. I was probably too triumphant about my ability and turned into some kind of culinary know-it-all.

It was my one skill though. I successfully fed my husband for twenty years, my son for eighteen. Both are well-nourished specimens. I looked after them perfectly, even if they're now abandoned.

It's only been two days. I'm sure Pete won't have starved in my absence, his survival instinct will have kicked in. As for James, I must ring him. I need to tell my side of the story, reassure him of my love. Until I can keep the tears out of my voice though, I won't make the call.

~

CRAIG

When did I last get home, kick my shoes off and just relax? Walking in the front door today made a bad day worse. This afternoon I see my home as it really is.

The stacks of audio and visual technology, ranks of black boxes, covered in dust. The computer games scattered on the floor are violent. The DVDs piled by the TV are violent or pornographic. The washing up stacked in the sink is probably a health hazard, and fuck knows when I last cleaned the bathroom.

This is not somewhere I could bring a small child.

I stumble to the sofa and sit down. There are many things I need to be thinking about:

What the fuck am I going to do?

How the hell will Mum take this?

What does this mean for my future?

What kind of mentalist calls their kid Wolfgang?

This is terrible. This is worse than terrible. I can't have a kid. I am a kid. No. I'm not a kid, I'm a responsible adult. I used condoms. I should sue someone. I should sue Julia for emotional distress.

Right, I'm getting angry now. That's good. Anger I can handle. So Julia says I need to decide what to do. Not many options though are there? Of course I have to get involved. What kind of wanker isn't involved in his son's life? I'll have to give her money I suppose.

Well, OK, I can probably afford that. Might have to cut back on something else.

I need some kind of practical involvement too. I have to see him, fill some kind of 'Dad' role I suppose. The mostly hands-off kind I hope.

Christ. This is meant to be cause for celebration. I'm meant to get nine months of pampering before I hit the reality of actually being a dad. It's not meant to be dumped on me like this. The stork's meant to deliver a bundle of joy, not a toddler.

The kid is cute though: blond hair, blue eyes, red cheeks kind of cute. Sort of like me in the baby photos Mum still coos over. He played in the corner the whole time Julia talked at me. He had that sort of stumble in the way he walked, like it was hard to pick up his feet.

Well, sometimes it is my son. Try doing it after fifteen pints of lager. Oh, bollocks, I have to be involved. I have to stop that innocent little boy growing up into a clone of me.

I don't know how to break this news to Mum. I can't think of any way to start that conversation. I don't even know how to feel about this myself.

This is torture, agony. My brain's crumbling with the pressure of the new information, the shift in perspective. I'm not sure I can cope with this physically, let alone emotionally. I can't tell Mum yet. I need time.

Time? Oh, fuck. Why the hell did I say I'd eat with Susan?

I grab a bottle of wine and drag myself across to her door. Dinner does smell good, even from here. She lets me in, thanks me for the wine, then flashes me a big smile.

'I'll have to ask you another neighbourly favour,' she says. 'I don't have a corkscrew…'

When I return with the open bottle she's dishing up. It's sort of comforting, like how Davo and I used to pop between the flats, helping ourselves to anything we needed to borrow. Not that Davo ever cooked me anything that looked this good.

I pour the wine and raise my glass but I'm stumped for a toast. Davo's 'Wine, Women and Drugs!' salute won't fit and I can't think of anything suitable.

'Thank you,' I say, after a pause in which she looks at me without speaking.

'Thank you,' she replies and takes a sip. 'Very nice.'

I've munched down a huge forkful. Hadn't realised I was so hungry.

'No, this is very nice,' I say.

I continue to cram my food down while she takes on the weight of the conversation like a challenge.

'I got a job,' she says. 'At a café down in Kings Heath. And I've made an appointment to see your solicitor tomorrow.'

I nod and try to smile in the right places but I'm really focussed on the food. I need it. She serves me seconds without asking and tops up our glasses. I like this woman.

'No pudding, I'm afraid,' she says as she clears the table once I've polished my plate. 'Should have gone to the supermarket really.'

'No problem,' I say and nip back to my flat to raid the stash of chocolate bars for a selection to take round.

My mobile blinks at me from where I left it on the kitchen counter. One missed call, it tells me: Mum.

It's as if she knows I'm avoiding her. How could she know? I open another bottle of wine and take it and the chocolate back to Susan's. I leave the phone where it is.

'More wine?' Susan asks leaving the 'are you sure?' to her tone of voice.

'Why not?' I say.

I'm calmer now and feel as if I might be able to cope. Physically at least. Mentally I think more alcoholic cushioning is going to help.

We sit on her sofa. The one that never recovered from Davo tipping a curry over it. She's snapping chunks off a Dairy Milk, savouring it like a delicacy. I'm chugging Smarties, tipping my head back with the tube to my mouth, the sweets rattling as they fall against my teeth. A muffled knock keeps coming from upstairs. I look at the ceiling, but she doesn't mention it so neither do I.

'So,' Susan says as she folds the wrapper over her half-eaten chocolate bar, 'has the comfort food done its job?'

'I do feel human again. Great chilli by the way.'

'No problem. Just let me know, any time you need it.'

'You'll regret offering. I think I'm entering a traumatic period of my life. I wouldn't want to become dependent on your chilli to get me through.'

'I'll cook you a vat of it,' she says. 'You can fill your freezer. Now, is there anything you want to talk about?'

~

SUSAN

I don't know when I last had a night like that, or even if I ever did. Poor Craig's in such a mess but it was

48

the most wonderful thing. He listened to what I said. He asked for my opinions and he listened to them, thought about them, asked questions as if I had wisdom to share. I really don't think that ever happened before.

'I don't know what I'm going to do about this kid,' he said. 'I can't be a dad, I don't know anyone who's a dad. Trying to do my job's about all I can cope with.'

'You're in shock, you shouldn't make any snap decisions,' I said.

'But how will I ever work out what to do? I don't even know if I can live with having to see Julia again, let alone look after a kid with her. And, no offence, but it's mad that you're the one I'm talking to. Without Trev, or even Davo though, who else have I got?'

I resisted my maternal urge to take control, to fix things for him. That was the kind of behaviour my James recoiled from, even when he was too young to be embarrassed by me.

Craig seemed happy to have my sympathy though. It was as if talking made him stronger. James and I never talked like that.

I must stop thinking of Craig in the same context as my son. He's not that many years younger than me. He talks to me like a peer, although he caught himself and moderated his language. I wouldn't mind if he swore. His situation demands a strong response.

His own mother sounds as if she must be older. He talked about her with such affection, so concerned about how she'll react to the abrupt arrival of a grandson. 'She wanted me to do well at work, that was her top priority. Said there wasn't anything I

49

couldn't do and she'd see me boss of my own firm one day.'

God, the weight of the expectations of others. It makes me glad I've rejected them. 'A grandson won't be a disappointment for her, you know,' I said. 'I'm sure children featured in her dreams for you.'

'Yeah, at least nine months after marriage though.'

I laughed, but I don't need to have met that woman to guess the distress she'll suffer. Her golden boy's in trouble, his life tarnished. If I could tell her what he's done for me – how his manners, his attitudes, his recognition of me as a valuable member of society has buoyed me – then she'd know. Surely she already does. Craig can never be a disappointment to her. He's a triumph.

I wouldn't recommend becoming a parent at his age of course. Not based on my own experience. Teenage parents don't have it so bad. If you've barely started your life yet, what matter if you delay for a while? Of course, they may not be so well equipped to deal with the emotional and financial strain as say, parents in their thirties. But, early to mid twenties? No, I'd say that's the worst time to have a baby on your hands. You've just started out. You've seen the opportunities and excitement. You reach out to grab them and you find a baby in your arms instead. Get over the sentimentality and face the facts. There are things you will now have to put on hold. Then you find yourself, like me, itching to join the party again when you make the break from parental responsibility, but everyone else is twenty years younger than you.

Not that parental responsibility ever escapes you. Even now, when I'm determined to put myself first for once – to focus on what I want, what's best for me – even now I couldn't put off the call to my son any longer.

'Hello?' he said, clearly suspicious of the fact my new mobile number wasn't recognised on his phone.

'Jamie, it's Mum here.' I always feel the need to confirm my identity on the phone, as if I might not be recognised otherwise. As if my son might not recognise his mum.

'Where the hell are you? Me and Dad have been going nuts.'

'I'm sorry. I told him to tell you I'd call when I could.'

'When you could? It's been four days. How could you think it was OK to not let anyone know where you are for four days?'

He's so like his father, my son. Even in his concern for me he couldn't hide the aggression, the implication that I'm an inconvenience.

'I wanted to call, but I've been busy.' It was a struggle to keep my voice neutral. 'I wanted to get my new flat set up and get a job so you know you don't have to worry about me. How are things with you?'

'Me? Oh yeah, I'm fine, what with my Mum going walkabout and my Dad in meltdown. Yeah, just fine. Couldn't be better.'

'Good,' I said. I've never found his sarcasm amusing. 'Your Dad's not coping then?'

'Mum, he's in his fifties. He's never done a thing for himself his whole life. He says he had no idea you were going to leave. He's in shock. What did you expect?'

'Well, I made everything quite clear to him. I don't want to see him again. I'm going to see a solicitor about getting a divorce.'

'Divorce? You can't do this to him. He'll be broken.'

'He nearly broke me, James. I've got to go or I'll be late for my appointment. You've got my number now so you can call me if you need me. You, not your Dad.'

'But, Mum, where are you?'

I had to smile at that. My little boy was never clingy, never a mummy's boy, never homesick. Now he's off, living his own life at Bristol University, wrapped up in even more layers of self-absorption and now he starts whining for his mum.

'I'll tell you when I'm more settled.' I didn't want to keep it from him, but I also didn't want Pete immediately tracking me down.

'Fine. You do that. Walk away as if this family means nothing.'

The line went dead. Ending a mobile phone conversation by hanging up doesn't have the acoustic impact of slamming a landline down, but the finality of the action certainly resonated in my heart. I hadn't expected James to fully understand my decision, but his lack of any concern for my situation and well-being was disappointing. He was the one link with my old life I hadn't wanted to lose, the one person worth holding on to. My husband and friends were easy to let go because they had only filled those roles superficially. My son, however, I loved. He was just too angry to love me back.

CHAPTER FIVE

CRAIG

Still haven't shaken off the mother of all hangovers.
Think I must've drunk most of the wine I took to
Susan's. Even the cushioning of a bellyfull of chilli
couldn't save me.

Course it might have been the tequila nightcap that
did it. The four hours sleep before my alarm went off
didn't do much to repair the damage either.

I stopped at Khan's on my way into work for my
recovery supplies of Coke, aspirin and a Kit Kat (eat
Kit Kat first, wash aspirin down with Coke) and
actually got to the office before Amisha.

As promised, she'd sorted out my contract
paperwork and the files were in order. So now I'm
indebted to her. Great. At least talking with Susan's
got things straight in my head.

However I feel about Julia, and however stupid I
think his name is, I want to get to know my son. I
played with him for a few minutes yesterday, knelt in
the debris on the café floor, and it was obvious he
was great. He took to me straight away too – clearly
has good taste.

I do my job: emails, phone calls, smile in my voice, promises I'll deliver on. This firm is lucky to have me. Yeah, Amisha is good, but so am I and next time it'll be me moving the contents of my desk into a private office.

I pass the open door to hers on my way out to lunch. She's on the phone so I wave to get her attention and mouth, 'Thank you'. She smiles back. Nice teeth.

I said I'd meet Susan after her appointment and take her for a drink. She seems to have slotted into my life and filled the Davo-shaped gap. Think Davo'd be shocked by his replacement though.

She's waiting for me at the entrance to the cathedral square. She looks younger with her hair loose instead of clipped back. Almost blends in with the emo students, except, on her, the clothes aren't ironic.

'Suits you,' I say and gesture at her head.

'Thank you. I'm thinking of having it all cut off though. If I can get an appointment this afternoon I might just do it.'

'Wow. We'd better hit the pub. You need some Dutch courage.'

She's got an armful of papers again, leaflets and info about divorce by the look of it. I buy her a glass of white and a lemonade for me. Stomach's still dodgy. Must stop keeping tequila in the flat.

She chooses a table in the window where we can watch the desk jockeys battle the Goths for benches in the graveyard.

'Popular spot,' Susan says.

'Yeah, its all right here since they cleaned it up. Used to be pretty rough.'

'Really?' she replies, not sounding that interested. She's looking around the pub. 'This place is huge.'

'Used to be a bank.'

How did I suddenly become a tour guide? How do I even know this stuff? I change the subject before I come out with any more fascinating facts, 'How was the solicitor?'

'OK. She gave me lots to think about.'

I don't want to ask her about her marriage, seems too personal. Even though she's now fully up to speed on the details of my life, knows more about me than my own mum.

'Good,' I say. 'Well it's a big decision.'

'No, leaving him was the big decision. Divorce is just tying up loose ends.'

Fuck. I'd never have guessed Susan was made of steel. I'm impressed. She tells me about her plans to get her hair cut and buy new clothes. We discuss the shops she should try – endless Saturdays following Julia around have left me with a detailed knowledge of what can be purchased where.

'I think I'll come shopping tomorrow,' she says. 'Devote a full day to it.'

'Good plan. Think I'd better call Julia. Ask if I can see her and Wolfie tomorrow.'

'That's a good idea. I know you'll do the right thing, you're such a nice man.'

'Nice!' I say, slamming my glass on the table. 'Susan, no man ever wants to be told he's 'nice'. Brave, sexy, strong, good-looking, witty – anything but nice.'

'Well, you're all of those too, of course,' she says. She's laughing at me.

~

Amisha wanders over when I get back to my desk.

'Everything OK with those contracts?' she asks.

'Great, thanks. Really good of you to do that for me.'

'No problem. Everything else OK too?'

Typical woman, after the gossip. Well Wolfie is not about to become the latest water cooler chit chat. 'Yeah, fine,' is all I give her.

'Was that a client you were with in the pub at lunchtime?'

What is this? Is she my stalker now? That's the last time I sit at a window table anywhere.

'No, er, that's my next door neighbour. She had an appointment she wasn't looking forward to so I said I'd take her for a drink afterwards.'

'Oh, that's really nice of you.'

Nice! What is it with women? You try to be pleasant, behave like a decent human being, and all they can do is insult you. I turn to my computer and Amisha takes the hint and disappears.

Gav sticks his head over the partition separating us and winks, 'Flirting with the boss, eh, Craig?'

'Fuck. Off.'

~

SUSAN

This morning I ran a brush through my newly layered hair and hit the shops. I'd been shopping in Birmingham before, with Jo; but it was never so satisfying. I never returned footsore and laden with bags. She would drive us here, park the Volvo estate in what she deemed the best car park, and lead the way around the shops. Marks and Spencers, to stock up on basics; Rackhams if anything with more class was required. She led me between the two on a tight lead so I could only glance at the tempting windows of the High Street fashion chains. Their names were familiar to me from TV and magazines, the trendy clothes were beyond Jo's comprehension and denied to me.

If I'd kept my own car I could have got here alone, but Pete didn't think it worth keeping my runabout once James no longer needed ferrying to and from school and sports clubs. He wouldn't have liked the thought of me out on my own without the responsibility of James's schedule to clip my wings. I'm here alone now though. The treasure trove of Birmingham's retail opportunities is open.

Underwear was first on my list. The only kind I owned was easy-care cotton in plain black or plain white. There had been some overly sexy, complicated and impractical bras, knickers and suspender belts in my old wardrobe – all presents from Pete. He's a man with a habit of giving presents that were more for him than for the recipient. Needless to say, they're landfill by now.

Given I'm the only person who'll see my new underwear, I looked around the lingerie departments and wondered what kind I really wanted. I've always known that the right bra can make a big difference – outside and in. It's one of the early entries in 'The Book'.

My first bra – 1981

Mum took me shopping for my first bra today. I feel so grown up with it on. I won't have to wear vests like a kid any more. She didn't let me choose it though. Just took me straight to the display of boring boxes at the back of the shop. I wasn't allowed to look at the glamorous, satiny bras on padded hangers. I was only allowed to choose between two styles, both ugly. I look great with it on though, especially if I pull my T-shirt tight. The boys at school are bound to notice me now.

They didn't notice me. Not when there were other girls whose lacy, black bras were visible through their white school shirts. No, I wasn't the kind of girl who got noticed like that.

Male attention isn't what I want from my underwear any more. And easy-care cotton has its attractions. I wanted something fun though, something pretty, something to make me smile when I get dressed in the morning. I chose a selection in pale sorbet colours, the bra straps embellished with touches of lace, the cut of the knickers covering the worst of the pregnancy stretch marks that trace their own lace work across my belly.

Next I looked for work clothes. A new wardrobe for my new job. Both Mark and Andy wore jeans and shirts, so I supposed I could do the same. I tried on denim in a range of styles – slim fitting, boot cut, rhinestone studded. Anything other than the high-waist slacks fit of the jeans from my old life. The matronly type which added years to my age and inches to my hips.

As I checked myself out in the fitting room mirrors I even convinced myself the skinny legged version looked OK. I didn't buy them though. I chose a straight cut pair in both blue and black denim and a selection of pretty tops to go with them.

I was enjoying myself, riding the wave of my splurge and humming along to the pop music piped through the shops. I added a black knee length skirt, a wrap over floral print jersey dress, and two pairs of light ballet pumps – one pair cream, the other red. All clothes which would have made Pete frown. With several bulging bags in each hand, I felt fantastic. No matter that my newly acquired funds were being drained; from next week, I'll be earning my own money. Mine: to do with as I please.

Back home, I unpacked my purchases, snipped off tags and smoothed out creases. I emptied all the old clothes from my tiny wardrobe and drawers into three piles: charity shop, rags and dustbin. When the new clothes were stowed as safely as possible in the flimsy furniture which seemed about to revert to its flat-packed state, I sat on the bed with the wardrobe doors open and admired them. My cheeks ached with the grin I'd been suppressing all afternoon. Not even the thumping noise from upstairs could upset me. No wonder people get addicted to shopping; this afternoon was the most fun I think I've ever had.

I suppose wedding planning came close. All the things to choose: dress, flowers, food. But I had to defer to Pete's opinions. I had to listen to Mum's thoughts. This was the first time I've indulged my own taste without needing to consider anyone else.
I couldn't resist and got changed into the blue jeans and a top with purple flowers embroidered around the scooped neckline – the outfit I plan to wear to work on Monday. I did a circuit of the flat, collecting plates from the kitchen and delivering them to the bedroom. I felt fourteen, not in my forties. I felt as if life really is starting again.

~

CRAIG

OK, I can do this. He's just a boy. A little version of me. He is mine for fuck's sake. I can be alone with him without breaking him, losing him or anything bad happening.

'Come round to my parent's on Sunday,' Julia had said. 'Spend some time with him.'

We said some other things too. Well, I did. To be fair to her, she's showing remorse. And surely I'm entitled to let off a little steam?

Her parents live in a big house in Selly Park and it was really awkward when I got here. I'm still struggling to be civil to her. But the boy's great. Full of cheek and wanting to play. With me. As if I'm the best person he ever met. So I sort of started to enjoy it. Especially as her stuck up old folks weren't around.

Then Julia says, 'Would you take him to the park for a couple of hours? I could go and get the rest of my things from Trev's.'

'But, I can't look after him. Not on my own.'

'Don't be stupid. You babysat my nephews enough times with me. You're good with kids.'

'But he doesn't know me.'

She ignored me, bent down to Wolfie and said, 'Darling, wouldn't you like to go to the park with Daddy?'

Wolfie just looked at me. His eyes showed no emotion. I have no idea how much kids this young understand but I really felt for him. Surely he'd connected the word 'Daddy' to Trev, surely he'd bonded with Trev, and now that bastard had walked out on him just like he'd fucked me over.

'Looks like it's just you and me then,' I said to Wolfie once Julia had clipped him into the buggy, loaded me with a bag, and waved us off.

I used to pick up Julia from her parent's place and we'd go to Cannon Hill Park. We'd throw a frisbee and have drinks at the Arts Centre bar. Can't exactly do that with Wolfie.

He seems to like the noise of the buggy wheels rattling over bumps in the pavement so I push faster and he giggles until he gives himself hiccups. Now there's panic in his eyes. I really don't want him to start screaming. I haven't been in charge of him for five minutes yet. I check the bag and find a drink.

'Here, try this, mate,' I say and hand him the yellow plastic cup with its no-spill spout extended.

'Deuce,' he says.

'Yeah, juice.' My heart feels like it's too big for my chest as his eyes lock onto mine.

He sucks at the drink, dribbles of the juice spilling down his chin. We sit and look at each other for a while, him comfy in the sports-styled seat of his buggy, me crouched by his side. I'm taking it all in, the thick mop of blond hair on his oversized head, the big, round, light brown eyes, same colour as Julia's, the plump cheeks, red lips. Despite all these differences from my own thinner, darker, stubblier face, I still think I see some hint of me there.

I don't know what he's thinking.

'Cow,' he says and dangles the cup over the side of the buggy.

I catch it before it hits the pavement and rummage through the bag for anything that might be called 'cow'. I find things that alarm me, like nappies, and things that I'm sure can't be what he's after, like a plastic tub with biscuits in it. No 'cow' but he doesn't look too bothered so I get us on the way again.

I keep up a running commentary as we walk. 'Take a look at these cars, Wolfie. Lexus, Jaguars. You're in luxury land here, lad.' A dog being walked past us gives me plenty of conversational material. 'Aww, look at the doggie, he's a cute one isn't he?' I'm

61

panicking. I have no fucking idea how to talk to this kid, veering between cutesy baby talk and man to man banter. I'm lost.

Yes, me and Julia used to take her nephews out for the day sometimes and I was good with them. But they were older, they spoke more, they were toilet trained. Wolfie is much harder work. He either seems to be ignoring me, off in his own world, or he tilts his head up to look at me above the back of the buggy seat and says cryptic things.

'Dagger,' was the last one.

'What's that? What is it you want? Oh, 'Jaguar', right? Well, maybe when you're older if you're very, very good.'

There are a lot more people around once we get to the park, a lot more kids in buggies and prams. I check out the adults, looking for some clues on what I'm meant to be doing, whether I'm getting it right. There are women on their own, ignoring the child they're pushing while they chat on their mobiles. There are men on their own who have stopped pushing while they stare at a group of lads playing footie – shirts versus skins. It's cold for that yet. There are couples who gaze at the child with them as if it's a miracle, as if there are no other children.

While I'm looking around, working out what to do, Wolfie's getting bored. He's starting to whimper and I have to act fast. I really don't want him to start screaming. I can imagine some busybody interfering, deciding I've abducted him and calling the police.

I unclip the racing seatbelt holding him in the buggy and lift him out. It's the first time I've held him. I cradle his little body against my chest and he reaches one chubby hand out to touch my cheek.

'Sorry, mate, should've had a shave.' My voice has gone all soft like when I'm talking to a girl and I really want her to like me. I really, really want Wolfie to like me.

I give him a smile and let myself squeeze him a little tighter, feeling the warmth, weight and solidity of him. 'So, are we going to do this?' I say. 'You and me? Man and boy?'

He starts to fidget under the pressure so I go cross-eyed, which makes him laugh, and I carefully put him down. I'm panicking. This is huge. What the hell was Julia thinking to let me out with him? What kind of a mother is she?

Wolfie bends to inspect the grass I've parked the buggy by and I snatch him back up. Fucking goose shit.

Awareness of all the dangers in the park overwhelms me. There's the young girl wobbling towards us on her roller blades. The bounding spaniel. The overshooting football. The cyclists riding too fast on the paths, the lake which would probably poison him if he fell in, the lone man sitting too close to the kid's playground. Shit, I've brought the boy to a warzone.

He fidgets again, oblivious, so I put him down away from the grass and he totters a few steps along the path. I steer the buggy round to walk beside him, his bodyguard through the chaos and constantly thinking, 'Don't have a poo. Wait til you get home, lad.' I do not need to expose my lack of knowledge about how to work a nappy in public. There's far too big an audience here today. Most of south Birmingham has congregated to watch the first episode of the Craig and Wolfie show.

Despite myself, I love this park. My dad used to bring me here when he was well enough. We rowed boats on the lake, played crazy golf, ate ice creams from the van where there's always a queue whatever the weather.

It's not a battlefield. It's a good place to be. There's space to run around, squirrels and ducks to watch. There are trees and flowers, even if it's mostly old blossom and fallen petals crushed into the mud along with bits of litter.

'Hey, Wolfie, what say we make this our place? You and me? I'll row you across the lake, I'll kick a ball with you. What do you think? Is it a date?'

He's ignoring me of course. Why listen to the ramblings of a bloke with tears in his eyes when there are ducks to chase?

We wander about for a while. Things catch his attention, then lose it. I only take my eyes off him to scan for danger, like the bloke selling cartoon character helium balloons. I do not need for the boy to start screaming like a brat for one of those.

I realise it's probably time to head back and bribe him into the buggy with the biscuits. I hardly recognise myself as I leave the park. No jay walking, no texting as I walk. My attention is fully focussed on the task in hand. I am responsible for this boy's safety and it's a job I'm not sure I'm qualified for.

Julia opens the door when I ring the bell. She has mascara smudged on her cheeks but she gives Wolfie a huge smile and he reaches out to her. I didn't think I was the jealous type, but I hate seeing his interest switch immediately to another person. Especially when I don't trust the woman he's interested in.

'When can I see him again?'

'Um, maybe you could come round after work sometime,' she says.

It's not good enough. 'Tuesday.'

'OK, Tuesday. He goes to bed at seven so make it before then.'

I don't want to hang around talking to her, I've got too much to think about so I make to leave.

'Bye then, Wolfie,' I say.

'Say 'bye bye' to your Daddy,' Julia tells the little boy in her arms.

'Bi Dar,' Wolfie says with a casual wave.

I don't think my heart will ever be the same again.

CHAPTER SIX

SUSAN

I suppose it was silly of me to arrive quite so early this morning. No wonder I'm tired. I wasn't sure how long the bus would take though and had been awake since five thirty. So I stood at the Tall Trees door for half an hour before Mark and Andy arrived to open the café. I watched the street come to life: shutters opening, traffic building, bin lorry collecting.

Mark rubbed bleary eyes as he walked up the street but found a smile when he saw me. 'Morning, new employee. Ready to join the team?'

'More than ready,' I said. 'It feels like the first day of the rest of my life.'

'Bloody hell. Andy, I think her expectations may need to be managed downwards.'

Andy unlocked the door, tapped a code into the burglar alarm panel and didn't say anything. I decided neither of them were morning people and tried to keep my excitement in check. Andy set me to work wiping the tables.

'We keep it simple for breakfasts,' he said. 'It'll go quiet around nine thirty and we'll clean down again, put the table cloths on and reset everything for elevenses. With luck, there'll be a steam of customers through lunch into late afternoon and we clock off around five. As you know though, the stream sometimes dries up.'

He was confident of his subject, but hadn't looked me in the eye. I found the cutlery and menus and started to work. Andy disappeared into the kitchen from where I could hear Mark clattering around. The scent of bacon soon wafted into the room and Mark's laugh rang out. He was obviously perking up.

'Oh,' Andy said when he came back into the main room.

'What? Is it OK, have I done it OK?' I glanced at my handiwork wondering what he didn't like. I'd laid all the tables, fanned out green paper napkins, and propped breakfast menus against the slim glass vases containing a single white gerbera stem which I'd shared around the tables. I thought it looked good.

'Yes, no, it's fine. It's just...we don't normally do it like that. Or that quickly.'

It wasn't quite a compliment and I wasn't sure what had upset him – the fact I'd altered his system or that I'd worked so fast.

'Sorry, I'll change it if you tell me how,' I said.

'No, don't be silly. It's fine. It's good. Um, I was just going to say, do you want a bacon bap? Mark always does us one first thing.'

'That's so kind of you, but no, thank you, I'm fine. I already had breakfast.'

'Well, if you do want to eat here in future, you know, feel free. And you can have lunch, of course.'

He was nervous again, giving me a tight smile, using those chopped up phrases.

'Thanks,' I said and reached up with a napkin to wipe a smear of ketchup from his chin. Boss or not, his nerves brought out the mother in me.

He blushed and took the napkin from me, using it to scrub at the place I'd touched.

'I only want to make sure everything looks perfect for the customers,' I said in the voice I used to put on to encourage James to finish food of which he wasn't fond.

'Perfect. Of course,' Andy said and went to the door to turn the 'closed' sign to 'open'.

The morning passed more quickly than I've ever known. I took the breakfast orders – takeaway sandwiches and tea for builders, plated fry-ups for those in no hurry to get to work. I fastened orders to the board in the kitchen for Mark to know what to cook next and took turns with Andy to deliver the plates Mark prepared. From the fridge behind the counter I selected drinks, pulling against the suck of the seal to open the heavy door and closing it carefully to avoid disturbing customers with its slam. I flipped the lids from bottles of fizzy drinks with a confident flick of my wrist remembered from my days at the pub, and poured carefully around clinking ice cubes to control the foam as I filled glasses and added straws for the children.

'Got to show you how to work this thing,' Andy said over a hiss of steam from the coffee machine.

As predicted, we did get a quiet spell and I zoomed round and fixed up all the tables to Andy's blinked amazement.

'Tracey would have needed reminding,' he said as he bent to wipe fingermarks from the glass fronted counter.

'I'm not Tracey,' I replied. I felt like Superwoman.

I took an early lunch perched on a stool in the kitchen and watched Mark chop vegetables, his movements fast and precise.

'Everything going OK, darling?' he asked.

'Just great,' I said. Because it was.

~

CRAIG

I couldn't sleep last night. Too busy thinking about Wolfie. Missing him. Was useless at work all morning too. Gav assumed I'd been out on the lash or scored with some girl. Asked inane questions all day.

'What was she like then, Craig? Bit of a goer? Seeing her again?'

For once I was glad to get into a meeting and away from him. Not that I got an easy ride in the conference room. Not with Amisha giving me evil stares from across the table. I remembered her comment about how loud Gav and I talk and assumed the disapproval was because she'd overheard Gav's teasing.

I couldn't exactly tell either of them the truth. I'm not sure what's happening with Wolfie and Julia myself. Last thing I want is advice from Gav, a man whose longest relationship lasted one week, and only then because the poor girl was trapped in the apartment next to him in Ibiza. I don't want sympathy from Amisha either.

Can't talk to anyone from work. And all the gang I go drinking with are only mates from footie. Not long-standing mates, mates who know things about me and understand me. They're not mates like Trev was. We used to tell each other everything. Bastard. I told him everything. There was one fucking important thing he forgot to tell me.

It must have started while she was still with me. He must've been fucking her then. He wouldn't have believed Wolfie could be his otherwise. He was just as good as me at maths and biology at school.

I get in from work and collapse on my sofa. Mondays are always shit. Work is always crap. No-one wants to be there. Not after a weekend of doing the things they really want to be doing. Bus journey was the usual bollocks. It's raining. And my head is going to explode with all these thoughts and feelings. Stuff I can't process, can't deal with. I need... I need to... I don't fucking know what I need.

I pick up the phone and dial. It's answered on the first ring.

'Hello?' she says. The tentative voice is so familiar it breaks my heart.

'Hi, Mum. Are you busy? I was thinking of popping over.'

~

The house is warm when I let myself in. I leave my wet coat in the hall, kick off my shoes and push open the living room door. She hasn't heard me come in. She's glued to EastEnders, Alfie Moon's head larger than life size on the 37 inch flatscreen. A Christmas present from me. A present she insisted was too much, not necessary for her, not when there's only her to watch it. A present she loves. I've seen her stroke it when she turns it off. Fetch a duster if there's the slightest hint of a mark on the screen. All because the lady loves EastEnders.

The dramatic end comes, the drum beats and the credits roll.

'Hi, Mum.'

'Craig,' she says and turns to me with a smile. 'Have you had your tea?'

It's a loop too far on the emotional rollercoaster. My throat closes up. My eyes are wet. I can't answer.

'Craig? What is it, darling?'

I slump onto the sofa. It's too soft, the cushions take you prisoner. I can't bear to watch as Mum inches her way forward in her armchair. She tries once, twice to get her arthritic knees to obey, to let her stand. A movement I've watched a million times. She won't accept a helping hand.

So I don't watch. I stare straight ahead at the gas fire, its flames turned down low, the swirls of the textured wall paper, the framed photos of me fixed to the chimney breast. Me in a mortarboard, graduating with a grin. Me in my footie kit, holding a trophy I can't remember winning. Me, over and over and now I know how to tell her.

'Mum,' I say as she manages to find her feet. 'I've fallen in love.'

CHAPTER SEVEN

CRAIG

I guess the thing about becoming a grandparent is that it can't be anything but good news. It won't be you having to do the hard work this time. It won't be you who'll be short of cash because the kid can't go without. And it won't be you taking responsibility. No, it's me who's got to get used to that idea.

Of course Mum was pleased. Once we'd got over the initial confusion where she thought I was telling her I was gay. Maybe 'I've fallen in love. I can't wait for you to meet him,' wasn't quite as clear as it sounded in my head. She's definitely watching too many soaps. I've taken literally tens of girlfriends home to meet her. I have given no-one any cause to think I might be gay.

'No, Mum,' I said. 'I haven't got a boyfriend, I've got a son. He's called Wolfie, he's a year and a half old. I've only just found out about him, but he's great. I know you're going to love him too.'

She went quiet. I'm not sure how the shock of discovering you're a grandparent ranks alongside thinking your son's gay. I showed her the snaps on my mobile of Wolfie standing in the park, looking at the ducks. I knew he was too cute, that she wouldn't be able to resist him. She's embarrassed me enough times in the supermarket by stopping to tell random kids how adorable they are.

'Tell me what happened,' she said.

So I told her.

'You remember Julia?' I said.

Mum pursed her lips. She had not approved of Julia.

'The silly one? The one you got rid of ages ago?'

I had to break it to her. That I hadn't got rid of Julia, Julia got rid of me. I didn't mention Trev though. Mum still asks about him and I just claim that we're both busy, too busy to keep in touch. She loved Trev. That bastard might have hurt me but I sure as hell wasn't going to let him hurt my Mum.

I explained Julia's mistake, the revelation that I must be Wolfie's dad, my shocked acceptance of this because, well, the boy's face is the image of my baby photo hanging over the fire.

'Tell me about him,' Mum said.

What could I say? He walks a bit, talks a little. I don't know whether he's talented - sporty or smart. I don't know what makes him laugh. All I know is that I looked in his eyes and now I'm in love.

'He's great,' was all I could say.

She hugged me when I left. Harder than in a long time. Her head only comes up to my chest and she rested it there while she squeezed her arms round my waist.

'Gotta go, Mum,' I said.

She unhooked her arms and laid one hand flat against my cheek. 'Be a good dad to him won't you, son?'

I had two buses home and another sleepless night to think about that one. Does she think I know too much about having a bad dad? Mine wasn't bad. Not while he was around.

I drifted through today at work, left on the dot of five and now I'm ringing the doorbell with no decisions made about how I intend to live up to that promise.

Julia's dad answers the door. Instead of stepping back and inviting me in, he steps forward and joins me outside.

'Mr Gibbs,' I say and put out my hand.

I've forgotten his first name. All my mind can supply is a vague recollection of him telling me 'Call me ...,' while giving me a look that said 'I'm watching you, you reprobate.' Guess he never liked me. Makes up for Mum not liking Julia.

He shakes my hand, in both of his. He keeps me anchored to him as he speaks. 'Craig, I have to tell you: I believe my daughter has treated you abominably. I admire you for handling this so well.'

He's a professor at the University and his accent lets him get away with sounding like he's from the 1940s BBC.

'Well, it's been a shock,' I say, 'but you don't need to worry. I'm going to do everything I can for Wolfie.'

'Of course, of course,' he says as he lets me into the house.

So that's how I'm going to be a good dad I realise as Wolfie's voice leads me towards the kitchen. I'm just going to do everything I can. Just everything. No sweat.

~

SUSAN

After three days of unaccustomed hard work, it was no surprise I was too tired to remember my manners this evening. I was warm. Cushioned. Swaying. More asleep than awake. Deeply relaxed. I heard twitters from birds, their wings beat the air and claws scratch the wood of a bird table. From much further away, the urban hum of traffic reached me. Tyre against tarmac. Like white noise, it lulled me.

Then – closer, much closer – the sound of glass against stone. And a swish, as if cotton rubbed against cotton. My ears sent a signal to my sleepy brain to point out that, no matter how weary my body, my eyes should open to assess what was happening.

I dragged myself into wakefullness, fighting my brain free of its cotton wool coating. I blinked to adjust to the bright light and remembered where I was. A swing seat in their garden. I was their guest and the condensation-laced glass placed on the patio by my feet told me my nap hadn't gone unnoticed.

Guilt contracted my throat as I reached for the drink. The clink and bob of the ice and a slice were as refreshing to my eyes and ears as the sharp, tangy liquid was to my thirst. I'll take two minutes to collect myself, I thought, then face the consequences of my lack of etiquette.

Andy and Mark didn't need to invite me to eat with them. And I'd tried to decline the invitation. But my introduction to waitressing had left my feet throbbing, my legs drained of energy, my resolve too weak to resist kindness.

'It's a beautiful evening,' Mark had said, as he turned the sign on the Tall Trees door to read closed and stretched his arms above his head. 'Perfect for drinkies in the garden. You will join us won't you, Susie? Stay for supper.'

No-one calls me Susie. Well, no-one since school. Mark adopted it straight away though and, delivered with his panache, I like it. It makes me sound like someone who's a lot more fun. Not someone who's feeling her age and falling asleep on his patio.

Perhaps slightly more than two minutes passed. I jolted awake again at the sound of the legs of a chair scraping against the patio stone.

'Oh, Andy,' I said, and straightened the glass which had become precariously tipped in my sleepy hand.

'Sorry, did I wake you?'

'No. I'm sorry. That was rude of me. You two are being so kind.'

He shook his head to dismiss my apology and started to peer at the flowerbeds. The spring bulbs had died back and green shoots sprouted on lavender bushes while new leaves and buds filled out the rose bushes. It was an attractive combination of disarray and new growth. Nothing like my old garden where Pete had insisted on stripes rolled into the lawn and a barricade of conifers around us which he trimmed twice a year to his exact specification.

Andy put the plate he was holding down on the patio. It looked like a side dish of vegetables – some carrot, a cabbage leaf, slices of courgette.

'It's so peaceful here, so comfortable. The birdsong, the sun on my face – and I'm exhausted. Guess I'm not used to the working life.' I was gabbling, but he wasn't even trying to keep up his end of the conversation. He just forward and craned his neck to look at the shrubs. 'And I'd hate you to think I'm the kind of guest who turns up empty handed. I mean, normally I'd bring wine or chocolates or something if I'd been invited to dinner.'

'It's OK,' he said, and turned to look at me. 'Mark did practically kidnap you.'

'He's not an easy man to say no to.' I smiled my relief that Andy was finally making an effort. 'Have the two of you lived here long?'

'No. Well, Mark has. I moved in a couple of years ago.'

'How lovely,' I said. I'd have guessed the two of them had been together longer. 'Well, it's a beautiful house and this patio is perfect – a complete sun-trap.'

The house hadn't actually looked much from the front. A Victorian end of terrace on a cramped road near the café. Once inside though, it stretched down a long hallway – front room, back room, kitchen and out to the garden.

White gloss paint highlighted original features and the walls wore careful décor in warm colours. It was tidy and clean and not what I'd expected from two men living together. It certainly couldn't be mistaken for a family home.

'Ah, here he is,' Andy said.

I turned to look but Mark hadn't appeared. Andy had taken his plate of vegetables to a hydrangea that was flopping on to the far corner of the patio, its flowerheads preparing to burst open. He took a piece of carrot from the plate and held it out as a tortoise shuffled from the shade of the leaves.

'Oh. I did wonder what you were doing.' I was relieved he wasn't quite as mad as his behaviour had suggested.

Andy rubbed the tortoise's scaly head as it munched the carrot. 'Come and say hi to Nigel.'

I got out of the swing seat, with difficulty, and bent down to look at the crepey neck sticking out of the ridged and patterned shell.

'Sweet. Have you had him long?'

'Oh, we don't own him. If anything, he owns this garden. Here - d'you want to feed him something?'

'How do you mean?' I asked and offered the cabbage leaf towards Nigel's beaky lips.

'He belongs to the house. Mark inherited him when he moved in, and the people before said they'd been here thirty years and Nigel pre-dated them.'

'Wow, a sitting tenant. Well, I'm pleased to meet you, Nigel.'

He was ignoring the leaf and taking more interest in the soft cream leather of my shoe.

'Doubt that was always his name but as he pays no attention to anything you say anyway, I guess it doesn't matter,' Andy said, distracting Nigel with another carrot stick. 'Anyway, if you've woken up fully, Mark should have something for us to eat.'

'I feel so guilty. He spends all day in the kitchen. The two of you must come to eat with me one day. Although, I don't have a sunny patio or a resident tortoise to offer you.'

'Don't worry about it. Mark loves food. Always has. Eating it, cooking it, talking about it. Put him in a kitchen and he's as happy as – well, a tortoise in the sun.'

~

CRAIG

I rip off my football boots and hurl them against the changing room wall. The spikes leave a satisfying

78

scratch in the paintwork. I've probably lost myself my place on the football team. I'm one of the most committed players for fuck's sake. There every week, always available for matches, reliable in defence of the left wing. So why the shitting hell have I just told the captain to go fuck himself and been thrown off the pitch?

OK, it's not much - Wednesday night training, Saturday morning five a side. Not exactly La Liga. But it was my routine. My regular mid-week stress busting exercise. My Saturday reason to get up despite the hangover. And yes, Nick has always been a wanker. Fancies himself as a superstar striker and the rest of us as his slaves. But I have always put the team first and resisted the huge temptation to share my opinion of him publicly. Until today.

It's not like work was a breeze either. Amisha's getting stuck into her new job which, thanks to a 'reshuffle', has me and Gav reporting directly to her. And I see now all too clearly why she got the job. She has Big fucking Ideas. Ideas that she is not hesitating to put into action. Ideas which are about to see me spend three days with her at some crappy conference - manning a stand, pressing flesh, charming new customers. I am part of marketing, not sales. I am not a sales stand dolly.

Does she not understand that business men go to these shows to have the promotions girls chat them up? Any business that's done is incidental.

Yeah, OK, Amisha will be able to schmooze the potential clients, charm them with those big eyes and glossy hair and maybe negotiate some deals while she's at it. No one'll want to talk to me. Not unless I catch them off guard, distract them with talking about sport or something. Ask them if they play football. Ha!

Worse still, I'll have to stay in the hotel with her for two nights. Not like she's going to want to go out on the lash is it? She'll probably want to 'go for a meal' and 'get an early night'. Fucking fantastic.

So I am not in the right frame of mind to put up with Nick condescending to me because I missed a couple of passes. I did not want to watch him sodding about, showboating up the pitch in his gold coloured boots like he's fucking Ronaldo or something. Football training is meant to be about maintaining your fitness, practising skills, gelling as a team before Saturday's match. It is not meant to be about that wanker pulling a dangerous tackle on me then demonstrating his celebration dance when he's lucky enough to dodge Smithy in goal too.

I was right to put him straight about it. Probably only said what the rest of the team were thinking. Smithy definitely agreed with me.

'Nick,' I said, 'you are the biggest wanker I have ever had the bad fucking luck to share a team with.'

'Fuck off, loser,' was his eloquent response.

I had taken hold of his shirt at that point. I was not going to let the bastard turn his back on me. I was not finished making my point.

'No, Nick, you're the loser. You're the embarrassment to this team. You are an arrogant fuckwit.'

I think I presented a reasoned argument.

'No, Craig, I'm the reason this team is second in the league.'

Admittedly his response had some truth in it. You can't argue with the numbers and it was goal difference keeping us above the third placed team and in line for promotion. No excuse for being an arrogant fuckwit though.

If he hadn't at that point attempted to remove my hand from his shirt with a dismissive flick of the wrist, I probably wouldn't have actually punched him. Unfortunately he did. So I did.

Of course I'm regretting it now. I'm twenty five, not five. I deserved to be sent off the pitch. I assumed I was not welcome at the post-training beers. It is quite clear to me why I am not in the squad for Saturday's match.

Four years I've been in that team and this is the first Saturday I haven't made the squad. Haven't missed many Wednesday night beers after training either. Wonder if Smithy'll still call me to go drinking on Friday?

If I'm honest it's not about football. Not about conferences or even Amisha pulling rank. It's about Wolfie. And Julia and Trev and the whole fucking mess.

Most of last night was brilliant. Wolfie gave me a huge gummy grin when he saw me. Those gappy teeth just break my heart.

Julia was getting him ready for his bath when I got there. He saw me, recognised me and offered me his red boat. We had a great game of splashing each other with the bath toys, until he started to get cold and screamed.

He let me wrap him in a towel and hug him warm again though. Then Julia showed me the required skills for nappy changing and Wolfie sat on my knee while we looked at a book about a puppy sniffing things. It was actually funny. I guess you need to be in a toddler's company for that kind of thing.

Julia was trying to keep her distance, let me have some time with Wolfie I guess, but she kept putting her head round the door and reminding me not to get him excited before bedtime. I got a night, night kiss and cuddle from him and let her put him down.

Afterwards, Julia and I talked. We were in the room that used to be her mum's interior designed kitchen-diner. It looked like someone had fly-tipped a mound of coloured plastic over the floor.

Julia started to tidy up the chaos Wolfie had created, chucking the bits and pieces of his toys and games randomly into boxes.

'Well, Craig. Have you decided what you want to do?'

Everything about her seemed tired, from the slowness of her movements to the whine in her voice. If she was amp'ing it up for me, she didn't need to. I had decided.

'I want to be involved. I want to be a proper dad to him. I want to see him two or three times a week and we'll agree how much money I should give you towards supporting him.'

'Good. Thank you. I know it's been completely rubbish for you, finding out like this, but I know you won't regret anything about Wolfie. He really is wonderful, even if, well, it's not ideal is it?'

'No, but we'll make the best of it. He deserves that.' I was so mature I could've been vintage Cheddar. 'Just one thing, Julia, his name: why the fuck did you call him Wolfgang?'

She stopped packing plastic into boxes. She stood up, very slowly and turned to face me. She almost made eye contact but couldn't hold it.

'Don't you remember, Craig?' she said. 'There's at least one other person you know called Wolfgang. Trev named him after his dad.'

~

SUSAN

My body is not used to long hours of constant activity and I was ready for my day off. I've enjoyed the work though and, while I don't have much to compare them against, Mark and Andy are great bosses. Even when I struggled to get the hang of operating the coffee machine, Andy didn't lose his temper as Pete would have done.

The machine made me nervous. It looks so aggressive: highly polished chrome, spitting steam and macho engineering. But Andy was patient about showing me how to tamp down the coffee grounds, adjust the pressure and steam the milk correctly. The loud rattle of the beans grinding set me on edge, but he was so supportive. He thought up different ways to explain the functions to me and suggested methods by which I could remember what went into each type of drink. He made sure I got into the routine of checking the temperature and wiping the steam spout every time I removed the milk jug. It felt as if he might be a friend I could confide in. I almost mentioned the contrast.

I didn't though. I didn't start a sentence with the words 'My husband…' Even after all my recent successes, everything I've achieved that I didn't think I could, that is one thing I'm really proud of. I did not acknowledge Pete. The achievement of my learning to operate the coffee machine was in no way publicly connected with any reference to Pete. It's my triumph. It doesn't matter to Andy that he's a better man than Pete. Why should it? Of course he's a better man.

Maybe he's not so rich, or tall. But in every way that actually matters Andy is superior. I'd describe him as 'nice' but Craig would tell me off. He's certainly nice-looking; it's obvious what attracted Mark to him.

It's also obvious what first attracted me to Pete. I've always been nervous, ready for criticism: convinced that anything I'd done, I must have done wrong. So of course confidence was going to be the quality I most admired in others. Right from the first time.

My first kiss 1983

I can't believe it's finally happened. After weeks of sitting behind Ian in maths lessons, gazing at the back of his head, feeling wobbly in my stomach whenever I heard his voice answering a question and not daring to actually speak to him – he spoke to me! Tonight, at the Hallowe'en disco, he spoke to me, danced with me under the flashing lights and then, outside in the dark – he snogged me!

I want to remember every second of it. His breath was warm on my face and he smelt of cigarettes. My hands were on his waist and his body was slim and firm. He was kissing me normally to start with but then he wriggled his tongue in between my lips. I didn't know whether to be shocked or delighted! It was exciting, even if the taste of the ciggies made me feel a bit sick. And he was squeezing my right boob as well. It felt like it went on for about half an hour but I guess it can only have been a few minutes. He let go, said 'Night then' and walked back to his mates. They were all giggling and a few of them patted his back and shook his hand. What if he's always fancied me too? I don't know what I'll do when I see him after half term.

What a fool I was. It didn't take long to discover that actually Ian's mates had dared him to snog me. I was the one they all laughed about, 'Silly little Susan - with her obvious crush on Ian. Like he'd ever look at her!' He was good enough to put me straight about it himself. I suppose he got fed up of me trailing after him, trying to talk to him. So he stopped one day, in the middle of the school playground, and said, 'It was a joke, Susan. A stupid joke. I'm not interested in you – now stop following me around.'

I don't know if there's a better way to destroy a teenager's fragile self esteem. I certainly withdrew completely during those last couple of years at school. I didn't really talk to any of the girls who'd been my friends before then, didn't go out, did just enough work to not draw any attention from the teachers. I stayed at home and filled the role my parents had cast me in: pathetic Susan, can't be trusted to do anything except cook. And I assumed that those confident, charismatic men I couldn't help admiring would only ever be a fantasy part of my life. I never believed that one of them could be seriously interested in me.

So when I met Pete, five years down the line, of course I was attracted to him. And, when it actually seemed his interest in me was sincere, I was flattered. Blind to the fact that while the interest may have been sincere, his intentions weren't. He'd chosen his prey well. I gave in immediately to his domination. I stuck to the letter of the laws he laid down, never questioned his decisions. I believed he was right to have me stay home and wait on him and James, that I couldn't want anything more. Even when it was apparent that his life was more interesting, I didn't complain. Even when I suspected there were other women, I thought myself fortunate. Until James left for university and I began to wonder if that was really the case.

The solicitor explained the complexities of divorce to me last week. How, if both parties agreed and were separated for two years, the actual divorce was a straightforward formality. If there was any hurry, dispute or contention however, things could be complicated, drawn out, and expensive. I'd made another appointment to see her this afternoon and knew that, before I could instruct her on how to proceed, I needed to speak to Pete.

I guessed he'd be in. Since he decided he could afford his early retirement at the start of the year, the only time he leaves the house for long periods is to play golf, and none of his golf buddies are free on Thursdays. He's too young to have taken the decision that the offer he'd received for his electronics business was too good to turn down; that rather than continue in an advisory capacity – or find an alternative job – he'd much rather stay at home and enjoy the fruits of his labours.

I dialled the number. I won't store it in my new mobile phone. It's not a number I intend to call often. Even keying in the sequence of digits was strange. The number itself is indelible in my memory, but isn't one I've often dialled. I was always the one at the receiving end, picking up the phone to hear why Pete would not be returning home at the time he'd been expected. Replacing the receiver while wondering how much of the excuse he'd given was the truth.

My finger hesitated over the green call button. I was standing in my flat, looking out at the road below. The tight, pale buds on the trees are unfolding to reveal dark leaves and soon they'll screen my view of the litter strewn pavement. Then my view will be of greenery again, just as it was back in Alcester where the kitchen window looked out to the wide garden: a vista of shades of green punctuated by regular splashes of floral colour.

Of course I was always in the kitchen so that was my view. I tried to guess where Pete would be at that moment. Probably the sitting room, in prime position for a view of the TV.

I wondered whether the room would be tidy, or whether in my short absence it would already have become as dishevelled as the pavement below me. From James's description, his Dad had gone into meltdown. As I've never known Pete lose control to any significant extent, I didn't know how to prepare myself for the conversation.

I pressed the green button. There was a pause while the line connected and then the echo of the ring at the other end sounded back to my ear. It rang five times before the answer phone clicked into action. Pete's voice spoke to me, the message recorded years ago, the tone of voice full of assurance that all was well in his world.

'Thanks for ringing. No-one can take your call at the moment so why not leave us a message – someone might call you back!'

I paused after the beep. It seemed wrong to speak to that ghost of Pete from the past. On the other hand, I wanted to speak to Pete now. If he was there and using the machine to screen calls, I wanted him to know it was me.

'Pete, it's Susan,' I said, still feeling that need to identify myself. 'There's something I wanted to…'

The phone was snatched up and Pete spoke, 'Susan, where are you? What the hell do you think you're playing at?'

I had hoped the worst of his anger would have passed by now. That I wouldn't have to deal with the rage, only the recriminations.

'Susan? Susan? Are you still there?'

His voice had changed. After the initial bluster, I could hear it now, the crack in his confidence.

'Yes. I'm here, it's me. I want to talk about what we're going to do.'

'I'll change,' he said, speaking fast. 'I know, I understand I haven't been the husband you deserved. But now I've stopped work I'll be here, don't you see? We'll be together like we always should've been.'

I didn't know how to respond. I'd already told him that wasn't what I wanted. I had already done the hurtful bit, the rejection, when I left. Hadn't he been listening? Did he think I was just being dramatic? I am not the dramatic type. Nor am I vicious. I couldn't keep saying it, over and over – hurting him again and again. I couldn't say that us having more time together sounded like torture to me. But this needed to be clear. I knew what I was doing. I sat down.

'Stop it. Stop saying things will be OK for us. Things haven't been OK for a long time and I don't believe they can change. I've left you. I don't want to be married to you any more. I want a divorce.'

'We'll get counselling,' he pleaded. 'We'll go to Relate. I'll promise you anything, Susan. I want you back.'

'You promised me the world when you married me. It's taken until now for me to realise how much of the world you've kept from me. Counselling would be pointless because I don't want to be married to you any more.'

Being that tough was horrible. My free hand was clenched in my lap, beating against my thigh as I deliberately caused him pain. I wouldn't have been able to keep it up but it didn't matter because his pleading swung back to anger so fast I suspected him of putting on an act.

'Fine,' he spat. 'Let's forget it all. We'll throw 20 years of marriage in the bin. You can have your divorce but you needn't think you'll get anything from me. It's my money that's paid for everything. If you took cash from the joint account to fund your running away I'll have it all back and more.'

I knew there was no point talking to him about it, the solicitor had advised me to try and keep things calm.

'I didn't take any of your money. I used my own.'

'Your own? Where'd you get that from? You never had any money.'

I didn't want to get drawn further in to the argument, so I just said, 'I'm seeing a solicitor. You'll hear from her soon.'

I pressed the red button and put the phone back in my handbag. As it slid into place in the inner pocket designed to hold it, the case clinked against something metal: the abandoned wedding ring I'd stowed there as I rode in the van towards Birmingham.

CHAPTER EIGHT

SUSAN

After my conversation with Pete, I packed a sandwich and caught the bus even though it was hours too early for my appointment. I had to get out of the flat. As I waited at the bus stop I noticed that the green leaves outside my window are the only soft thing in this landscape.

Across the road, the once fancy brickwork of the derelict factory is crumbling. The traffic is constant, as though everyone needs to be somewhere else. Advertising hoardings praise telephone companies or tempt with the glamour of alcohol.

The bus carried me to the city centre and I got off at the Bullring markets. The studded Selfridges building loomed above me like a monster slug as I fought my way past stalls piled high with international fruit and veg. I climbed upwards past the plate glass of shops towards the statue of the bull: one hoof raised, nostrils flared and brows taut. The adopted icon of this city shows no fear. The statue captures aggression, power, an untameable spirit. It does not appeal to me.

Shoppers milled past, laden with bags. They chattered on mobiles and cut across my path as though I were in the way: an irritation. They were possessed and confident. Not like me.

I walked on through the city up towards the stone grandeur of the civic buildings. The morning's cloud was burning off into one of those glorious days the weather can deliver in late spring, when people are tricked into thinking summer's arrived. I climbed broad steps already collecting sunbathers, towards the smooth architecture of the Council House and the faux weathered columns of the Town Hall, past Queen Victoria looking down her nose while her cloak draped her pedestal. Her statue doesn't appeal to me either.

My energy was defeated before I could climb further steps up to the once futuristic Central Library. Craig had pointed me in its direction when I'd asked, certain I'd find any book or dvd I needed there: something factual about divorce or entertainment to distract me.

My mind was too full of it right then, that, and the reality of my financial situation. I hadn't admitted to Pete that my running away money had been a bequest from a forgotten great aunt who died last year. Five thousand secret pounds which had been sitting in a newly opened account while I gathered courage and laid plans to leave. I didn't want to count how little was left after the deposit and first month's rent on the flat, the van hire and new clothes were paid for. So I lost myself in the crowd colonising the steps to eat their lunch. I chose a spot away from the middle, behind the fountain, near to a statue of a forgotten politician. The sculptor had caught him down from his pedestal, relaxing on the steps with the general public. A lone bronze figure, he sat among the neon vests of workmen rubbing shoulders with office staff kicking off high heels or loosening ties.

I perched on a step near the statue's feet and watched as a crocodile of school girls wandered through the square, their teacher snapping at the front. The girls were made identical by their neatly tied headscarves and long black robes; the garments designed to repel observation drew my eyes towards them. I turned my face to the sun and listened to the thwack of skateboarders taking jumps from the lower steps, interrupted by clock tower bells chiming quarter hours.

Bronze pages from the politician's speech were strewn about the steps there, abandoned as if he knew the city would one day favour a bull over his ideals. *'Votes for all'*, declared one sheet. Well, I was with him on that one. Everyone's opinion counts for something, even mine. *'Demand for change'*, I agreed with that too. Change is in fashion for me right now. *'Full employment'*. I smiled, this speech could have been written to inspire me, until I got to *'Prosperity restored'*. Well, as I perched there, Birmingham's prosperity didn't seem to be in doubt, I could almost feel the heat generated by chip and pin terminals as the crowd bought its lunch or splashed out on treats.

For me though, prosperity was now endangered. If Pete did manage to deny me any share in his money or possessions, then wealth would be in short supply. I'd been frittering my lump sum; not planning long term. If I really had to support myself from scratch then I wouldn't be able to continue working at Tall Trees for minimum wage. I needed to find out about benefits, tax credits, so many things which were alien to my former pampered existence. It couldn't be fair to deny me a share of the money could it? My work in our home was worth something. It was the only job he'd allowed me.

I hadn't permitted myself to cry after I spoke to Pete. Leaving the flat immediately for a public place had been a tactic to keep me from brooding and remorse. Craving sympathy, my first instinct had been to call James. I hate that he thinks I'm the baddie in this drama and there's no one else who might understand. I put the phone away in my handbag though. The fact is that he hasn't tried to call me now he has my number. He has already taken his father's side. I rewrapped the sandwich I'd only nibbled at and braced myself to see the solicitor.

~

CRAIG

I was actually glad when Steve turned up at my desk yesterday and asked me if I wanted to play for his cricket team today. I didn't care that Gav immediately started with the jibes, sighing deeply and shaking his head while he said, 'Oh dearie, dearie me, Craig. First you're flirting with the boss, now you're hanging with the geeks. Is it that you want to become a corporate clone?'

I think my response of, 'Fuck off, wanker' put him straight. If he could see me now though, in the whites I've borrowed from Steve which are about an inch too short in the leg and several inches too narrow in the chest, I would have to agree with him that I do in fact look like a geek. I abandon the shirt and stick to my own plain white T and head off for a chat with the skipper.

My recent interview experience ought to have left me well able to present my cricketing abilities to him in a positive light. Perhaps my recent interview disappointment has sapped some of my confidence though.

'What's your skill level?' he asks.

I mumble something like 'I used to bat OK sometimes.' Luckily, he just seems glad we've got eleven men out.

He wins the toss and chooses to bat. Steve's one of the openers so I take a seat on a shady bench in front of the pavilion and have a chat to one of the other guys on the team. He's called Adam, he's probably ten years older than me, and he has a small boy with him.

'Your son?' I ask and smile at the little lad as he conducts an imaginary air fight between the two toy planes he's holding.

'Yeah, that's Sammy. He likes coming down here, but it's a long day for him.'

I nod. It's going to be a long day for me too, what with the hangover from last night's home alone drinking session. I am not looking forward to standing out on the square in the bright sun.

'I only see him alternate weekends. Probably won't be able to play every match this season, isn't really fair to drag him down here every time.'

I turn to Adam with interest. This man knows stuff I need to know. I still haven't told anyone but Mum and Susan about Wolfie. There is the possibility that if Steve hears the gossip, it'll be all round the office on Monday. But, on Monday, I'm going to the convention in London with Amisha. I wouldn't have to witness the vultures circling.

'I've got a son,' I say. It all pours out of me. This Adam bloke, who doesn't know me from, well, Adam, gets the full story: the cheating girlfriend, the bastard friend, the two year silence, the announcement of Wolfie. Adam raises his eyebrows when I tell him Wolfie's name. When I explain the circumstances of the origin of the name, his eyebrows go into orbit.

'God. You poor bastard,' he says.

I bat ineptly, adding a huge two runs to our total before being bowled.

I redeem myself a little after tea, taking a stonking catch and stopping a couple of boundaries. When our defeat has been conceded, Adam buys me a pint in the clubhouse bar.

'Look, mate,' he says. 'It won't be all bad you know. Once you and Wolfie get to know each other I bet you're going to love having a son. But what you really need to do is get things straight with his mum.'

'Hmm,' I say. The whole Wolfie distraction has meant I've had no time to decide how I feel about having Julia around again.

'Take my number. Give me a call sometime and we'll get together with the lads. Sometimes it's hard to find something to do with them, specially if it's raining. You don't want to end up as a sad dad down McDonald's every Sunday.'

He pats my back and wanders off.

Steve has overheard the conversation. 'Didn't know you had a kid, Craig.'

'No, it's new news to a lot of people.'

There. It's done. The water cooler gossip can flow.

CHAPTER NINE

SUSAN

This morning I posted the forms the solicitor had given me. It's all so official. The dry facts and details of our marriage listed out: who did things, who earned what, whose name is on which documents.

I actually quite enjoyed the ordered and rational approach: stripping out all the emotion and concentrating on bare facts in clear black ink on crisp white paper. My future is in her hands now. If she can't get me a good settlement, I'll have to rethink my plans.

Mark and Andy were already at Tall Trees when I arrived, both leaning against the counter eating their bacon baps. Mark unlatched the door to let me in.

'Well, Susie, you've been with us a week now and Andy and I were discussing whether or not to make you permanent.'

I couldn't tell from the look on his face whether he was teasing me. My panic about what I'd do if they did ask me to leave must have shown because Andy butted in, 'What Mark means to say is that we'd like to make you a permanent member of the team. That is, if you're happy to stay on.'

I could have hugged him, but restrained the impulse and said 'I'd love to,' while giving him a huge smile. Even that made him blush.

'Great stuff,' said Mark. 'Andy'll sort out the paperwork. We probably need to send you on a food hygiene course – that's simple enough. We'll even work out if we can offer you a teeny bit of a raise. God knows, you deserve it.'

I think I outperformed myself preparing the tables after that incentive. And I found myself turning on the charm for the customers. I flirted with the builders as I poured their tea. I cajoled babies into behaving while their mums drank coffee. I chatted to Mr Bates who comes in every day. Mark and Andy didn't know his name, but I've got various bits and bobs of his life story out of him over the last week and always remember to ask about his daughter and how he's feeling. He never wants Andy to serve him anymore. Andy even confided that Mr Bates had complained about my absence on my day off.

'I could work six days a week like you and Mark, you know.'

'No, you mustn't,' he replied. 'Well, not unless we have an emergency or something. Running this business was our stupid idea. We should be the ones to wear ourselves out.'

Today was exhausting. The weekend brought in extra customers who'd been out shopping, their bags cluttering the spaces between and under tables and creating an obstacle course for me.

'Perhaps this sunshine's bringing everyone out for a good time,' Mark mused as I helped him dry up at the end of the day. 'I am well and truly overheated.

I'm going home for a cool shower and an even colder beer.' He took off his apron, ran his hands through his hair, called 'Laters' to Andy and left by the back door.

'See you Monday then,' I said to Andy as he set the burglar alarm and locked the front door behind us.

'Actually, I'll come your way,' he replied and walked with me towards the High Street. 'I could do with a walk to stretch my legs a bit. Fresh air, you know.'

'Sounds good.'

'Oh, um, would you like to join me?'

'Gosh, no,' I replied. 'I wouldn't want to intrude. You carry on.'

'No, really. I'd, um, like you to come.'

His anxiety was appealing. After all those years with domineering Pete, it was so refreshing to be in the company of a man who didn't just assume things.

'That would be lovely then, thank you. Where are we going?'

He'd turned down the High Street towards the entrance of the park I'd noticed from the bus. A sign named it as Highbury Park.

'It used to be the grounds of Highbury Hall,' Andy said, confident again while he was talking about facts he was sure of. 'The best bit is the arboretum, down the bottom – are you OK to walk that far?'

I nodded and we followed a broad path cut through an area of woodland along a line of tall, straight, shimmering poplars which marked the boundary of the park. Their bark was folded into creases like comfortably wrinkled skin. After a few minutes, we reached a level, lawned area where people sunbathed, played football or threw toys for dogs to chase. Birds were competing to drown each other out with rapid chirps and chatter.

'Popular spot,' I said.

Andy didn't reply. I realised conversation was not required and kept quiet as we walked on past a duck pond where mallards and moor hens drifted across rather murky water. There were fewer people as we got further from the High Street and I caught snatches of birdsong like overheard conversations, similar to how I picked up snippets of what the customers were talking about at their tables in Tall Trees. One bird warbled as if she were a soprano warming up with arpeggios until the interjection of a crow's rough caw interrupted her. The leaves on the trees standing in clumps or groves along the path murmured in the wind, as if they had nothing important to discuss. The sensation of fresh air on my face was refreshing after a day cooped inside the warm café, like rinsing my skin with a cleansing tonic.

'Here we are,' Andy said after ten minutes or so.

The area we'd entered was a stretch of lawn punctuated with a variety of mature trees: pines in differing shades of green grouped together in an area beyond which the tall, deciduous trees were coming into leaf. The spacing between them varied, with some clustered and others scattered, making the landscape seem wild rather than formal. Andy led the way to a noticeboard and showed me a map listing all the latin names. An avenue of Sequoiadendrom Giganteum Wellingtonia loomed ahead of us, currently only a fraction of their final height if the facts presented were to be believed.

'This is wonderful,' I said as I took in the range of evergreen hues from greyish sage to blueish purple. 'I would never have believed I'd find something like this right in the city.'

He turned and treated me to that nice smile. 'Oh, Birmingham's full of surprises like this. Lots of pockets of secret greenery.'

'Really? Wow. Where I live it's so relentlessly urban, I hadn't imagined it could be like this.' There was some traffic noise from a nearby road, but the birdsong here was slower, calmer – as if the influence of the trees was soothing everyone.

'You're up the Moseley Road, aren't you? Any reason you chose there?'

'The price,' I said and my bluntness made him blush again. 'No, don't worry. I'm new to Birmingham. I didn't know where I wanted to be really. Maybe I'll move in the future.'

'I see,' he said.

If he wanted to ask more, he held his tongue instead. Even after a week of working together, and the lovely evening round at their house, I hadn't discussed many personal details with Mark and Andy. They'd both been incredibly friendly, but without prying. Perhaps they were waiting for me to volunteer details. In any case, we'd stuck to general chat about food, weather, the customers. It wasn't as if my sparsely completed application form had provided much detail either, although I had listed my name as Mrs Susan Clarke.

Andy and I wandered over to a bench which was still catching some sun and sat back, admiring the trees. Only a gentle breeze sighed through the pine needles, the boughs bowing under their weight, the dipping motion mesmerising. The trees cast patches of shade across the grass so that, from our position in full sun, my vision of what was happening around me was obscured.

'If you tell Mark I brought you here, he'll groan.'

'Not his type of thing then?'

'Not at all. Relentlessly urban suits him perfectly. He calls me a tree-hugger.'

'Charming. Well I haven't seen you actually hug any trees, so I'll fight your cause with him.'

'Thanks, but I don't think you'll change his mind.'

He said it with fond resignation; they were clearly so comfortable with each other that this space for different interests was a good thing, not a threat. I didn't reply.

The knowledge that there was no way Pete would ever have been happy to let me go off and enjoy a hobby or anything without him reinforced my certainty that I was doing the right thing. We sat in silence for a while listening to the quiet rattle of pine needles before Andy spoke, his voice soft, 'Still painful, then?'

'What?' I asked, no clue what he was talking about.

'Third finger, left hand. You keep scratching that groove where your wedding ring used to be.'

'Oh,' I said, immediately stopping my right hand from scratching at the unmistakeable notch worn into that finger by the ring.

'Don't worry,' he said. 'I know all about the symptoms of being married too long. It will pass.'

'You're divorced?' There was perhaps slightly more surprise in my voice than good manners would have allowed.

'Yeah, is it that unbelievable that someone would marry me?' His tone was just on the jovial side of offended but I had to make amends.

'Of course not, no. I just, um, I just didn't know.' I'd become the one sounding anxious. It wasn't clear if he'd been married to a woman before he'd come out as gay, or if it had been a civil partnership with another man. I certainly didn't want to ask such a personal question, or say anything mentioning gender which he might think rude. He and Mark were such a good match I'd assumed they'd been together ages, so I shut up.

'Not the kind of fact you trot out on first meeting someone, is it?' he said.

His voice was kind and I smiled my gratitude at him. 'No. I'm still coming to terms with it all myself. I'm not actually divorced yet.'

'I see,' he said, nodding as he stood up and stretched. 'Time to get moving again.'

He led the way through the corridor formed by the line of sequoias, the trees only an arms' breadth apart. I trailed my fingers through the needles on the branches to either side and registered the strange lightness of that hand which was no longer laden with the gold band. My eyes had suggested the texture of the foliage would be soft, like fur, but it was sharp, rough and oily to the touch. I drew my hands back to my side.

When we returned to the High Street, Andy waited with me at the bus stop until he saw the 50 approaching. 'If you want to talk about it, you can you know.'

I thanked him and got on the bus. He stood and watched until it pulled away. I chose a seat and laid my resin-scented hands in my lap. I deliberately didn't scratch at the phantom wedding ring.

~

102

CRAIG

Sunday morning and I'm picking Wolfie up to take him to meet my mum. This is almost guaranteed to be a fucking nightmare.

Julia's mum lets me in. 'Hello, Craig. It's nice to see you again.'

Yeah, right, I think, 'cos it isn't like you used to hate me, convinced I'd led your precious daughter astray. She was extremely familiar with drink and drugs before I met her, thank you very much. What I actually say is, 'Good to see you too, Mrs Gibbs.'

God, I wish I could remember these people's names. I sound like a child calling them Mr and Mrs Gibbs.

'Call me Wendy. We are going to be seeing rather a lot of each other again, after all.'

Yeah, wonderful, can't wait.

'Thanks for making me welcome. Is Wolfie ready?'

Oh, I'm on fire with the perfect behaviour thing. Then he appears, clattering down the stairs trailing a stuffed dog.

'Dar!' he says and I scoop him up and squeeze him because I have to get him close. He is so completely gorgeous with his chunks of blond hair sticking up and his eyes shining.

'What's this bruise?' I ask Julia who comes down carrying a bag of Wolfie's supplies. 'He's got a huge lump on his head.'

'Kids fall over, Craig. No drama. He screamed for ten minutes, now he's fine.'

'Why weren't you watching him?' I demand.

'Chill out, Craig. I'm his mum, I know what I'm doing. I'm looking after Wolfie perfectly well. There's no need to be overprotective.'

'She's right,' says Wendy. 'Wolfie's fine. He has to take a few tumbles so he learns what not to do.'

Oh, great, now I'm getting a whole parenting class from this pair of witches.

'Right, we'll be off then. Ready to meet your other nanna, Wolfie?'

He grins at me as Julia attempts to bend his arms into the sleeves of his jacket. She smells good up close. That familiar perfume. And she's washed her hair and put make up on.

'You going out?' I ask.

'Just up to the shops. Call my mobile if you need me.'

She doesn't quite meet my eye. We haven't yet agreed the details of how much I'm going to pay for Wolfie's support. I know she's not working at the moment and decide to keep a sharp eye on how many new clothes she appears in - any money I give for Wolfie I want spent on the lad, not her wardrobe.

Outside, I get Wolfie strapped into the buggy and we head for the bus stop. Selly Park to Cotteridge isn't a long journey but, with the walk at either end, it's going to take the best part of half an hour. I give Mum a quick ring to say we're on the way. She is stupidly delighted to hear from me.

The bus arrives before I've thought through the logistics of getting the buggy on to it. Course I've seen buggies on there before, but I usually walk straight past, or head for upstairs. I don't look at how the parents get the buggy on and into position. Well, I say 'parents', it's usually a woman on her own. I really have to reconsider whether I can afford a car.

I bump Wolfie up on to the platform the driver has lowered for me and manage to get him parked in the buggy and wheelchair bay. I only run over the toes of one woman. I'm pleased with myself, but Wolfie is not. He starts to scream, holding out his arms as if pleading to be allowed out.

'Not just yet, mate,' I say and bend over to pull funny faces which don't entertain him. The other passengers are looking at me. His voice really is impressively loud and I contemplate gagging him somehow before he bursts everyone's eardrums.

Then I remember the stuffed dog Julia had shoved in the tray below his seat. Pulling it out and making it appear by surprise from behind me manages to distract him enough to keep him quiet until we reach our stop.

I reverse the manoeuvre to get the buggy off, even more ineptly this time. The driver is drumming his fingers on the wheel, itching to get going towards his tea break no doubt. Well, sorry mate, I know I should be wearing L plates and will probably never get my licence to drive this buggy, but I'm the only dad he's got. You've got to feel for the lad, haven't you?

I can see Mum watching from the window as we approach her house. It's the most neglected looking one in the terrace, with weeds for a front garden and a broken gutter. I really should do more for her.

She appears at the front door, hands clasped together and beaming. She's dressed up too - lipstick, the lot.

'Well, well, Wolfie,' I whisper as I release him from the buggy. 'Your Nan never makes this much effort for me. Think yourself lucky, lad.'

'Oh, Craig,' Mum says. 'Just look at him.'

I'm not sure I've seen her this happy before. She's beaming at Wolfie, reaching out to touch him, then withdrawing her hand and holding it to her lips. The boy toddles into her sitting room; Mum hobbles after him.

'Good God, Mum. What have you done?' The room looks like it's been transformed into a toy shop.

'Don't blaspheme in front of your son,' Mum tells me. 'All I've done is bought him some toys.'

'Define 'some'. You can't afford all this.'

There's a box full of Duplo bricks that Wolfie has already upended across the carpet, as well as piles of jigsaws, books, a train track and two huge teddy bears.

'I got it all in the charity shop, love. Don't worry, Helen next door put the plastic bits and bobs through her dishwasher and the teddies through the washing machine so they're all clean.'

Hygiene had not been my concern. How could she think it was? She's seen my flat. I don't know the words to express what I'm actually feeling.

'Thanks, Mum,' is the best I can do. I'm nearly crying again. Is this what fatherhood does to a man? Turn him into a fucking cry-baby?

'Don't be daft, love. I wanted to get him something. If he's going to be visiting a lot he needs some toys here. I mean, you can't take him to your place, can you?'

'Er, yeah I can,' I say, but I don't want to be ungrateful so I let it go.

Mum lowers herself onto the edge of the sofa near where Wolfie has started to rummage through the bricks. He turns to face her and displays that heartbreaking gummy grin. That's my boy, you already know how to charm the ladies, don't you?

'Look, Craig,' she says. 'He loves his Lego, just like you did.'

Yeah, thanks, Mum, like I really need more reminders of my inner geek right now. I kneel down to free Wolfie from his coat and give him his cup of juice. He looks into my eyes again as he drinks, almost as if he's asking me 'Am I getting stuff right here, Dad?' Yes, my boy, I think you've got your nanna on side. Nice work.

She's even got child-friendly food in for lunch. I cut Wolfie's mini sausages into chunks that he smears into ketchup and manages to get almost all of it into his mouth. I should thank Helen next door, Mum must have been driving her mad with questions about what she should do to prepare for our visit.

After lunch, I persuade Wolfie to take a nap on the sofa, wrapped in the blanket Mum usually arranges round her knees. I go back to the kitchen where Mum is pouring us some tea.

'He's wonderful, isn't he?' she says.

'Yeah,' I reply and give her a hug. I don't hug her often enough. Right now I'm really glad to have her support.

'Wolfgang's a funny name though, isn't it? Don't know what Julia was thinking of.' She frowns. 'Didn't we know a Wolfgang once?'

I don't reply. I'm hoping her memory won't get there.

'Oh, yes, I remember. Trevor's dad; German fella wasn't he? Not a name you hear much in Birmingham.'

Bingo, Mum. Jackpot. Now I'm definitely going to cry.

CHAPTER TEN

CRAIG

Bollocks. Fuck. Wank. I've overslept. I've got about forty five minutes to get to New Street to meet Amisha for the train. I shave quickly, which means I cut myself in several places. The water in the shower hasn't even heated up by the time I jump out again. I throw shirts, ties, jeans and T shirts into a bag along with a handful of toiletries off the bathroom shelf. The bus has now got twenty five minutes to do its thing.

As I'm pacing around the bus stop, willing the bastard to arrive, Susan comes out of the flats.

'Morning, Craig,' she says. She looks all fresh and well rested.

'Hi, Suze. Tell me, am I still bleeding?'

She peers at my chin as I lift it for her inspection. 'No, you'll do. Here comes your bus.'

'Thank fuck for that. I'm going to be away a couple of days so I'll see you soon OK?'

'OK,' she says, doing a sort of smirky smile like she's trying not to laugh at me. 'Oh, by the way, how's Wolfie?'

I can't help myself. I grin. Even the memory of that cheeky face makes all the stress I'm putting myself through this morning completely irrelevant. 'Wolfie,' I say, 'is fucking amazing.'

I don't even feel guilty for swearing. Strong language is needed. She waves me onto the bus where I can't take a seat, I have to stand near the driver willing him to put his foot down, begging with traffic lights to stay green.

I leap off the instant the door begins to open at the stop in town and run for the station. Crowds of stupid fuckers mill about and get in my way.

I can see Amisha going through the ticket barrier as I get to the concourse. She obviously thinks I'm a no show and has decided to leave without me. I fumble in my pockets for my ticket as I dodge through the crowd, producing something that satisfies the guy on the gate to let me though without examining it closely. She's on the steps down to the platform as I catch up.

'...misha,' I gasp.

'Craig,' she says, turning to me with a flick of that glossy hair and a display of the dazzling smile. 'Thought you weren't going to make it.'

Rate my heart's banging at, I might yet not make it. I just nod and smile, trying to hide how out of breath I am. I even manage to do the gentlemanly thing and take her bag from her when we get to the platform.

'Oh, thanks,' she says. 'We're in coach B, up here look.'

I still can't speak. Without the weight of her bag, she's moving fast and I have to persuade my legs into a higher gear to catch up with her. I haul the bags up the step to the compartment and the door pings to

109

behind me as the conductor blows his whistle. Perfect timing.

Amisha has found our reserved seats and I use one final burst of energy to lift the bags into the overhead rack before I collapse beside her. I am totally fucked. I need food, sweet tea and sleep.

'I thought we could use the time to plan our strategy for the convention,' Amisha says as she takes a notebook from her handbag and arranges her pens on the table like she's preparing for an exam.

I try not to look horrified but, frankly, I've lost all muscle control, my face is acting independently of my mind.

'Is everything OK?'

'Mmm, yeah, course. I just..., have you had breakfast? I could really do with breakfast.' I'm looking around, hoping there'll be a sign saying 'buffet car this way'.

'I could drink a coffee,' she says.

'Coffee. Yes. That is a great idea. I'll be right back.'

The train has already picked up some speed so I'm not too steady on my feet as I walk down the carriage. I meet the ticket collector at the end.

'Can I buy coffee on here?' He points back in the direction I just came from. Great. Amisha is definitely hiding a smile when I wobble back past her. So I'm incompetent, useless, idiotic. Tell me something I don't fucking know.

I get to the onboard shop and have to wait to be served because the bloke behind the counter is doing an announcement on the intercom, listing all the types of coffee he can make, as if us twenty first century city dwellers might still be impressed by the excitement and glamour of choosing between cappucino and latte. Wanker.

By the time I get back with her coffee, my tea and some Danish pastries, Amisha has written a page full of notes. Thankfully, she snaps the notebook closed as I put her coffee down, and starts making a performance out of adding milk and sugar. She uses her long fingernails to delicately peel back the foil from the little milk pot. She pushes her sleeves back to expose slim wrists before shaking the sugar sachet with a jangle of bracelets, neatly ripping it open and depositing the contents in the cup. The routine is completed with a flourishing swirl and tap with the plastic stirrer.

I realise I'm gawping. I add my own milk and sugar with no drama. 'Pastry?' I offer.

Her face betrays temptation as she looks at the packet, lips pursed. I know she wants it.

'Perhaps I could have a little bit?'

'Knock yourself out,' I say and devour mine in three bites.

She tears a small piece off and nibbles at it, licking her lips in between bites. The way this woman eats is fascinating. I've never seen anyone be so delicate about it. But everything about her is delicate - the petite body, pretty face, nice manners. I guess she's what Mum would call a 'proper lady'. Never thought I'd find myself thinking that was something I could admire.

'So, were you out on the lash last night then?'

Her question shocks me. The words are all wrong in that delicate mouth, but the flash of cheeky wit in her eyes is irresistible and I have to laugh.

'Just overslept a little. I hoped you hadn't noticed.'

'Nope, you were busted the moment I laid eyes on

you. Not quite your usual well-groomed self this morning.'

'Bugger. Does this mean you're going to punish me by giving me tedious jobs to do all day?'

'Punish you?' she says, and those eyes are definitely teasing me now. 'No, I don't think that will be required. I have set us some performance targets though.'

She opens the notebook again and starts droning on about figures and networking opportunities. Just when I thought she had the potential to be interesting.

~

SUSAN

Guilt nagged me all day. After Craig described Wolfie as 'fucking amazing', I couldn't stop thinking about James. Craig's the only one I've even mentioned his name to and, although I've been thinking of him, everything is so busy and new that, for the first time since his birth, James hasn't been my top priority. It's a strange sensation. As I rode the bus to work I convinced myself that by not even saying 'I have a son' to Mark or Andy, I was denying James's existence. It was if I was ashamed of him.

I'm not ashamed. James is, in his own way, 'fucking amazing'. I just haven't ever felt the strength of emotion that would lead me to describe him like that. Of course I bonded with him, felt a mother's love for him. But he was always obsessed with his dad. Nothing I could do was ever right or good enough. Once he was weaned I might only have been there for his convenience. Of course I'm happy to fill that role, but he's an adult now and it can no longer be my primary purpose. It's still an important part of who I am though, and I hated feeling as though I'd been denying him on top of having caused him anguish by leaving his dad.

The café was busy right through the morning into lunchtime. On a journey to ferry used plates back to the kitchen, I bumped into Mark who was trying to peek into the main room without being seen. 'Whoa!' I attempted to right the stack of crockery that threatened to slip out of my arms.

Mark pulled me through the doorway and craned his neck round the corner again. 'Yep, I'm sure of it,' he said.

'What?'

'It's him. Food Snoop! It must be.'

'Who?'

I put the plates down and wiped my hands. He leant against the wall inside the door as if his own legs couldn't support him and looked at me in amazement. 'You don't know? He's the restaurant critic, for the local paper. If he gives a place a good review, its profits can triple overnight.'

'But this isn't a restaurant,' I said as I checked the slips to see which order he was meant to be working on.

'Doesn't matter. If he likes it, he'll write about it. If he hates it – he'll destroy us!'

'Which customer are we talking about?'

Mark glanced around the door again. 'Black shirt, balding, table four.'

'You'd better make it good then,' I said and waved table four's order at him.

'Arghh, I can't do it, I just can't!'

'Everything OK?' Andy appeared in the doorway and frowned at Mark.

'Nooo. It's a disaster. I can't cook. Why did you ever tell me I could cook?'

Andy turned his frown towards me.

'Food Snoop,' I said.

'No. Where?' Andy asked, glancing behind him into the main room. Whatever he saw made him take charge of the situation. 'Right, Mark, we don't actually know for sure. What have they ordered?'

'A garlic prawn salad and a mushroom omelette.'

Andy put his hands on Mark's shoulders. 'The garlic prawn is your speciality. You are an expert at making it. Exactly the right balance of flavours and textures: not too oily, plenty of texture. The omelette is a classic which you do incredibly well. Now cook them, chef. And Susan, could you make sure everything's perfect out there? That's your speciality.' For the smile he gave me, I'd have done anything.

I did a tour of the room, making sure every occupied table had what they needed and every empty table was cleaned and reset. When the bell rang from the kitchen I nipped in to get the order. Both Mark and Andy were wearing serious expressions.

'Maybe you should deliver it?' I said to Andy, infected by Mark's nerves.

'No, Susan. It's you the customers love,' he said. 'When you put the plates down, make sure they face exactly this way, ask the people if they need anything else, more drinks…, oh, you know what you're doing. Go on.'

I felt responsible for the success of the business as I carried the food to table four. Mark had excelled himself. Delicious scents wafted up and each dish was beautifully arranged to entice the fussiest appetite. I put the plates down, positioned as Andy had directed, and asked the couple if they needed anything else.

'No, thank you,' said the woman. The man had already picked up his knife and fork.

As I turned away from the table I could see Mark peering out from the kitchen, a tea towel pressed to his mouth. I gave him what I hoped was a confident wink and began to clear table one where they'd finished their lunch.

We were all relieved when the lunchtime rush was over and we had time to take a quick tea break.

'Well?' Mark said.

'He said 'Thank you very much' and left a generous tip,' Andy replied.

'Oh, might not have been him then. Why would he tip if he's on expenses?'

'Maybe he was so impressed by Susan's service he wanted to reward her. It happens all the time.'

'It does?' I asked.

I usually let Andy handle the bills and payment, maths not being top of my skill set.

'Yes. I suppose we should have said – we usually save all the tips up for a month and then share them out. Is that going to be OK with you? I mean, some places let each waiter keep their own and you're definitely generating more for the kitty than me,' Andy said with a grimace.

'It's absolutely fine,' I said. 'So, I'll get a sort of end of the month bonus?'

'You certainly will, star waitress,' Mark said. 'And if you've any sense you won't take it straight to the pub and drink it like Andy does.' He put an arm across Andy's shoulders and ruffled at his hair.

I think the relief made us all a little giddy. 'No,' I said. 'I'll probably use it to buy my son a present.'

They both looked at me. Then they looked at each other as if to agree who should ask a question, or whether anything should be said at all. It seemed that Andy's will held longest as it was Mark who spoke. 'Didn't know you had a son, Susie. How old is he?'

'Eighteen. He's at Bristol University. He's called James.'

'Wow,' Mark said. 'You do not look old enough to have an eighteen year old son. Tell me your secret, Susie. Do you use an amazing face cream?'

He teased me about my beauty regime while Andy shook his head and returned to the main room.

~

The rest of the day passed without excitement. I travelled home, washed my face and sat down on the sofa to call James. I'd begun to fret that he wasn't just sulking about our last conversation but that I'd wounded him too deeply and he really did want no more to do with me.

'Mum,' he said, his voice tight. 'Dad told me what you said to him. How could you be so cruel? Don't you know what you've done to him?'

'Jamie,' I said, but he wasn't in the mood to listen.

'I've had to come back here, to make sure he didn't do anything stupid. Are you trying to mess up my life too?'

'No, darling. I'm not trying to mess up anything, I just need to…'

'And that witch Jo was round when I got here. Cornered me in the kitchen and asked loads of questions about where you are. I mean, what are we supposed to say?'

'Oh, sweetheart, I'm sorry. I wasn't able to talk to anyone, you can't imagine how I've agonised about

116

this.'

'Dad's the one who knows about agony.'

James obviously didn't want to talk to me. He was not interested in my point of view. He'd well and truly taken his dad's side and I may never redeem myself.

'I'm sorry you felt you had to go home to look after him. You mustn't miss too many of your lectures though.'

'Term's over, don't sweat it. It's just my social life you've knackered and Dad's heart you've broken.'

I didn't know what else to say. There was no point me pleading my case, he wasn't interested in how his dad treated me, or over how many years. All he cared about was that his precious dad was hurt.

'If you're not ringing to apologise, don't bother, OK?'

He hung up on me again. It's not the first time someone's been unjustly angry with me. I'm not sure I'll ever get used to the feeling of helplessness though.

My first detention 1984

I'm so upset about what happened today. I've never been in trouble at school before and it's so unfair because I shouldn't have been in trouble today. Millie Walker and all her lot were making fun of Mr Turner, the physics teacher. I mean, he's a complete dweeb but he thinks he's God's gift and that we all fancy him. No-one would fancy him. So how he thought Millie was serious when she started asking him loads of questions about what it was like to be a physics teacher and did he find teaching her fulfilling, I don't know. All her gang were giggling and the boys were joining in too, making dirty comments about how they'd 'full fill' her. I was trying to ignore them, until Mr Turner twigged and said, 'Now Millie, you're not being entirely serious, are you?' in that pompous voice of his. 'Oh,' she sighed,

'I was just asking for my friend Susan, sir. She's the one who really wants to know.' He hit the roof, wanted to know if it was true, if I'd put her up to it. He wouldn't listen, and neither would Mrs Benn. I had to stay back in detention for a whole hour with Millie and mum was mad when I got home. Life is so unfair sometimes

.

CHAPTER ELEVEN

CRAIG

All the promotions material was at the stand when we got here, so it didn't take long to get everything ready. By the time the show opened half an hour ago, I'd even had time to sort my hair out so I didn't look like the arse end of a fucking badger. Can't believe Suze told me I'd do. She could have mentioned I might want to look in a mirror when I got the chance. Train toilets are frightening places as it is, what with the fear of the door opening while you're mid-stream. Catching sight of myself in the mirror was like the moment they reveal the monster in a horror film. No wonder Amisha knew something was up.

She's being friendly enough now though. Looking very professional in her tight little skirt and the kind of jacket that lets you know she's got boobs, she just doesn't need to show them off right now. The name badge pinned to her chest is encouraging the old blokes to take a look though. Maybe we didn't need promotions girls after all.

Plenty of business women here anyway, checking out the stands. Amisha brought a couple over just now saying, 'My colleague will be able to help you with that information. Craig, perhaps you could talk these ladies through our audit package?'

She's perfectly capable of talking them through it herself, she only wants to make me work. She is punishing me. Can't wait for this session to be over. I really fancy a beer.

One of the seminars has started so there's less traffic at the stand.

'Are we on target then, boss? I've got three definite contacts and those women you sent over were really enthusiastic.'

'Yeah, I thought they would be,' Amisha says and tries to hide a smile.

'What?' I ask, and the penny drops. 'Fucking hell! You're pimping me out!'

Through her giggles I just about make out the words 'You are so like, my bee-atch!' She thinks this is hilarious and is bent double laughing at her joke.

'That's sexual harassment,' I say, but I can't hide the fact I think it's pretty funny.

'No, Craig, that's marketing.'

'Is this why you brought me then? I thought you wanted to lord it over me, boss me about a bit, put me in my place.'

'God no, I wouldn't do that. I wouldn't have brought Gav either though, he lacks the required attributes.' She's raising one of those cheeky eyebrows at me again. I don't get this woman. Is she actually flirting with me now?

'Attributes,' I say. 'Is that what they're calling it in business circles these days?'

I'm quite glad that some bloke has stopped to look at our piles of leaflets and I can go and chat to him.

I've never felt this out of my depth when talking to a woman.

The level of interest in our stand is on and off through the rest of the afternoon. We're near the entrance to the seminar theatre so get the passing trade whenever a session finishes and a wave of people surge out. Amisha is definitely targeting the men and leaving me to approach the female punters. To please her, I turn on the charm and make my flirting as over the top and funny as I can.

While I've got a woman from a packaging firm in Leeds hanging on my every word, I hear a familiar voice shout, 'Hey, Craig Man!'

I look around and a waving arm catches my eye across the crowd of passing people. 'Davo,' I shout back. 'How's it hanging?' Never guessed he'd be here and I'm about to excuse myself from the lady from Leeds but he's moving on with a crowd of suits. He mimes international sign language for 'I'll call you. We'll go for a drink' and he's gone.

'Friend of yours?' Leeds lady asks.

'Yeah,' I say and get back to sealing the deal. 'We can tailor an end-to-end solution to identify savings across every department…'

I haven't actually spoken to Davo since he left Birmingham about a month ago. He doesn't know about me not getting the job. He would never even guess about Wolfie. He hasn't rung me; I haven't rung him. We were living in each other's pockets for a few months there and now, well, it wouldn't bother me if he doesn't ring.

~

Amisha and I are checking into the hotel and I can see the lights on the beer pumps through in the bar.

They know how to tempt a man. There's even a waist-coated barmaid stood there, taking a glass down from a shelf. She could be pouring that drink for me.

Amisha breaks into my daydream asking, 'Shall we meet for dinner?'

I knew it. She does want a 'nice meal' and an 'early night'. And not even the fun kind of 'early night'. I glance at my watch. It's six thirty and I want to call Wolfie before he goes to bed. I know he can't speak sensibly on the phone yet, but I really want to hear him call me 'Dar' again.

'I need to make a phone call,' I say. 'How about we meet in the bar at seven?'

Ten to seven and I've got that pint in my hand. I doubt Wolfie understood me telling him I'd be over to see him on Thursday, he seemed to think he was talking to Bob the Builder, or that he was Bob the Builder or something, but it made me happy to make the promise.

'So, is your girlfriend missing you?' Amisha asks as she appears next to me at the bar.

'Huh?' I ask.

'I thought it must have been a girlfriend you were so desperate to call, after I've been making you fake all that charm this afternoon.'

'Er, no.' I realise that if the whole office is gossiping about me having a son, Amisha is going to be out of the loop. I catch the barmaid's eye and ask Amisha, 'What are you drinking?'

I don't know if she does drink. I'm completely ignorant about Asian religions and culture. I don't even know if she is religious or if it's an easy opt-out thing like Christianity.

'Dry white wine, please.'

Answered that question then. I carry our glasses over to a table and take a deep breath. 'I was calling my son,' I say.

She doesn't falter in the sip she's taking of her drink and puts her glass down before she says, 'I didn't know you…'

'Yeah, no one did,' I interrupt. 'Even me. When you found me sort of dazed and confused in the foyer that day, I'd just found out.'

The thin arches of her eyebrows don't move. She looks at me with those dark chocolate eyes and says, 'That must have been hard. Is he very old?'

I tell her some stuff about Wolfie, but none of the messy stuff about Julia and Trev. I show her the snap on my mobile and she says 'Aaah,' like women always do. She's amazingly sympathetic and I find myself telling her all about how great it feels when Wolfie looks at me and smiles. She squeezes my arm and says, 'Let me get you another drink'.

We sit in the cushioned booth in the corner of the hotel bar for about an hour and a half, me talking about the wonder of Wolfie, her talking about her nephews and nieces. Several drinks are purchased, but no food. She's sitting close to me, leaning forward and some strands of that glossy black hair have caught on my sleeve.

Hoping it doesn't sound too much like a corny chat up line I ask, 'Would you like to have children?'

She smiles - the muted version, not the dazzling one. 'One day I guess. I'm concentrating on my career for now.'

'So there's no boyfriend back in Brum who'll be seething about all the men you've been flirting with today?'

'No, no boyfriend.'

My ignorance pricks at my conscience again and my mouth engages before my brain, 'Oh, you don't have to have one of those arranged marriages do you?'

This time she laughs. 'No, no arranged marriage. My parents aren't that traditional. They just want me to earn a lot.'

'Right, that's good. You hear nasty stories about Asian girls whose brothers beat them up because they're seen hanging around with black men.'

'Oh, my brother wouldn't beat me up for that, don't worry.'

I don't want to ask what her brother might do if he saw her hanging around with a white guy. What I want to do is stroke the lock of hair that's fallen over her face, find out if it feels as silky as it looks. I'd quite like to touch her skin too. She's wearing one of those sheer tops again. I can see the lace on a camisole underneath and there are a lot of things it makes me think about doing.

I haven't had sex in too long. Davo leaving messed up my social routine and opportunities to pull. Wolfie arriving messed with my libido. So now, the first time I find myself alone with a beautiful woman, I'm so turned on I know I'm not thinking straight.

Amisha is my boss. Amisha is only interested in her job. Amisha is not an appropriate woman to attempt to shag.

I stand up and say, 'We should get that meal.'

~

SUSAN

I sleepwalked through yesterday at work. Both Mark and Andy asked me if everything was OK. 'Fine,' I said. How could I tell them the son whose existence I'd just revealed actually hates me, doesn't want to speak to me.

Admitting it to myself hurts as much as if someone had scooped out a huge part of my chest. Leaving Pete wasn't a difficult decision. Not when I sat down and worked out the pros and cons. If I'd known I was also closing the door on James though, that would have been a con too far.

One of the most hurtful things is that it seemed as if turning his back on me wasn't a difficult choice. We may never have been that close, but I thought the mother-son bond might have counted for a little more.

Andy and Mark are wonderful, really fantastic bosses. And Craig's been a complete sweetheart. But I wish, desperately wish, I had even one close female friend to talk with about this. Just one woman who'd listen, understand what I felt, empathise with my situation.

So Jo's been round looking for me. It didn't surprise me. She'd be after the gossip, wanting to be the first to know. If she was really interested she'd have asked if I was OK a long time ago. She probably had a good nose around the house while she was there to get plenty of ammunition for her critique of my life.

I found it almost impossible to get up this morning. The thought that I didn't have to go to Tall Trees, that all there was to do was potter around the flat – which doesn't need cleaning because, guess what, not living with Pete, the place stays clean – it meant that today had no purpose. I don't know when I last didn't have purpose. There was always something needing doing, for Pete, or James, or the house. Now everything's all about me, and I don't know what I need.

It's all very well Andy saying I shouldn't work more than five days a week. What am I supposed to do with the other two? If the café was open seven days, I'd happily work them. I feel worthwhile when I'm there. Hopefully that was the food critic from the paper. I hope he loved Mark's food and writes something wonderful about Tall Trees. I hope the guys have to expand and I can work for them forever.

If only forever was actually a long time. My marriage was supposed to last forever. In fact it only really lasted a couple of years. Once James was born Pete knew I was trapped and his treatment of me deteriorated. I was really no more than a slave to keep house for them, not a partner. Not even a companion. He thought he'd still control me now he's retired and at home all the time, but he can't. Not now James has left home and I've decided I won't put up with Pete's behaviour any more. Not now I've tasted the alternative.

I tried to have a lie in as the noisy neighbour upstairs keeps me awake until late most nights, but my mind was too active. I got up, cleaned the already clean flat and did my laundry. Swept the landing Craig and I share, though I doubted he'd notice. Began to think about whether I should get myself a computer or something to occupy myself with before deciding it would probably be best to wait until I can ask someone like Craig what type of thing I should get anyway. I'd cooked, eaten and cleared up an early evening meal, then decided to take my recycling down to the bin cupboard before it got dark.

I opened my door to hear footsteps on the stairs and, hoping it would be Craig, I waited on the landing with a smile on my face. It wasn't Craig. It was a stocky, heavily bearded, Asian man who glanced at me with hooded eyes and didn't respond to my mumbled greeting.

He rounded the corner and continued up the next flight of stairs, his bulging holdall grazing the walls as he hurried onwards. I waited, and heard the door of the flat above mine open then slam shut. My noisy upstairs neighbour. Relieved that Craig had been the first person I'd met at the flats, I locked my door carefully behind me.

I'd been back in the flat half an hour when the doorbell buzzed. To tell the truth, I was scared. No-one's visited me, only Craig and he just wanders across and rat-a-tat-tats. My first instinct was 'Pete!' Then I calmed down. There's no way he could find me.

'Hello?' I said into the entry phone.

'Susan? Hi, it's Andy. I was, um, passing, and thought I'd pop by to say hello.'

'Oh, OK. Do you want to come up?'

'Is that all right?'

I pressed the button to admit him downstairs and went to the door, glad I had made the effort to sweep and clean. Seeing him in the stairwell was strange, like meeting someone where you least expect them. He looked taller. I stepped back to let him into the flat.

'Welcome,' I said. 'You're my first proper visitor. I don't think the next door neighbour really counts.'

'Thanks.' He glanced around in a way that was obviously trying not to be too inquisitive.

'Would you like a drink? I've only got tea though.'

'Well, actually, what it is, um…' he left a long gap. I suppose the double anxieties of being on unfamiliar territory and his conversational nerves were conspiring to steal his tongue. 'I was heading towards the pub down the road from here – The Old Mo, do you know it? No, well, they do a lot of real ales and they've got a beer I wanted to try and I wondered, um, if you wanted to join me? If you're not busy of course.'

'As it happens, I'm not busy,' I said and smiled at him as though he was my saviour.

I'm not much of a pub person, but getting out of the flat as a distraction from my pain was the best thing anyone could have offered me at that point. I nipped into the bathroom to tidy myself up a bit, put on a little make up and we walked down the road.

It's a traditional-style pub, not one of the monsters that had intimidated me when I first arrived in Birmingham. Not that I would have had the nerve to walk into this place on my own. Not as a lone woman. Andy held the door for me and advised which of the beers I might like to try as we stood at the bar.

'Sorry,' he said. 'I can be a bore about it. Our fridge is full of some lager Mark buys that's had all flavour extracted from it, and I really fancied a decent pint tonight. Cheers.'

He lifted his glass and sipped. The head of the beer left a line of foam above his top lip, the bubbles bursting against his stubble.

I took a sip from my glass. It was a light amber colour, rich in flavour but not too fizzy. Much nicer than the bitter Pete drinks.

'Do you like it?' Andy asked.

I nodded and smiled as the anxiety lifted from his face. We sat at a corner table below odd bits of brass cluttering the walls, and chatted about what I'd missed at Tall Trees.

'Mark's obsessing. If that was Food Snoop, his column's in tomorrow evening's paper. It'll be unbearable until Mark sees a copy.'

'Aren't you worried too?'

'Course I am, but it won't help if we're both overwrought, will it?'

'No, you make a good team,' I said.

'We've had long enough to get used to each other, and anyway, you've completed the team – brought all the customer care skills we were lacking.'

I smiled even more at that. The fact my contribution was valued was exactly what I needed to hear. He went to buy another round of drinks and, while he waited, I noticed how the bar staff moved around behind the bar, the casual physical contact between colleagues which couldn't be more different from the way Andy and I were behind the counter at Tall Trees. He always avoided touching me and gave me plenty of room to work. His every move was considered and careful. He never laid a hand on my shoulder or leant over me as the staff did here.

I was a little surprised when our conversation became more personal when he got back with the second drink. He wasn't prying; he didn't ask me any pushy questions. He's just so kind that I found myself admitting I didn't know anyone in Birmingham and had been feeling a bit miserable before he arrived. I didn't admit that 'a bit miserable' really meant heartbroken, desolate loneliness. I didn't supply any details about why.

It was still early when Andy walked me back to the door of the flats and waited while I punched in the entry code. 'Thanks,' I said. 'I really enjoyed this evening, it was just what I needed.'

He had his hands in his pockets, shoulders hunched, 'I'm glad, I, um… I wondered…'

As he struggled towards what he was trying to say, Craig hurried up the path.

'Hi Suze, how's it going?' he said as I stepped out of the way to let him in.

'Fine thanks, Craig. Oh, this is Andy, my boss. Andy, Craig lives next door.'

Andy didn't move from his position half in the shadows, Craig swapped his bag into his left hand and leant to shake Andy's hand saying, 'Good to meet you, mate. You coming in or going out, Suze?'

'Coming in,' I replied and stepped through the door Craig held open. 'See you tomorrow, Andy. Thanks again.'

He nodded and turned away.

'How was your trip?' I asked Craig as we went upstairs.

'Fucking disaster. Tell you another time, OK? If I don't lie down right now I'll die.'

~

CRAIG

I drop my bag and fall on my bed. Nightmare, absolute fucking nightmare. And most of it had gone so well.

We'd had another good day on the stand, busy with traffic, lots of interest. The team from the stand next door invited us to go out for a drink and some food with them. Great plan, I thought. They seemed like decent blokes.

So we were sitting in the restaurant, we'd had a few beers, the atmosphere was relaxed and convivial. I was chatting to this one guy who was a Wolves fan, but we were only winding each other up – nothing malicious. I noticed that Amisha was getting giggly. She was talking to one of the guys, a smarmy wanker in a sharp suit, and he kept topping her glass up with wine. When I saw him put his arm around her shoulders, I thought I'd better check if she was OK. She wasn't. She was drunk. So I had a word, which didn't make lover boy too happy.

'Come on, Amisha,' I said. 'Time to get you back to the hotel.'

'She's fine here with me,' he said.

'No. She's coming with me.'

She managed to focus on me and gave me the smile that's usually dazzling. With half-closed eyes it didn't have the same impact. 'Craig,' she said and stretched out her arms to me.

'Home time,' I told her.

We walked back to the hotel, well, she stumbled back. I had to put my arm round her to stop her veering off in to the bus lane. She was clinging onto my shirt and slurring, 'I didn't like him much. I'd rather have talked to you. I'm glad I'm talking to you now.' She wasn't making much sense.

When we got to the door of her room I said, 'Make sure you drink loads of water before you go to sleep. I'll see you in the morning.'

I swear that's what I said. I was fully intending to leave it there.

She was doing the low wattage smile thing at me. In the dim light of the hotel corridor, her half-closed eyes actually looked damn sexy. So when she leant forward and gave me a goodnight kiss it was surprising in a pleasant way. An extremely pleasant way.

One goodnight kiss turned into a full blown snog with enough body contact for there to be no way she can have missed my erection. Then she pulled away, said 'night night' and left me leaning against her door panting in frustration.

When I went down to breakfast there was no sign of her. When I checked out they said she'd already left. When I got to the convention hall, she was in full on professional mode again.

'Look, Amisha, I…' I started to say, thinking I'd better break the ice, offer an apology, do something.

'Right, Craig,' she interrupted. 'Last day. Let's see if we can't double those figures.'

So I had a crap day, what with her refusing to talk about anything but work and bossing me about all day, the guys on the next door stand giving me evils, and me feeling shitty about the whole thing. I mean, I meant to be a gentleman and rescue her from that idiot who was trying to take advantage. Then I go and take advantage myself. Complete wanker.

Finally, it was over and we packed up and got the train home. We had one of those pairs of seats, the ones where you're tucked in behind four seats round a table and it feels as if the two of you are enclosed. Close together. Private. So not what I needed.

I didn't try to make conversation. I was thinking, 'Fine. If she wants to pretend it didn't happen, that's fine.' I wasn't even looking at her, just wondering how long I should leave it before plugging my headphones in. Then she said, 'I'm sorry about last night.'

Her voice was so quiet I had to turn to her to make sure she had said it. She glanced away, couldn't hold the eye contact. So I said, 'Don't worry about it. Everyone does silly things when they're drunk. I should probably have stopped it.'

She was quiet for a while, looking out the window. But then, 'I'm kind of glad you didn't,' she said. 'It was nice.'

Well, shit. What was I supposed to say to that? I didn't know if she was flirting with me or what. So I said, 'Yeah. It was.' And she gave me the full beam smile, reached over and squeezed my knee. Definitely flirting.

'You're a great guy, you know.'

'Um, you're nice too.' Hell, what was I supposed to say? This wasn't just any fantastic-looking girl. This was my boss talking.

'I was worried you might try and slap some sexual harassment thing on me,' she said.

I didn't know if she was joking with me or not. It was dodgy ground. Very dodgy. So I said, 'Well, it was all pretty consensual, right?'

'Right,' she said. 'So, um, do you fancy going for a drink when we get back to Brum?'

It was like one of those game show challenges – make the wrong decision and you're going home empty handed. But how could I win? Of course I wanted to go for a drink with her. If there was the potential for more of those kisses and anything that might be the next course on the menu, I'd go anywhere with her. But she's my boss and getting involved with her seemed dangerous. Offending her by turning her down also seemed dangerous. Then I remembered my get out clause.

'Oh, I promised Wolfie I'd go and see him tonight. If I don't go straight there from the train, I'll miss his bedtime.'

Brilliantly played. I'd managed to avoid saying either yes or no. She could be neither offended nor encouraged by the fact I had a prior engagement.

'Fine,' she said. 'Maybe another time.'

I hope the panic didn't show in my eyes. That one required a yes or no answer. Yes or no.

'Yes,' I said. 'Great.' Damn.

I tried to relax, play it cool, but there was an old git in the seat behind me who kept clearing his phlegmy throat. He sounded like he had fruitcake and claret wedged in his gullet and I wanted to turn round and fucking strangle the wanker to help him clear it.

After what seemed like several months, the announcement for Birmingham came on with the earnest instruction to make sure you have all your belongings with you before leaving the train. I did not have all my belongings; my peace of mind and sense of humour were AWOL. We were late into New Street so by the time I got to Julia's parents' house I had a total of ten minutes with Wolfie.

It was good though. The one good thing about today. Once I'd put him down to sleep, Julia said, 'D'you fancy a coffee?'

Well I was tired so I took it at face value and said yes. Once we were sat down though I noticed that she was all dolled up again.

'Going out?' I asked.

'No. Just thought I'd make an effort. I get a bit fed up with always having Wolfie's dribble down everything I wear.'

'Not sure I'd mind that,' I said. 'It would mean I

was seeing him more often.'

'Well, you could, you know.' She inched her chair closer and that was it. Forget feeling tired. Forget all the stress of the day. I was in full on defensive mode again. Julia was definitely coming on to me.

What the fuck is wrong with these women? Why can't they let a bloke be?

CHAPTER TWELVE

SUSAN

Craig and I left for work at the same time this morning. 'You've got that spring in your step again,' he said, as the echo of his footsteps followed me down the stairwell. 'Raring to get to work and now I know why.'

'I like my job,' I said. 'Why wouldn't I want to get there?'

'And the little flirtation you've got going on with the boss has nothing to do with it, right?'

'Flirtation? Andy's not flirting with me. He's gay.'

'Really?' Craig frowned as he held the door open for me. 'Damn, there's a bus coming, gotta run.'

And he was gone. Leaving me to pull the door clicked shut as he raced to the stop on our side of the road. I followed at a slower pace, waited for the lights to change at the crossing and stood at the stop across the way until a bus arrived to carry me in the opposite direction.

I dismissed Craig's teasing; he'd hardly seen Andy last night, a meeting during which Craig himself had been rather distracted. Really, the argument with

James was troubling me too much for Craig's words to even register. As the bus carried me closer to Tall Trees though, I became more and more nervous about what it might say in the newspaper, and how disappointed we'd be if we weren't in it after all. I made myself focus. There was nothing I could do about James today.

Mark and Andy were subdued. Mark made mistakes all morning, failing to read the orders I wrote out correctly. Andy could hardly look either of us in the eye. Fortunately, it was busy, so I could concentrate on the customers, ensuring they had everything they needed, making sure neither Mark nor Andy missed anything critical. By lunchtime, we were all wound so tightly we were talking in clipped sentences and finding it hard to smile.

My feet ached and my apron bore stains of uncharacteristic clumsiness. Andy was silently chewing his fingernails down, while Mark let food burn, swore a lot and had to start several orders over. At two o'clock, he couldn't take it any longer.

'I have to get it,' he said, as he strode into the main room and thrust his apron at Andy.

He opened the door so forcefully it stuck on the floorboard it always grates across. Andy stepped forward to ease it closed but then threw an apologetic look at me and followed Mark into the street. They'd never left me alone in the café before and I reached out to steady myself against the counter as panic rose up. There were only customers at two tables. They didn't look in imminent need of anything. I relaxed a little, stepped behind the counter into Andy's normal position, and found myself, like him, biting a fingernail.

Eventually I couldn't ignore the fact that one group had finished eating. I stirred myself to clear their table, dropping cutlery on the floor as I tried to pile plates on my arm. I managed to ask if they needed anything else and was attempting to operate the till when the door screeched open again.

'Susie,' Mark shouted, bursting into the room and grabbing me round the waist. He planted kisses on both cheeks and squeezed me tight. 'We did it!'

I looked to Andy, who nodded and held up a crumpled newspaper. I grabbed it from him and scanned the headline: Side Street Surprise. Underneath, a disguised photograph beside the by-line 'Food Snoop' was almost recognisable as our visitor from Wednesday. Most noticeable were the four stars printed next to the Tall Trees contact details.

'Four stars, Susie, count them,' Mark crowed.

I smiled up at Andy, who had moved a little closer. 'Well done,' I said.

'Couldn't have happened without you,' he replied and gave my shoulder an awkward squeeze.

The group of women who wanted to pay looked perplexed, but Andy swung back into action and smoothed out their concerns. 'Forgive us,' he said. 'It's not every day you get in the paper.'

The boost to his confidence showed in his smile. I watched him chat to them, explaining what had happened, charming them with his modesty and willingness to share the plaudits with not only Mark, but me too. I moved to reset their table and Mark came back into the room, talking on the phone.

'Yep, course I'll send you a copy. Yep. Here he is.' He handed the phone to Andy. 'It's Mum,' he said.

'Hi.' Andy smiled into the phone as he listened. 'Yeah, great news, isn't it?'

He turned away to the window as Mark danced back towards me, grabbing me into a waltz and calling out to the remaining customers, 'Did you hear our good news?'

The couple smiled at him. 'I guess it's our congratulations to the chef, not just our compliments,' the man said.

'The chef needs his team. Without my star waitress here, and my brother over there running the show, I'd be nowhere.'

I tripped over his foot as he span me round, stunned by the revelation that he and Andy were brothers, not lovers. The heat in my face confirmed that I'd flushed bright red. I pulled away from Mark and fanned myself with a hand, pretending to be breathless from the dancing, not startled by his words.

'You OK, Susie?' Mark said. 'Gone giddy with excitement?'

I nodded and went to the kitchen to run myself a glass of water. I was holding it to my cheek to cool my blush when Andy came in. Not wanting him to guess at my confusion, I gulped the water down.

'Our mum's even more excited than Mark is,' he said.

'I can imagine.'

'Are you OK?'

The concern in his voice was overwhelming. How could I have been so stupid as to make assumptions that because two men were close, because one could cook and one was kind, they had to be gay? And Andy'd started to tell me about his marriage, but I'd

139

been trying so hard to be modern and accepting I'd assumed it was a same sex couple. Everything was now up for question. Mark was flamboyant and well-dressed, but did that mean he was gay? Andy was quiet, nervous and drank real ale, but did that mean he was straight?

I just nodded at Andy. Confusion plus embarrassment meant I couldn't speak. I was glad when Mark bounced back in and the difficult moment passed.

'So, who's for closing up early and going to celebrate?' he asked.

'Close up? We can't do that,' Andy said. 'We might get people coming down who've seen the paper. Can't not be here.'

'My brother, the business brain!' Mark replied, giving me a wry smile and Andy another hug. 'But we will celebrate; you too, Susie. Down to Moseley the minute we close and the champagne's on me.'

I'm not sure the article did bring in any additional customers during the rest of the afternoon. Milla, the owner of the jewellery shop next door came in to congratulate us. She perched on a stool at the counter, exposing a lot of leg and chatting to Andy about how he should display the cutting from the paper in the window while she sipped the coffee he'd made her. I watched them as I looked after the other customers, trying to assess from Andy's behaviour whether he was interested in her as anything other than a fellow business owner.

I don't know why I was doing it. I was trying to reorient my assumptions I suppose. But Mark noticed and teased me when I delivered a tray of used cups to the kitchen.

'Oh, that one's no competition,' he said. 'Had her eye on Andy for ages, but she's just not his type. You don't need to worry about her.'

'What?' I asked. 'No, I don't..., I didn't mean to... I wasn't doing anything.'

'Darling, don't fret. I'm only teasing.'

His smirk told me he wasn't.

When closing time came, I tried to excuse myself from the celebration, but Mark wouldn't listen. He linked an arm through mine and marched me to the bus stop.

'It's on your way home. I insist you come with us.'

'But I look a state,' I said. 'I'm not dressed to go to a bar.'

'You look lovely,' Mark replied. 'Doesn't she, Andy?'

My blush returned. I hoped they'd never guess my mistake about them, but Mark wasn't going to give up on his assumption that I was interested in Andy. Fortunately, Andy was back in one of his nervous moods and didn't reply. He walked behind Mark and me, hands stuffed deep into his pockets.

We went into a bar in Moseley. I'd noticed it before, from the bus as I passed by. It looked off-puttingly trendy, with groups of confident, arty types clustered around tables outside, drinking bottled beer and smoking. Mark strode to the bar and ordered champagne while Andy and I trailed after him.

'Here,' Andy said, touching my elbow. 'Let's sit down.'

He drew me towards a leather sofa and I sank into its squashy cushions, slipping my feet out of my shoes under the low table in front of us. Mark came back from the bar with the bottle resting in an ice bucket in one hand and three glasses carried by their fragile stems in the other. It was too early for the bar to be busy yet, but people at the few occupied tables he passed turned to look. He was certainly making a performance of it.

'Give it here,' Andy said and poured the fizz into the glasses Mark held out. Once we were all holding one, he proposed a toast, 'To Tall Trees.'

'And all who sail in her,' Mark added.

We clinked glasses and drank; well, I sipped, Mark gulped and Andy swilled the liquid around his mouth experimentally.

'No,' he said, 'I still don't like champagne.'

'Philistine,' Mark replied. 'All the more for Susie and me then.'

He topped up our glasses while Andy went to the bar to buy himself a beer. Mark got even more talkative as the champagne took effect. His dramatic gestures as he described his plans for the dishes he'd like to put on the menu threatened the safety of the spiky flower arrangement on the shelf behind his armchair. Andy smiled, only murmuring the occasional comment about what the clientele of a suburban café might and might not be expected to embrace.

'Oh,' Mark said, his attention distracted, 'there's Josh. I have to show him this.'

He leapt up and bounced over to the bar to accost a man who'd walked in, pulling the folded up page from the newspaper from his back pocket to wave in Josh's face.

'Was he always this excitable?' I asked, trying to make my voice convey how entirely natural it was that I would think Andy knew the answer based on a lifetime's knowledge of his brother's behaviour.

'Pretty much, yeah. You should have seen him when he was at college. Not a day without a drama.'

'You're lucky to have a brother you're so close to. Plenty of siblings wouldn't be able to share a house and work together the way you do.'

'Yeah, it works most of the time. Well, it has to now we've got our finances so tied together.'

I nodded; financial worries were just one item on the list of things I didn't want to think about. Mark returned to attempt to persuade us to join him and Josh on a trip up to town. Quite certain I'd had enough excitement for one day, I refused with more conviction than I'd managed earlier. Mark drained the champagne from his glass, leant down to ruffle Andy's hair and left us behind.

We sat in awkward silence for a while, Andy sipping his beer, me playing with my champagne flute. I was about to say that I'd better be going, when Andy glanced at me and said, 'I could show you something interesting, if you like?'

~

CRAIG

Bollocks. What is the point of getting an early night if you can't sleep? Half an hour I've been lying here. I need rest, I need oblivion. What I need are dreams. Dreams in which sexy women want only to make me happy.

No.

Dreaming about women would be a bad idea. I've had my fill of women and their fucking games. Dreams in which my sporting talents are recognised would do. Perhaps I could take the winning penalty for England in the World Cup final? Not much to ask, is it? Just a little bit of escapism, that's all I want.

Surely I deserve it after the week I've had? A week in which today has been the fucking icing. I mean, it was after midnight when I stopped thinking about Julia last night, so the stuff with her qualifies as part of today's disaster. Then I make it in to work – feeling like shit – and have to pick my way across the Amisha minefield while dodging sniper bullets from Gav all the way. No wonder Call of Duty was not my Playstation game of choice tonight. I'd like to see how the SAS would have handled what I survived today. Surprisingly though, no one was talking about Wolfie. Steve hadn't started any gossip. I don't know whether Amisha will.

A few beers with the footie team would've been perfect. Especially as they were the excuse I used for not being able to go for a drink with Amisha. 'Meeting the boys,' I said, 'same every Friday – can't let them down.' Except I have let them down. I broke ranks when I told Nick what an arse he was. I'm not in the squad for tomorrow morning and I wasn't copied in to the Friday afternoon 'Beers?' email.

I hear Susan's door being unlocked, then closed and locked again and grab my phone to check the time. Illuminated blue digits tell me it's eleven thirty. Even Suze has a better social life than me. Wonder if the boys went for a curry? My stomach's complaining that marmite on toast was not enough when it was expecting the usual Friday night feast. I'm not getting up though. I know there's nothing worth eating in the cupboards and can't be arsed to go across the road.

I punch the pillow into shape and squeeze my eyes shut. I am having an early night. I am getting the rest my body requires. I will awake with clear resolutions to all of my problems. So why the fuck can't I get to sleep?

~

SUSAN

Andy promised something interesting, but he delivered somewhere so enchanting I hardly believed I was still in Birmingham. As we got up from our seats, they were instantly taken by a group of stylish, animated young people and the silence between Andy and me as we left the bar and walked along the main road seemed uncomfortable in comparison.

In the fresh air, I could tell that the alcohol had affected me. I didn't dare attempt conversation for fear of gabbling on in a way which would irritate him or seem silly. Instead I gazed at the windows of the dry cleaner, the delicatessan, the charity book shop – all closed for the day, except for the betting shop where posters were displaying incomprehensible odds of success for upcoming sports events. Traffic rumbled past us as people made their way towards their city centre nights out.

As I was thinking of something to say about the neighbourhood he touched my arm and guided me into an alleyway in between two shops, just wide enough for a car. Although I had no reason not to trust him a few nerves prickled the edge of my tipsy haze. I've seen too many films where bad things happen in city alleyways and this one didn't look promising.

The sun hadn't set, so it was light enough, but I tried to stay alert as we left the safety of the main road. Andy continued to walk confidently ahead and pulled his keys from his pocket. I gripped my handbag tighter under my arm and followed him.

From half way down the alleyway, the atmosphere started to change. The engine noise from buses and cars faded and there appeared to be more light. I'd anticipated parking spaces, bins, old fittings from the shops left out to rot; something like the area behind the café. But behind these buildings, in addition to those things, was a gate set into green painted iron railings. And Andy was unlocking it.

He turned to smile at me. 'Welcome to Moseley Park.'

He held the gate as I stepped through then locked it behind us, the clang of the ironwork strange now that the urban hum was silenced and birdsong sounded above me instead. He led the way down a tarmac path, broken and rutted by time and tree roots. It wasn't the only sign of human presence though: I picked up the thwack of a ball against racket strings.

'Is it a tennis club?' I asked.

'It's so much more than a tennis club.'

We walked further down the tree-lined path, rounding a corner where flashes of neon and white sportswear and a red clay court startled my eyes. I'd already adjusted to the muted shades of the trees and grass. I think Andy noticed my confusion, because he smiled again and said, 'Although some people do use it just for the tennis courts of course.'

He lifted a hand in greeting to one of the players who looked up as we passed. We walked onwards, downwards still, across a wide lawn to the edge of a lake with evening light glinting from its smooth surface. Smooth until ducks, disturbed by our presence, waddled from the lawn back to the water with a chorus of quacks. A long-legged dog, graceful as a racehorse, picked its way along the muddy lakeside and sniffed for adventure.

The lake was big; in fact, the whole park was larger than I would have imagined could be hidden away behind the high street. We sat on a bench by the water's edge and I gazed around. We were much lower than street level, which probably helped with insulation from the noise, and between the trees was the occasional glimpse of red brick – large houses on surrounding streets enclosing this magical space. Once the lake surface settled from the ducks' passing, it acted as a mirror to clouds and the outlines of the trees surrounding it. Only breeze-driven riffles marred the reflection.

'It's amazing,' I said.

'Sssh,' Andy replied, 'it's a secret. It's a private park; only those in the know can come here. Along with their valued guests, of course.'

He looked far more at ease sitting on that bench, much more at home than in the trendy bar. He wasn't anxious when he talked either, and the frequent silences weren't awkward any more, they were calm pauses in which we listened to the birds and watched the changing light on the lake. The leaves of the trees which overhung the water moved gently in the slight breeze, displaying varying shades of green as they moved from sunlight into shadow or dragged over the wooden boards which edged the lake shore.

A line of fuzzy grey cygnets sailed across the water, but stopped to look as a chugging sound like a steam train starting to move sounded from the other end of the lake. It was an adult swan taking off from its watery runway, its feet dragging and wings pumping as it gained height.

'Who do you think lives in those houses?' My gaze had followed the swan's flight and I could see that the windows of the highest stories of the surrounding buildings had a view of the park in addition to their own large gardens.

'I've no idea who could afford them. Not that they come up for sale often; it'd be an estate agent's dream to get one of those on their books – probably some of the most desirable property in Birmingham. I went in one once, for a party.'

'You have friends who live there?'

'No, um, my ex-wife, it was someone she knew.'

I feared I'd unwittingly ruined the atmosphere, but he moved on quickly.

'That's how I found out about the park. I saw it from their patio and it was an ambition of mine to become a key holder ever since. You have to pay, of course. So it's only worth it if you live nearby. Not that Mark would care, but his house is close enough.'

I looked up through the jumble of branches overhead and let my gaze follow the complex edge of the canopy which framed the skyline in a palette of colours from sunlight yellow to blackest green, the frills and spikes of the varied species more like a coastline drawn on a map than a horizon.

'So moving in with him made a dream come true for you.'

'Yes, it was the silver lining to a particularly black cloud. And living together meant we finally got the café started. If we hadn't been spending so much time together, it would probably have stayed as one of those vague dreams we chatted about after Christmas dinner or something. We wouldn't each have realised quite how serious the other was. We wouldn't have made it happen.'

He was totally relaxed, leaning back on the bench with legs outstretched and crossed at the ankle, the scuffed toe of his brown shoe tracing a lazy circle in the air, no cloud of a frown on his forehead. We both watched as a moorhen popped out from the nest of twigs it was building among half-submerged branches. I was so pleased about how well things were working out for Andy and, with the buzz from the champagne still distracting me, my defences were down. I wasn't ready for him to ask, 'What about you, Susan, have you found your silver lining yet?'

I doubt he was expecting me to cry in response, but he handled it brilliantly. He brushed off my gulped apology and rested one hand on my back, stroking lightly as I searched my bag for a tissue. When I finished blowing my nose, and dabbing my eyes, I found I still couldn't look at him. The silence between us was uncomfortable again. I have been crying over my situation in the privacy of my flat, and since my last conversation with James the tears have always been close to the surface. But in public, apart from a sniffy moment in the solicitors', I've kept things together. Until then, when I had to spoil what should have been one of the most positive days of Andy's life with my tears.

'You must be hungry,' he said. 'I know I am. Come on, let me buy you dinner.

'

CHAPTER THIRTEEN

CRAIG

It's seven o'clock. Seven o'clock on a fucking Saturday morning. I'm wide awake. I don't have a hangover. I'm not late for footie – I won't even be going to footie. This is utter shit. I need food, greasy plate-loads of food.

Suze's at the bus stop across the road, so I dodge a dawdling taxi, returning the driver's not so friendly gesture, and join her.

'You were out late,' I say.

'Sorry, did I disturb you?' she asks, and she's blushing, actually blushing like a guilty schoolgirl.

'I happened to hear your door go; but of course now I want to know where you were and who with, you dirty stop-out.'

Her eyes take on a panicked glaze, and I'm just starting to think that I've overdone the teasing, which would be typical of the way I'm managing to upset every woman I talk to at the moment, when she says, 'I wish I'd listened to you the other day.'

What's that? Someone actually valuing something I said, wishing she'd paid me more attention. Now this is more like it, Suze. 'Why's that then?'

'You didn't think Andy was gay when you met him. You didn't jump to the silly conclusions I did and I got myself in such a pickle yesterday, when it should have been such an exciting day.'

'Andy, that's the guy who's your boss? And from the way he looked at you I guessed he wanted to be considerably more. Obvious. And, if I may say so, you look very pretty when you blush like that.'

'You're a terrible flirt, Craig. Didn't your mother tell you it'd get you in trouble?'

Trouble is an understatement for the mess I'm in. I can see her bus approaching though and stick out an arm to flag it for her. 'Already has; and getting worse by the minute. Are you on your way to work? I might tag along. I assume this establishment sells bacon?'

'The as of yesterday, four star rated Tall Trees serves one of the best breakfasts in south Birmingham.'

'Four whole stars and a side order of sexual tension between the staff? This I have to see.'

I'm impressed by the story she tells me about the food critic as we take our seats. I've read that column sometimes when there's been a copy of the paper left on the bus and he can really rip into a place if he didn't like the food. So my stomach's growling looking forward to breakfast.

'There it is,' she says, pointing at an estate agents' in Moseley, 'the private park, you get in down there.'

'Are you sure?' I can't see where the secret park she's describing would be, and it's the first I've heard of it anyway. 'Do you have to say the right magic word before it appears, then do a funny handshake to get in?'

'It does look a bit like a fairy land, but no, it's utterly real. You just need the key and Andy has one.'

'Funny how I hear about nothing but Andy these days,' I say and give her a nudge. She's blushing again, but I know she loves it.

'Really, Craig, you've got to promise me you won't say anything cheeky like that in front of him. I already made things uncomfortable enough between us last night. The poor man's only trying to be nice to me. I'm certain there's nothing else going on.'

There she goes again: calling men 'nice'. Just not the case, Suze; but I keep my thoughts to myself. After all, women can be scheming bitches too.

'So, how was your week at work?' she asks.

'Very nice,' I reply.

~

SUSAN

I was grateful for Craig's company on the bus, although I was nervous about him making inappropriate comments in front of Andy. After my crying fit last night, we'd left the park and looked for something to eat. Moseley certainly seems to be the place to go for food, there are Indian, Moroccan and Thai places among others; all with enticing menus displayed in the windows. All were busy though: full of laughing, chattering groups and Andy seemed to pick up on my reluctance to go in. I have a slight phobia about being in that type of environment.

My first date with Pete – 1986

I still can't believe Pete Clarke actually asked me out. He's always been nice to me at the pub, but when he asked me to go out to dinner with him I thought it must be a joke. I've been in a panic all week, not knowing what I should wear and wondering what we'd have to talk about. I just really can't believe he wanted to spend the evening with me.

He did though. He took me to a place called Francine's where they do this thing called Nouvelle Cuisine. Pete says it's all the rage. Tiny portion though. I'm so glad I was with him as I wouldn't have known what to order, the whole menu was in French. And there was this group of business men sitting behind us who kept staring at me and making comments about my skirt.

Pete was brilliant. He told me I was looking lovely and that's why I was getting so much attention. He was a complete gentleman for the whole evening. He opened doors for me and poured my drinks. He was wearing this great red leather jacket too.

After the meal, we went back to his car parked outside and instead of just opening the door for me, he bent down and kissed me! It was amazing, I didn't think anything like that would ever happen to me. If only that group of men hadn't been leaving at the same time. They all started wolf whistling and laughing at us. I hate gangs of men like that.

I've been anxious around exuberant groups in bars and restaurants ever since. I always feel as though they're laughing at me.

Fortunately, the busy restaurants didn't seem to appeal to Andy either. 'How about we get a take away and go back to Mark's?' he said as we glanced in the windows of a crowded Italian place.

'Are you sure? You should be celebrating this evening, not pandering to my moodiness.'

'I want to celebrate by eating a meal with you. I don't mind where. Now, do you like Chinese?'

The take away was busy as well, with a queue of people waiting for their orders to be prepared. A tv set fixed to the tiled wall was tuned to a game show which held the attention of the man behind the

153

counter, and the amount of shouting from the kitchen suggested things weren't running quite as smoothly as they could. We sat down to wait on the worn, plastic covered seats lining the edge of the room. Andy touched my arm and indicated the newspaper the woman I was sitting next to was reading. She had it open at Food Snoop's column.

'What do you think he'd score this place?' he whispered.

I watched the woman's face to see if she gave away her opinion of the review but her number was called and she flung the paper aside to collect her food. Andy retrieved it and folded it neatly open to display the right page, before pretending to casually put it down in the line of vision of the man waiting beside him. I had to giggle at his cheek.

Our number was called and Andy jumped up to collect the bulging carrier bag. 'How much food did we order?' I asked.

'I have a master plan,' Andy said, 'I intend to leave some food in the fridge so that when Mark comes home drunk tonight and looks in there, he'll find something vaguely sensible to eat. For a chef he can make some poor choices, and we need him on top form again tomorrow. That woman who read the review will be in for sure.'

The evening was still warm as we walked back to Mark's house tucked away in the maze of residential roads off the main road in Moseley. I confessed I'd lost my bearings.

'Well, this is still Moseley,' Andy explained, 'but we're just as close to Kings Heath so it's an easy walk to Tall Trees. The bus you get along the main road makes it seem further than it is if you use the back streets.'

'That's the Moseley Road then, that main road? That's what it says on the front of the bus.'

'It's the Alcester Road by the time you're in Kings Heath, but yes, it's the same road.'

'Alcester? But that's where I'm from.' I didn't like the coincidence of the road being named that.

'Really? It's a lovely place…' He started on an anecdote about when he went walking near there once, reminiscing about the ancient buildings and quaintly cobbled Malt Mill Lane lined with tiny cottages.

'I lived on the new estate on the edge of town. It wasn't quaint.' I should have responded more politely, but the sudden reminder of what I'd so recently left behind unnerved me. It was as if the person I was there had intruded on my evening here.

Andy seemed to take the hint and changed the subject. 'Well, there's lots of roads named for other places like that in Birmingham: the Coventry Road, the Stratford Road; perhaps they were old coach routes or something.'

So I've ended up living on the road which would take me directly back to Alcester. At least the bus doesn't go that far.

Andy put the food in the oven to warm up and left me on the sofa with a glass of white wine in my hand. As I looked around I realised the house wasn't quite as well-kept as my first impression had assumed. The flat surfaces of the living room were scattered with newspapers and magazines, the screen of the TV wore a sheen of dust and one of the speakers for the hi-fi stood on top of a haphazard pile of books, with one thick spine bearing the title 'Feng Shui for

Modern Living'. I really had got a lot of things wrong about these two and I couldn't help thinking about the other men in my life: Pete and James. How would they be coping without a woman in the house?

I heard Andy taking plates out of the oven and went through to help. 'This is a lovely house,' I said.

'Yeah, Mark bought at the right time. I don't know when I'll be able to get back on the property ladder – prices have gone up so much since I last bought anything. All my money's tied up in the café anyway.'

'Which I'm certain is a good investment.'

'Well, it's looking OK at the moment, isn't it? But I think I'll be Mark's lodger a while yet.'

We carried the food through to the dining room and began to eat, mixing the dishes and trying everything at once. Not how Pete would have done it. He'd have insisted on keeping his own meal choice to himself, not interested in anyone else's food. It was better than the Chinese take away in Alcester too, the vegetables and batter were crisp, the flavours of the individual dishes clearly different. Whatever was going on it that chaotic kitchen, it was working.

'I think even Food Snoop would have to admit he was impressed,' I said.

'Hmm, maybe. I didn't think much of their ambience though, could have done without the game show.'

'But the ambience here is good, I love the décor.' The dining room was painted a pale green, the bookshelves in there were tidy and the patio was just visible through the window in the last of the evening light.

'This is mostly Mark's interior design,' Andy said. 'Except for that.'

He pointed to the picture hanging above the fireplace. It was a watercolour of a horse chestnut tree. Each leaf was a different shade of green where the light from the sun lit it or was filtered through it. Stalks of pink blossoms were dotted across the canopy like the lights on a candelabra. The tree's many branches spread to cover the full width of the canvas, casting a patch of shade on the grass below where a man had been captured reclined on a rug, reading a newspaper.

'It's beautiful.'

'My ex painted it for me: a wedding present.'

'Oh, that's you then.' I couldn't imagine how bitter-sweet it must be for him to look at the picture, such a beautiful scene but with a heartbreaking provenance.

'Perhaps I should have guessed something from the fact that the man in the picture was alone,' he said. 'If it is me in the picture, I guess her view of me was of a man by himself.' He gave me a quick, tight smile. 'Anyway, she captured the tree well.'

I returned his smile, impressed by his bravery. 'I'm sensing you have a bit of a thing about trees.'

'More than a bit. I've been accused of obsession on occasion. If you'd asked me what I wanted to be when I was a boy, I'd have said tree surgeon, or maybe tree house builder, depends how young I was. And look at me now: ex-accountant turned café owner.'

I did look at him. What I saw was a kind, sensitive, nice-looking man, doing his best under difficult circumstances and, most importantly, staying positive. And I resolved to try harder myself.

~

CRAIG

Susan wasn't wrong. The breakfast is outstanding. Crisp bacon, meaty sausage, juicy black pudding, baked beans and mushrooms. White toast and brown sauce. The chef (who is definitely gay, can see why Suze got confused) took one look at me and seemed to know exactly what I needed. I'm not sure about the fancy stuff on the menu, but a solid full English like this – they'll do well.

They're not open yet, but didn't mind me coming in. That Andy's eating a bacon bap while he sorts out the coffee machine. Trying not to look at Suze. She's been flapping about laying tables but grabs a mug of tea and comes to join me.

'Did you see Wolfie in the week?'

'Yeah, he was ace.' I scroll to the latest snap of him on my mobile. He's wearing his Thomas the Tank Engine pyjamas and she does the gooey thing. My boy's going to be a heart-breaker. Much like his dad. 'Shame Julia's turned into a psycho-bitch, though.'

'What happened?'

'She sort of propositioned me, but it had a sort of threat to it too. I think it's driving her nuts living with her parents, and she's got the idea that I'm her ticket out of there.'

'Have you forgiven her for deceiving you?'

'She thinks I should have. But of course I haven't. If I saw Trev, I'd flatten him; I wouldn't be able to help myself. And I don't trust her. How could I? She says it's immature not to be able to put it behind us, that we should be able to move on from it, together. She kept saying the word 'together' like she was trying to brainwash me.'

Susan gave me her maternal look and poured more tea into my mug. 'Don't get forced into anything you're not comfortable with, Craig.'

'I haven't told you the best bit yet: when she realised that I wasn't going to play the game, that she couldn't seduce me or trick me into getting back with her, she started on about how maybe she'd go and live with her sister up in Manchester and wouldn't it be a shame that I'd miss out on seeing Wolfie?'

I grabbed the sugar bowl and stirred two heaped spoons into my tea. Poor Suze was frowning, as if she didn't know what to say but felt really uncomfortable not saying anything. I decided I'd spare her an update on the Amisha situation for now; it was less urgent anyway. I've got until Monday to work out how to play things with Amisha; Julia I have to face again tomorrow.

Today though, I'm not playing football, even though it's the last match of the season and a win would get us promotion. Can't say 'us' I suppose, if I'm not on the team any more. Guess I won't know how they do. And when I saw Steve in the week he said there wasn't a space on the cricket team this week, though they do need me next week for a match against a team from Harborne. So I have a whole day stretching ahead of me. Perhaps I'll go up town, buy Wolfie a present before I see him tomorrow. Maybe go round to Mum's later.

'It's eight thirty, Susan,' Andy says. 'Opening time.'

She gives me a sympathetic smile, goes to the door to unlock it and turns the sign round to 'open'. I push back my chair and go to the till to pay. 'Great breakfast,' I tell Andy. 'Top waitress too.'

~

SUSAN

The café was so busy today I hardly had a moment to think of anything but work. As I passed his door on my way home though, I wished I could do something practical for Craig. His ex-girlfriend sounds rather manipulative, and I know I would have stepped in if it was James in that situation.

But Craig's not my son, and I'm not sure I know any good advice anyway. My own son wouldn't take it from me right now if I did and would resent my intrusion.

I wondered where he was; if he was still with his dad, back home in Alcester. Exhausted though I was from work, I knew I wouldn't be able to rest until I'd tried to speak to him again, tried to smooth things over between us. I sank onto the sofa and called his mobile.

'Mum.' He made no attempt to disguise the sigh in his voice.

'Hello, Jamie darling. How are you?'

'Oh I'm just fine, Mum. It's Dad you need to ask about.'

'Sweetheart, I explained. I can't be responsible for him any more.'

'You're not interested in his health then? You don't care that he's in hospital right now?'

I didn't speak for a few moments. I couldn't. I didn't know what I was feeling or thinking. My reactions were conflicted: the instant denial that it was anything to do with me was undermined by the guilty knowledge that no one but me would take charge of this situation. I had to take care of my son at least, and to do that I was going to have to take care of his dad.

As soon as I was sure I had my voice under control, I asked, 'What happened?'

'He went to the golf club yesterday, drank too much and decided to drive home anyway, stupid arse. First thing I know about it was the police ringing the doorbell just after midnight.'

I could hear the crack in his voice, the small boy struggling to cope with the grown up drama he'd been plunged in to.

'What then, darling?'

'They said he'd put the car in a ditch, been taken to hospital. He's got a broken arm, loads of cuts and bruising, and he cracked his head which is what they're really worried about. When I got to the hospital he was muttering and dazed – I wasn't sure how much of that was the drink, how much the bang on his head. So they're keeping him in. Oh, and the police are gonna charge him.'

I couldn't worry about that. I prompted James to tell me what had happened next.

'I drove back over there this afternoon and they've patched him up. But he's covered in bruises and was saying I should bring him home even though the doctor didn't want to discharge him. Started banging on about his civil liberties. You know what he's like.'

I did. I knew all too well what Pete was like and couldn't imagine that if he was getting imperious with the hospital staff there was too much wrong with him. What I didn't like was the thought that James had to pick up the pieces of his father's behaviour because I wasn't there to do it.

'OK, darling. Can you drive over and collect me tomorrow? I'm only in Birmingham, not far. We'll go to the hospital together then I'll help you work out what needs to be done.'

So much for not going back. I dropped my phone on the coffee table and leant back on the saggy cushions. As I'd been talking, the knocking and shuffling noises from upstairs had started again and I thought back to my encounter with the man from that flat. His heavy bag, the way he glared at me. The thick beard and facial features similar to those I'd seen in news reports on TV. Those adverts advising citizens that if they have suspicions, they should voice them to save lives. I covered my gritty eyes with my palms, unable to really believe I'd be unlucky enough to live downstairs from a terrorist, but then luck isn't exactly on my side.

CHAPTER FOURTEEN

CRAIG

At last it's just me and him, running down the hill to the park. Well, I'm running. He's strapped in the buggy, fringe ruffled by the breeze. We're both shouting 'wheeee!'

It's going to be brilliant when he's older and I can put him on a bike, a skateboard, take him on a rollercoaster.

Susan said that yesterday, when she asked about my plans for the weekend and I told her seeing Wolfie would be the highlight. 'Make the most of all the first times,' she said. 'The first time he does something is so special, and if you get to be part of it, then think yourself very lucky.' It might be a few years before I get him on a skateboard, but I fully intend for it to be me who shows him how.

A point which I set Julia straight about while her mum was getting Wolfie ready to come out. 'I'm not interested in getting back together, I won't be guilted into forgiving you and if you move to Manchester Wolfie will be spending weekends with me,' I said before she could play any more tricks on me.

'I just want what's best for Wolfie,' she said, trying to be all innocent with her wet eyes and tremor in her voice.

'Yep. Me too.'

Thank fuck he played the game and didn't get clingy to his mum when I was ready to leave.

'So, Wolf-meister, we have all afternoon and the whole of Cannon Hill park to amuse us. What's your poison: swings or ducks?'

In the absence of a sensible answer from him, I chose swings. Julia's dressed him in ridiculous jeans with patches and straps all over them and it's clear he's not comfortable as I slot him into the safety frame round the seat of the toddler swing.

'Those are stupid trousers, Wolf,' I tell him as they ride up one leg while remaining caught on his shoe on the other. 'Think I need to take over buying clothes. Your mum's dressed you up like you're her doll. What we need is the proper equipment for extreme sports like riding the swings.'

Wolfie listens to me with a serious expression, before gabbling something I choose to interpret as 'stupid trousers'. You're not wrong there, I think as I straighten them out, but keep it to myself as it's obvious the woman pushing the girl on the next door swing is laughing at me.

I quickly get bored of pushing the swing, but Wolfie yells when I try to take him out, so I bung him back in and keep going. I'm still worried that if he throws a tantrum he'll scream for his mum and people'll think I've abducted him. But after fifteen minutes the repetition is doing my head in.

I make a game of yanking him out mid-swing, lift him over my head and in a few aeroplane swoops he's back in the buggy.

'Let's go check out those ducks,' I say and head round the lake for the main lawn.

It's heaving out here – family cricket matches, kick abouts, picnics, it's all happening. Lots of ideas for things I want to do with Wolfie sometime. I'm trying to stop him lobbing the entire bag of bread at the ducks in one go, when an all too familiar voice ruins my day.

'Craig, fancy meeting you here.'

I pick Wolfie up for protection, not sure if it's for my sake or his, and turn round. 'Amisha, good to see you.'

Actually, it is good to see her. She looks amazing in some kind of bright pink sari type thing and a pair of Gucci sunglasses are pushed up on her head pulling her hair back from her face. She's using that amazing smile on Wolfie, who's pulling some moves even I'd be ashamed to try. He's working the whole Lady Di-style head on one side, coyly lowered eyelashes look and Amisha's eating it up.

'Oh, Craig, he's adorable!'

'Yeah, I take full credit for that, obviously. So, what are you doing here? You're dressed for a party.'

'My nephew's birthday, we're having a picnic. My mum, sister and aunties are over there, would Wolfie like to come and have something to eat?'

Well, I don't know about the boy, but I could fancy some party food myself, and I can't risk offending Amisha again. Not after the raincheck excuses I'd given her about going for a drink. So we wander over and Amisha introduces me to about a million Asian women and before I can work out what's happened, I've exchanged Wolfie for a plate of food. He's sat in the middle of the group with a bunch of other kids, his blond head standing out and those terrible jeans an embarrassment compared to the outfits they're wearing.

'Do you always dress like this outside work?' I ask Amisha who's sat next to me on the edge of one of the many rugs they've laid out in the shade of a tree.

'No, just special occasions – parties and stuff.'

'And you're really related to all these people?' I realise that sounds rude the moment it's out of my mouth, but it's OK because she's smiling.

'I'll let you into a secret,' she says. 'Some of the aunties aren't really aunties.'

That sparkle in her eyes lets me know I can take advantage. I lower my voice and lean closer to her, 'Some of them do have more the look of uncles about them.'

She giggles. 'Shush. Anyway, try the pakora, I made them.'

I turn my attention to the plate of food. I have no idea what most of it is, but the smell is incredible. I start to eat and mime my approval to Amisha. She smiles and stretches her legs out in front of her, crossing her ankles. She's wearing an anklet that jingles as she moves her legs and I can't help noticing that her beaded sandals expose how pretty her toes are. The nails are painted pink to match her outfit and a toe ring glints in the light as she moves her foot. I can't remember ever paying attention to details like this.

Perhaps I'm harbouring a foot fetish. I just never realised because frankly, most girls' feet are hideous. Julia's certainly were – all bunions and blisters from shoes she couldn't even walk in.

I'm lost in these thoughts about food and girls when a yell that couldn't come from anyone but Wolfie interrupts me. I leap up and find him red in the face and bawling about something. It seems he hasn't yet learnt how to play nicely with other kids and has raised an objection about a toy car being taken from him. I'm under pressure now. I have to calm the boy and fast, before any of the nice ladies or my boss start to wonder if I have in fact abducted him from his real family.

'Hey Wolf man,' I say, 'you can't be the driver all the time. Come on now.'

He won't look at me, he won't listen, he's all scrunched up in fury and everyone's fallen silent. 'I'm sorry,' I say to the woman I think I remember was Amisha's sister. 'He's normally really well behaved. I think he's too hot today, and overtired.' I don't know what I'm saying, but it sounds good, like the kind of phrases I've heard somewhere before. Fact is, I don't know if he's normally well behaved. I don't know if he's too hot. I don't know what to do. I'm not even sure Wolfie's breathing at the moment.

I bend down and lift his rigid body off the rug. He doesn't turn to me like he's done before, he fights against me and nearly catches an auntie with a flailing foot. 'Don't worry,' she says. 'The terrible twos, yes?'

I decide I'd better get us out of there and mumble some thank yous to Amisha's family while I pin Wolfie back into the buggy, restraining him with the seatbelt. He's yelling and hitting at me, desperate to escape. I'm actually biting my own fucking tongue to stop myself yelling back at him. But I figure that exposing my inadequacy as a parent is more likely to make someone call the police.

167

'Think we'd better go,' I say to Amisha. 'Maybe a walk will calm him down.'

'I'll come with you,' she replies.

Fucking great; that's exactly what I need. 'Great,' I say.

The movement of the buggy does seem to calm Wolfie, who stops yelling although he gives me a murderous look when I hand him his drink. I glare back at him, trying to convey a telepathic message of 'we'll talk about this later'.

'You're great with him,' Amisha says.

Wow, I might actually be getting away with it. 'Yeah, well, just one of my many and varied talents.'

She laughs and bends with a jangle of bracelets to pick up the cup Wolfie's dropped on the pavement, but instead of giving it back to him she whispers, 'He's asleep'.

Brilliant news, he's worn himself out. I push the buggy over to a bench in the shade and pull the sun visor over him too. Amisha sits down, crossing her legs with a tinkle of bells from the anklet.

'So,' she says, 'are we going to go for that drink sometime?'

After the run in with Julia turned out so well earlier, I decide to play this one straight too. 'I like you Amisha. But the whole thing with you being my boss makes things difficult. And I've got so much going on with Wolfie coming into my life, I'm not sure that...'

She cuts me off. 'I didn't ask you to marry me. Don't get carried away. You sound as if you're breaking up with me.'

Bugger. I didn't get that one right then, best to apologise. 'Sorry. It just feels like everyone's playing games with me at the moment. And I can't win any of them.'

'Perhaps you should throw a tantrum?' she says, glancing at Wolfie who, thank fuck, is still asleep.

'I don't think that's a winner's game plan.'

'I really wasn't playing games with you. I wasn't being malicious, I suppose I wanted you to think I was fun to be with.'

She sounds sad and I look at her but she's slipped the sunnies on so I can't read her expression. 'But I do,' I assure her. 'And I think you're gorgeous, but I also think that you being my boss makes things way too complicated.'

She nods. 'Do me a favour? Don't let my mum hear you saying I played games with you. She chose the name Amisha because it means 'free from guile'. She wanted an honest, open, hardworking daughter. It's a hell of a lot to live up to.'

The cheeky smirk is back on her lips and I think I might have got through this unscathed. There's danger in a rejected woman though, so I just say 'It's a beautiful name for a beautiful woman.' Sometimes I'm so smooth I sicken myself. A subject change is called for. 'So where are all the men from your family?'

'You mean the ones who aren't masquerading as aunties?' She points, 'Down there, that cricket match is some of them.' We watch as a young man lopes in to bowl an exaggerated slow ball to the small boy facing him. 'That's my brother bowling, Dasbal.'

'Right, what's his name mean?' I say, instantly uncomfortable about the thought she might have an army of male relatives warming up to unleash retribution on me.

'Dasbal means 'possesses ten powers'.'

Fuck. Ten whole powers to kick my arse with. 'Lovely,' I say, glad that with the bench being in the shade and the match in the sunshine, he probably can't see who's sitting here so I can spy on him in disguise.

'Spin bowling is one of them, he took five wickets for his team yesterday.'

'Who does he play for?' I ask, already anticipating the answer.

'Harborne.'

CHAPTER FIFTEEN

SUSAN

James was waiting in the car park when I left the flat this morning. We've been apart for long periods since he left home for University, but somehow seeing him here made him even more unfamiliar. Or perhaps it was even more obvious how little I fit in to my new neighbourhood. I wasn't sure which.

His hands were shoved deep in his pockets, his shoulders were hunched. He couldn't have been more positioned to avoid a hug from his mother if he tried. It hurt to feel so estranged from my own son, as if recent events have changed us both too much.

I know I've changed; that was the point. But the burden of his dad's behaviour has changed my Jamie. Typical of Pete to be so selfish.

'You're living here?' James said as he looked up at the tall, red brick building. 'Not very you.'

'I don't think I knew what 'me' was before, darling. This is only a short term thing, anyway.' I didn't think it wise to let him see my flat; if he thought I was out of context in the city he probably wouldn't cope with the sight of me in a space more suited to his student friends. Our family home was full of chintzy designs, fringes and tassels – décor which now strikes me as twee and pedestrian. But Pete liked it, the style suited the successful, powerful man he saw himself as, and the submissive wife keeping it neat for him was part of the package.

It was a shock to see him in his hospital bed. He looked old. His hair was uncombed, he had a black eye and red swelling to the left side of his face. The broken arm lay awkwardly propped on his paunch, and crusted scabs of cuts and grazes marked the bare skin between the fresh bandaging and the frayed edge of the short sleeved hospital gown. His normally clean-shaven chin carried several days' worth of grey-flecked stubble.

'Didn't you bring him any pyjamas?' I asked James, and instantly regretted the critical tone in my voice. Of course James hadn't known what to do, he's been cosseted all his life the same as his dad.

When I reached the bedside, Pete and I just looked at each other. The aroma of antiseptic hung around him where normally there'd have been a cloud of cologne. There were so many things I thought about saying and so many reasons I didn't want to be there at all.

When I left him, I didn't think I'd have to speak to him in any meaningful way again. I'd escaped, finally taken full control of my own life. Now here I was, manipulated by him again and cursing my own automatic reaction to take care of him; but I refused to be cowed.

'How are you feeling?' I kept my voice businesslike and buried the concern and sympathy which had welled up as I met his eyes.

'Shit,' he said. 'And surprised to see you. Running back home are you?'

I paused. If that was how he intended to behave, then I wasn't going to feel guilt. 'No, I'm just doing a favour for my son. I'm here to help him work out what to do about you.'

'I think I'll be the one who makes the decisions, Susan…'

'No, you're the one laid up in hospital being charged with drink driving. I'll do what I can to protect James from having to pick up the pieces of that, but I will not be getting involved myself.'

'Jesus, Mum,' James said. 'Could you both be a little less embarrassing about this?'

A nurse stopped by the bottom of Pete's bed and glanced at his notes.

'Will he be kept in much longer?' I asked as she turned to leave without speaking to us.

'The doctor'll be round tomorrow morning, they'll decide then.'

She had my sympathy; I doubted Pete was being an easy patient to care for.

'What do you need bringing in?' I asked him. 'Jamie and I will go and fetch it, I'll help him with anything else that needs sorting, then we can drop your things in when he's taking me back.'

'You're not staying?' Poor James looked agonised; he'd clearly hoped I was back for good.

'No. I can't. I won't. I have work tomorrow anyway.'

'Work!' Pete's tone couldn't have been more dismissive, which was a good thing. It made it easier for me to stay strong.

'Yes, Pete. I have a job, and I am needed there

tomorrow morning. You will have to make your own arrangements.'

I was proud of myself as I left the hospital with James. We'd stayed less than twenty minutes and I'd managed to hold all my emotions in check. I didn't manage as well when we got back to the house though. As soon as I walked in the front door the neglect was apparent. Mud trailed up the beige hall carpet; the air was stale to no one had opened any windows in days; the curtains on the landing were still drawn. The home I'd tended for so long rebuked me for my absence.

I took off my jacket and hung it in the cupboard under the stairs, delaying the moment when I had to walk into the kitchen. I'd spent so many hours in that room, expended so much energy on cooking and washing – my efforts largely unappreciated. I had volunteered to walk back into my prison cell.

It was worse than the vision my feeble imagination had supplied of course. Dirty plates and pans were stacked on the worktops, crumbs and tea stains littered the tiled floor, the blind had been drawn up at an angle and the pots on the window ledge held only the dry remains of the herbs I'd grown there. All trace of my influence had been eradicated by Pete's disregard.

'What have you been eating, Jamie?'

'Take away mostly.'

I could see the pizza boxes stacked up by the bin, along with a collection of beer cans and bottles which hadn't made their way into the recycling box in the utility room.

'Is that all you eat when you're at Uni?'

'No. But it's different here. I can't cook my stuff.'

'Don't be ridiculous. It's only your expectations that are different.' I sighed. If my son was lacking in basic housekeeping skills then some of the blame must lie at my door. 'Why don't we get this cleaned up, then we'll get a bag of things together for your dad?' I sounded as if I was cajoling a nine year old, not sharing tasks with a nineteen year old.

It took us an hour to get the kitchen back into an acceptable condition. I didn't bring it up to the standard I'd have kept it at, but at least James would be able to use it to cook. Leaving him to make us a cup of tea, I went into the living room. The neglect showed there as well. The curtains were only half drawn and my hands automatically looped them into their matching tie backs and straightened the nets. More crumbs from TV dinners were collected around the armchairs and a pile of DVDs sprayed across the carpet by the television. I forced my hands into my pockets and remained standing by the window.

I'd lived in that house twenty years. No, I had kept that house for twenty years: cleaning and polishing, decorating and maintaining. All because that was what Pete wanted: it was his palace. I'd been away less than a month and already he'd let it go. All that time he demanded I kept things nice, and it turns out it mattered so little to him that he let it go immediately. He'd used it to control me, to keep me occupied and distracted. But the thing which had been important to him had been the control, not the result.

So many times he'd found reason to be critical of a perfectly good dinner I'd cooked, or picked up on a tiny fault or omission in the housework. Or if a visitor happened to admire something about the house, he'd find some way of belittling me, brushing it off with a comment like, 'Yeah, Susan had to be good at something I suppose.' And all the time he refused to let me spread my wings, to go out into the world and find out what I could do. He kept me there, left me tending to my cage which, now I'm gone, has no value to him.

James came in with our mugs of tea. I decided it was time to talk to him like the grown up he was going to have to be.

'James, do you understand why I left?'

He looked surprised and couldn't quite meet my eyes or respond.

'I should never have married him. I was your age; I didn't know what was good for me. My mum and dad always treated me as if I was a disappointment to them – you must have noticed that. So when your dad treated me as if I was a princess, I thought he was perfect. But once we were married and I'd had you, he turned out to be just the same as them: undermining me, holding me back, making me think I was good for nothing.' There were tears in my eyes, but I was determined to tell James the whole truth.

'I wanted to have more babies. Wouldn't you have loved a brother or sister? But he said no, didn't I think I struggled enough looking after just you and him? You're his little prince and he wasn't going to let me do anything that would dilute my attention or loyalty to the pair of you. When you left for Uni, well, I thought I might finally get some time for me. Your dad took his early retirement though, said he wanted me at home with him. Can you imagine? Twenty four hours a day with his demands and criticism. I'm in my forties, James, not my eighties. It's time for my life to start.'

He'd slumped onto the sofa, cradling his mug as he listened. For a while he didn't say anything, but then he took a sip of tea and asked, 'Has it then, has your life started?'

'I have a job where my bosses appreciate me. I have some new friends. My flat is not ideal, but it's OK for now.' I went to sit next to him. 'I wish you could be part of it though. Knowing I've hurt you has been the hardest thing.' The doorbell rang, making us both jump. 'I don't think I should get it. I don't live here anymore.'

James dragged himself off the sofa and I wiped my eyes and found a space on the messy coffee table to place my mug.

'It's Adrienne,' he said, and showed her into the room. 'I'll go and get Dad's things together.'

I was surprised how pleased I was to see her. Although I'd claimed to James that I'd made new friends in Birmingham, the reality was that they were really neighbours or work colleagues and were all men. Of the group of women I knew in Alcester, Adrienne was the one I most admired. She lives with her husband, Dominic, in a house a few doors down across the road and I always wished we'd been closer friends.

'I thought that was you at the window,' she said. 'Are you back?'

'No, just helping James.'

'Good. I couldn't believe it when Pete said you'd left, but I don't blame you one little bit. And now the silly bastard's in hospital. Dominic told me what he was like at the club that night. Obnoxious!'

I was amazed to hear her talk like that. She'd never expressed an opinion about my life in the entire time

I'd known her. Now her attitude brought a guilty smile to my face. 'Your French accent makes that word sound even more despicable.'

'Absolutely! He should be ashamed of himself, but I suppose he isn't. So, where have you gone? What are you doing?'

Her utter dismissal of Pete and interest in my life empowered me. It was the first time someone else who knew Pete had criticised him to me. I only wished she'd done it years before. 'But it's James I'm worried about,' I said, after I'd told her the rest of my tale, 'I can't bear him having to take on looking after his dad. He can't really even take care of himself. And look at this place.'

She looked around with a wrinkled nose. 'You need to be strong, Susan.'

~

I tried to keep her words in mind when James and I got back to the hospital. The thin cotton curtains were pulled around Pete's bed and I felt awkward about intruding. I no longer felt I had any right to cross into his personal space and I waited until James had drawn the faded pastel print fabric back along its rattling track before I stepped forward. As he took the bag of clothes, toiletries, electric razor and golf magazines from James, I noticed that Pete had tidied himself up a little and was sitting straighter in the bed. 'Can I have a word with your mum on her own?' he asked James.

James slouched off and I gripped hard on the strap of my handbag. 'I can't stay long, Pete. I need to get home…'

'I know, you have work in the morning. I'm impressed.' I couldn't detect any sarcasm in his voice.

'I don't like hearing you call somewhere else 'home' though.'

My tension increased. 'What did you want to talk about?'

'I've been an idiot, I know that. But the truth is I'm not coping without you. I never got myself in trouble with the police before. I never landed up in hospital. And you must have seen the state the house is in? I need you, Susan. I need you back. Tell me what you want me to do.'

CHAPTER SIXTEEN

CRAIG

Mum hasn't changed anything about my old bedroom. The poster of the 1991 Leyland DAF cup-winning Blues squad is still hanging in prime position over the desk with the broken drawers. More embarrassingly, the Britney Spears in bikini poster is still over the bed. I can't help thinking about how stunning Amisha looked on Sunday. That glimpse of smooth, brown skin between the tight little top and where the skirt of the sari started - sorry, Brit, but that was way more sexy than your over exposure.

Amisha was working her naughty secretary look today. Pencil skirt, tight top, high heels. Hot. Not that she acted like a secretary though, oh no. Frank, the Marketing Director, didn't know what had hit him when she presented her assessment of the conference and the number of expressions of interest we already have. He referred to us as the dream team. Ha.

I open the wardrobe to see if I did keep some cricket boots and pads. The stink released is enough to wipe any thought of sex from my mind. If I did keep some school sports kit, something's died in it. I rummage around and decide that actually, the whole lot should be binned.

'Did you find what you wanted?' Mum asks as I pop into the kitchen for a black bag.

'Found a lot of stuff no one would want.'

'Ah, nothing you want to keep for Wolfie then?'

'Don't think my rotting jockstrap'll make any kind of heirloom.'

I run back upstairs and bundle everything into the bin liner, ripping Britney down and adding her too. When I pop out to the back garden to leave the bag in the dustbin, Helen next door is getting her washing in.

'Hey, Helen. I never said thanks for helping Mum sort out those toys for Wolfie.'

'That's no problem, bab. Your mum says he's a sweetheart. Listen, have you got a minute?'

I walk towards her, picking dust and threads off my suit trousers. I can't help noticing that Mum's garden is totally overgrown, especially when I look over the fence at Helen's.

'Your mum says your job's going well. You certainly look like a successful young executive.'

'Yeah, things are working out all right at the moment.'

'Well, I hate to give you bad news, but I'm a little worried about your mum.'

There's a buzzing in my ears and I can't seem to focus. I can see Helen's mouth moving, but she's not speaking English. My heart's pounding away and I can't get a breath.

'...just think you should get her to see a doctor,' Helen says.

'Wha..?' is all I can say.

'It might not be anything serious, but I wanted to let you know so you can make sure, OK bab?'

'Yeah.'

No. Not OK. Not even a tiny bit.

~

Mum's dishing up the tea when I get back to the kitchen – pork chops, mash and peas. My plate is overloaded, she's hardly got anything. She carries our plates to the table and winces as she sits down.

'Are you OK?' I ask as I join her.

'Yes, love, course I am. Get it while it's hot.' She passes me the brown sauce.

'It's just that Helen said…'

'Oh, she didn't tell you about my little tumble! It wasn't anything to worry about, you know my knees are bad. I'm in my sixties, I can't expect them to manage steps as easily as they used to.'

The word Helen had used came back to me, the one I hadn't wanted to hear: confused. 'She said you didn't seem yourself, Mum.'

'Well I'd had a shock. Finding myself sat on the floor like that. But it's only a bit of bruising, nothing to worry about.'

I slice into my chop and dip the meat into the sauce but lay the fork down again without eating. 'Will you see a doctor though? Can I come with you? Just set my mind at rest, yeah?'

~

SUSAN

I am good at my job. It may only be waitressing but I'm competent and I work hard. Andy praised and thanked me several times today. Mark cut through to the point.

'What's up, Susie? Not your usual sparkling self

today.'

I took it as a criticism and apologised, but he stepped forward and placed a hand on each of my shoulders to hold me still. 'No, it's OK,' he said. 'I'm just worried something's wrong. Anything we can do?'

His kindness was hard to bear. The café was busy again today: regular customers gave their congratulations when they saw the framed review hung in the window and there were more lunchtime visitors than usual, perhaps drawn in by curiosity. Mark had been bouncing around the kitchen, singing along with the radio as he turned out plate after perfect plate. Andy smiled more than usual, his anxious frown only showing when he had to turn away a party of six because there were no free tables.

The thought of letting the brothers down was torture.

They've given me an opportunity, built my confidence, become my friends. Seeing Tall Trees becoming successful gives me a thrill too; I've started to feel part of the team there. But, no matter how kind they've been, I have to think about my true responsibilities. I may be good at my job, but it's only a job.

'I'm impressed by you, Susan. I really didn't think you'd manage on your own,' Pete had said.

'Whereas you,' I replied, 'you can't manage at all.'

Seeing him in that hospital bed, reduced to a patient, choked me. Adrienne had told me I had to be strong,

'You let him walk over you for too long,' she'd said. And she was right: I'd let him. I let him take advantage of me because I was grateful that he loved me. I allowed him to behave the way he did because I enjoyed his protection.

Now he needs protection. He needs to be taken care of while his injuries heal; he needs help with whatever comes from the drink driving charge. And our son needs me to lift that burden from him.

James and I didn't talk as he drove me back to Birmingham. He turned into the car park, pulled on the handbrake, but left the engine running. I thought about inviting him up to make him some dinner but he glanced at me and said, 'I'll be off then.'

I let him go without making any promises about when I'd call him or see him next. I hadn't decided what to do.

My first argument with Pete – 1987

I can't believe I was silly enough to disagree with Pete this evening. He really does only want what's best for me. Of course I don't need to go on the Christmas outing with the girls from college – they'll all be out looking for boys and getting drunk. I certainly don't need to do that. And it's so kind of him to offer to take me to the same bar another time.

He hates losing his temper, especially with me. He was so apologetic afterwards and kept telling me how much he loves me – how no-one will ever love me as much as he does. I need to try harder to deserve it because he really is the best thing that ever happened to me.

~

I nipped off from work as soon as I'd left everything straight tonight. Mark and Andy were in the kitchen when I went to get my mac, talking about what they needed from the wholesalers.

'Want to come with us, Susie?' Mark asked. 'Little bit of retail therapy with the bulk buy washing powder?'

I couldn't get out fast enough. The concern in the way Andy looked at me and Mark's attempts to cheer me up increased my guilt at the thoughts I'm having. Back at the flat, I couldn't settle. I pottered around doing bits of housework: a little ironing that was hardly worth getting the iron hot for, emptying the bins.

Craig was coming in as I dropped off my bag at the refuse cupboard downstairs. His shoulders were slumped and his 'Hey, Suze' lacked its usual vigour. We trudged up the stairs together and I accepted his offer of a cup of tea.

As he made the drinks in his kitchenette, I stood by his window with its view of the city. The light was fading and the street lights coming on. Everywhere were signs of life from illuminated shop windows to car headlights moving along the street below. Everywhere people were busy living their lives and I hesitantly mentioned my foolish thoughts about the man upstairs.

'Don't be daft, you've been watching the news too much. Course there's loads of Muslims here but there aren't terrorists. He sounds like your average useless bloke. Take it from me – I'm an expert.'

Of course Craig isn't useless. I got it out of him why he seemed down tonight – his mum's not well.

'Do you think I'm overreacting?' he said. 'I'll have to go with her to the appointment or she'll fob me off and tell me everything's fine. I don't know what I'd do if she's ill though. She hasn't got anyone but me.'

How could I give him advice? Not while I was stood there thinking that James was in much the same position with his dad, but James did have someone to turn to for help. James had me.

I turned away from the window and said, 'I think family always has to come first.'

CHAPTER SEVENTEEN

CRAIG

'Piss off, Gav,' I say as he mimics Amisha calling 'Craig, can I borrow you?' I walk over to her office and close the door as she indicates.

'Actually, I wanted a word with you too. Any chance I can get Thursday morning off?'

She frowns, 'Well, it wouldn't be very convenient, I was about to tell you we've been summoned to Head Office for a meeting on Friday. I thought we could spend Thursday working on a presentation for them.'

'Maybe Gavin could help you?'

'Maybe Gavin could. But it's not Gavin the board want to see at their meeting. That would be you and me.'

Bloody hell. The board want to see me? They've barely ever shown any interest in what goes on at this office and now they've asked for me and Amisha by name?

'You did really well in the interview for this job you know. People are talking about you. Well, and me. This will be great exposure for us.'

'Sounds it. But the thing is, it's my mum. I want to go to this medical appointment with her.'

Amisha's face changed. The calculating professional was replaced by total concern. She reached across her desk and put a hand on mine. 'Oh Craig, is she OK?'

'I don't know. That's why I'd rather be there.'

She agrees of course. She's way too nice not to.

I grab Gav's mug from his desk and wander to the kitchen to make us a brew. Steve's in there washing his Villa mug.

'All right?' we say in unison.

'Still on for Saturday?' he asks.

'Yeah, course. Are they a bit good, this Harborne team?'

Steve nods, and dries his mug, giving the fucking Villa shield a polish. I give our cups a quick swill and dump a couple of tea bags in them.

'They're top of the league. I imagine they'll beat us.'

That'd be right; it's all I deserve for touching Dasbal's sister. Shame Steve and the rest of the team have to suffer too though. 'Things busy in your department?' I ask.

'Bit of trouble actually.' He glances out into the corridor to see if anyone's around and I lean in to catch the gossip. 'Did you hear that the firm's lost its two biggest contracts? We're under pressure to look for savings everywhere. There's talk of job cuts.'

'Shit, no! I've just been called to a board meeting in London on Friday. You don't think they're going to hand me my cards, do you?'

'Not how it happens. They send an HR bod round to have a chat with you and next thing you know you're packing up your desk. Half the Edinburgh office have already gone.'

I ladle the sugar into our drinks wondering how I hadn't heard this on the grapevine.

'Keep schtum though, Craig. I shouldn't really have told you. The story's not meant to get out, OK?'

'Okey doke,' I say and mime zipping my lips. Then I unzip them and ask, 'Any chance of a lift on Saturday?'

We arrange the time and I take the mugs back to my desk, leaning over to hand Gav his. He's on the phone and sounds like he's arranging a meeting. After he's hung up he sticks his head over the partition between us, 'Wonder why personnel want to see me,' he says.

~

SUSAN

Leaving Tall Trees will be even more difficult than leaving Pete. I broke it to Andy and Mark first thing. I couldn't stand another day of them being kind even though it was the hardest conversation I've ever had to start. I haven't got a formal contract to work there, but thought it was only fair to give them a week's notice.

'But why, Susie? Aren't you happy here?' Mark looked devastated. Andy wouldn't look at me at all.

'Of course I am, I love working here. And I love working with you two. But I've got some family problems and I need to concentrate on them.'

The day was subdued, even though the number of customers seemed even higher than the day before. Mark didn't sing in the kitchen and Andy barely moved from behind the counter. He made a 'Waitress/Waiter needed. Apply within' sign and stuck it in the window below Food Snoop's review.

After closing time, as I was clearing all the tables down, I could hear their raised voices in the kitchen. I didn't want to intrude, but had to pop in to grab my things and overheard Mark hiss at Andy, 'Don't be a coward all your life.'

'I'll see you on Thursday, then,' I said and left.

I'd got as far as the bus stop on the High Street before Andy caught up with me. He was flushed and frowning. 'Susan, I wanted to…, could we…, um. Can you spare a few minutes to come for a walk with me?'

The guilt of how much I'd upset him cut in to me. In the last few days he's been relaxed and happy, now here he was, almost as anxious as when I first met him. 'OK,' I said.

We walked into the same park we'd visited before, heading down towards the arboretum in silence. Over the last week, the trees seemed to have bloomed into full leaf, and slices of sunlight filtered through and drew shadow lattice-work across the pot holed path.

Eventually Andy chose a bench he was happy with and sat down with his back to a topiary trimmed yew hedge. I joined him, placing my bag on the seat between us. We were surrounded by reminders that we were in the suburbs: the faint sound of traffic from a nearby road, a childish shout, a football being kicked and a dog barking. Everywhere people were using the space as an extension to their cramped interiors, living their lives in a public space. It wasn't as busy as on our last visit though; weekday routines were obviously keeping people at home.

Andy leant forward with his elbows on his knees and his hands clenched together. Then he turned to me and took hold of my right hand. 'I don't know how to say this, Susan, but I know Mark's right. I'll always have regrets if I don't say it. So, listen, I know you've never told us much about your personal life, and I may have assumed some things completely wrong, but it seems to me that... No, I know that you're a completely wonderful woman, and if you left your husband when you came here, no, if he let you go, then he doesn't deserve you. I mean, are you sure you're making the right choice to leave now? Because, well, like I said, I think you're wonderful and I realise that you might not think anything of me, but if I don't say so now, if I didn't tell you that I was wondering if there might be something between us now – while you're in this in-between stage – then I may never get to. And I wanted you to know that. Just in case it affected your decision at all.'

From the corner of my eye I could see he'd flushed even redder and that, while the hand which held mine was relaxed, the other was white knuckled as it gripped his knee.

Craig had been right: this kind, modest, hard working, quiet, beautiful man really did want to be more than my boss and friend. He'd managed to blurt out an impossibly long speech and was now hunched in on himself, not even looking at his beloved trees.

I enclosed his hand in both of mine and told him everything – about how Pete and I met, about all we'd done together, about James.

I told him how Pete had treated me, how repressed and submissive I'd been, how coming to Birmingham had allowed me to explore parts of my character I'd never known. And I told Andy how I felt about him.

191

'You opened doors for me, you and Mark. You gave me confidence when I had none. And you especially Andy, you've been so kind and gentle and looked after me in a way which has made me feel special – the exact opposite of everything Pete did. I think you might actually be perfect.' I sighed and let go of his hand. 'But I'm not, and I have to go back to my imperfect family and do what I can to help them because I'm responsible for them.'

We sat without talking until the silence began to feel uncomfortable. The fine needles on the nearest pine trees shivered in a breeze, while the fronds on others swayed as if to sweep me away. I picked up my bag and shifted to the edge of the seat, perparing to leave.

'Don't you deserve to be happy? Isn't that why you left him?'

'I needed to find out who I am and what I can do. I'm going back with that knowledge so I won't be as unhappy as I was before.'

His shoulders sagged even further forwards. 'Is there any point me insisting that I could make you completely happy?'

I stood and turned to face him. 'No. I'm afraid not. I have to do this for my family.'

I burned with guilt as I dragged myself back to the bus stop and left him sitting there, alone, in the shade of a tree.

~

James came to collect me again and took me back to Alcester for the day.

'It's got to be different,' I told Pete as I pulled my apron over my head and began to prepare lunch. 'This family has to operate on different terms, with me as an equal partner.'

'Of course, darling. I know you're Superwoman now, I'll be your trusty sidekick.'

He hasn't lost any of his charm, despite the bandaged arm and bruising. Over lunch I told him about Tall Trees and the review in the paper. I played down my role, praising Mark's cooking above everything. I hardly mentioned Andy.

'Perhaps you can get a job here in Alcester,' Pete said. 'Something part time maybe. I'm sure you can do better than waitressing though, you should be in charge of something – I could coach you.'

'Perhaps,' I said.

James cleared the meal up, while Pete came to sit beside me on the sofa, rather than on his usual armchair.

'Won't you stay tonight?' he asked, putting his good arm around my shoulders. 'I've really missed you.'

'I have to work at the café tomorrow.'

'Call in sick. Go on, what can they do? Sack you?'

'I don't want to let them down.'

He took his arm away and leant to lift the remote control from the coffee table. 'Ah, you're too soft, you are.'

No, I thought. I was too soft, in the past. Now I'm responsible, but assertive. 'I'll work out the rest of my notice,' I told him, 'then Jamie can come and collect me when the café closes on Saturday afternoon.'

'And what about the stuff you took to that flat?' His finger hovered over the power button.

'I can't get out of the contract, so we'll look into collecting it another time. Perhaps when your arm's better.'

'I won't be able to drive.' Pete's solicitor had advised him he was likely to be banned for three years. He pressed the button and the screen flashed into life, presenting us with a view of a pristine fairway and a golfer preparing his shot while his caddy stood by.

'No. So we'll have to get me a car.'

CHAPTER EIGHTEEN

CRAIG

It must be three years since I was at this surgery, and that was only for some injections so I could go to Turkey on holiday with Julia. Fucking disaster that turned into.

I want to get out of here before I catch something now. Bloody invalids, coughing and sneezing all over the waiting room. Bloody doctor sniffing constantly while he looks at his computer and not at Mum's knees.

'How are you getting on with the anti-inflammatories?' he asks. Like they're a new friend she might not have clicked with.

'Fine, but my son insisted we come and see you again because I had this little fall.' She's doing her telephone voice, like she has to be respectful to this wanker who's barely acknowledged her existence.

'Yes,' I say, with perhaps more volume than needed, 'Mum fell, and her neighbour was worried that she didn't seem quite herself afterwards.'

'When was this?' The doctor has taken the trouble to look at Mum now, his eyes travelling over her face.

She plays it down, like I knew she would. 'Oh, it was nothing really, I don't know quite what I did…'

But that's why I forced my way in here. 'Helen said you seemed confused, Mum. Best to let the doctor decide if it's important or not.'

There you go mate, what are you going to do about that? Take her temperature, apparently. And ask for a urine sample. Maybe Mum would have been better handling this on her own. She steps out to fill the little pot.

'Has she been confused any other time?' Doc asks me while she's gone.

'No, same as usual really. The knees seem to be getting worse, that's all.'

I look away as Mum comes back, really don't need to see her wee. Doc does some tests and says, 'You do seem to have an infection in your waterworks, rather common I'm afraid – and could possibly explain a little confusion, especially combined with the shock of falling. I'll give you antibiotics and also refer you to the hospital. I'd like the consultant to look at your knees again, maybe consider knee replacement surgery.'

'Surgery?' Mum yelps.

'Very common operation, nothing to worry about.' The doc's lost interest again – waterworks infection clearly not dramatic enough for him.

'Hold on,' I say. I'm determined to make him work for his wages. 'Can you tell us about this operation? I don't want to leave here with mum worried about it.'

The doctor sighs, turns his chair towards us and gives us a summary of the fact she'd likely be in hospital for a week, then need care while she recovered for a good few months. 'And the waiting list will be at least a few months long. It could make all the difference to your mobility though.'

'But I live on my own, doctor. I haven't got anyone to care for me.' Mum's voice has taken on a panicky tone.

'Hey, you've got me.' I'm not totally useless am I? 'I could do your shopping, get your meals together or something.'

'And you'd probably qualify for some kind of home help from the council,' the doc adds.

Mum's upset though. She takes her prescription and does her one, two, three to stand up. I help her put her jacket back on and open the door.

'So we'll hear from the hospital, yeah?' I ask the doc as we leave. He's already moved on though and just grunts in response.

~

SUSAN

I knocked on Craig's door when I heard him come home in case I don't see him again before I leave. The offer of another chilli for supper was so simple, so basic – it really didn't deserve the gratitude with which he responded. But we had a lovely evening: I cooked, he talked. He poured the wine, I talked. Perhaps I'll be able to develop this kind of friendship with Adrienne when I'm settled back in Alcester, now that she's broken the façade of reserve between us.

Being friends with Craig has never been hard work though. We accepted each other somehow, met a need in each other's lives and were lucky we got on so well; despite how unlikely the friendship is. With Adrienne, there was always the issue that she wasn't just a neighbour, she was the wife of one of Pete's golf pals. Appearances had to be kept up. And perhaps will continue to be. Even if Pete has promised to change how he treats me, I don't doubt he'll still be the same to his friends. Whether Adrienne and I will be able to develop anything more meaningful outside the network we're already held in remains to be seen.

Tonight though, neither Craig nor I could have hoped for a better friend.

'Knew it,' he said when I told him he'd been right about Andy. 'Are you sure about leaving though? If you don't mind me saying so, your husband sounds a right knob.'

I had to laugh. Craig's made my brief stay here so much more pleasant than it might have been. And I hope I've been some use to him.

'I'm sure your mum's health problems aren't as serious as they seem,' I said.

'She's so pale.' His voice was strangled with concern. He's so healthy, so young and full of life that it's hard for him to give her ailments the right perspective. 'And she stoops more. I've been taller than her since I was thirteen, but now, now she's so frail…'

'I'm sure once this infection's sorted she'll seem better. Come on, Craig, how old did you say she was? Mid sixties is nothing. Yes, she's ageing, but she's not ready for her grave yet.'

'But her arthritis is getting so bad. She had to work for so long – standing on the lines at Cadbury's, that can't have done her any good.'

'Maybe the op will revitalise her.'

'I'll have to be there though, I can't rely on anyone else to look after her right. But I'm with Wolfie two evenings and one day at the weekend, I'm at work all day – though there's trouble brewing there – I don't know how I can do it all. I suppose at least I haven't got footie any more.'

I didn't give him a hard time about the football incident. How could I? He knows he made a mistake, that he shouldn't have lashed out; but controlling his temper isn't going to be easy when he's under so much pressure. I only hope he's learnt not to use his fists to resolve things again.

In my mind, I can't help comparing every man to Andy these days. I can't imagine Andy ever being violent; actually, I've never known him show an interest in sport either. His approach to difficulty is to work out how to resolve it in a calm and mature way. I was worried that we'd be awkward with each other when I went in this morning. With my day off yesterday we hadn't spoken since I left him in the park and I'd been nervous as the bus took me towards Kings Heath, wondering what I should say.

But he took the initiative and surprised me with an apology. 'I shouldn't have said what I did, Susan. I hope I haven't made you uncomfortable about working here. I want you to see me as a friend still, anything else was just me being, oh, silly I suppose. You're only here a few more days, I hope you'll still enjoy them.'

We weren't quite as easy with each other as before, but then I have added to his problems. A couple of young women came in to ask about the waiting job but we could all tell at a glance that they wouldn't be right, they wouldn't fit in to the Tall Trees family. One spoke too loudly, her opinions broadcast across the café, highlighted with expletives. The other had no work experience and the panic in her eyes when

Andy described the opening hours suggested that early mornings weren't in her vocabulary.

Mark gave me several hugs, whenever I spent a quiet moment in the kitchen. 'Don't worry about Andy,' he said. 'You have to focus on what's right for you, my darling Susie.'

It's one of the things I think I'll miss most: the fond nicknames Mark and Craig have given me. They christened me into my new life and now I'll have to go back to being plain, old Susan and leave the new names behind me.

'The thing is, Suze,' Craig said as he left after dinner, 'I didn't expect to like you. I thought you'd be boring or cold. But you've been brilliant; the best neighbour I could hope for. I wouldn't even want Davo back now. I'll miss you.'

He hugged me too. It was different from being hugged by Mark. Mark is slim and his arms seemed to cradle me. Craig has gym toned muscles and applied them to full effect, crushing me against his broad chest. I felt true affection from them both though.

Craig and I knew there was no point making claims we'd stay in touch. His life moves at an entirely different speed from mine in Alcester, and I can't imagine Pete would understand why I'd want to be friends with a handsome twenty-five year old in Birmingham.

'Well, you know where I am,' was all he said in farewell to me.

And, 'I'll be thinking of you,' was all I had for him as I closed my front door. In the silence of his absence I heard the thumps on my ceiling. I'll miss Craig, but I certainly won't miss the man upstairs.

~

CRAIG

Chilli! Bloody hell, Suze, I can tell from Amisha's expression that she can smell the garlic coming off me and isn't impressed. OK, well she's had a hour and a half cooped up on a train with me to get used to it, now I just have to make sure I don't sit too close to any of the suits at this board meeting. The boss is in full on career woman mode this morning: sharp tailoring, shiny shoes and no hint of teasing sparkle in her eyes.

Which means I'd better not fuck up I suppose. And that as we're walking through the revolving door into the foyer of the London office is a bad time for my Mission: Impossible ringtone to sound. I grab the phone from my pocket and, seeing it's Gav, think I'd better take the call in case it's work related.

'The fuckers have totally fucked me!'

It is work related then, just not that relevant to the meeting. Amisha's signed us in at the desk and beckons me to follow her.

'They've taken my fucking job, Craig.' Gav's anger is making the line crack but I daren't hold the phone away from my ear in case his words leak out into Amisha's hearing.

'OK, Gav, calm down. Tell me quickly, and quietly, what's happened.'

Quickly and quietly are not words Gav is currently capable of comprehending. I've followed Amisha into an area where there's a table laid out with coffee, clearly the break out space from the meeting room. I nod and give a stupid thumbs up to her indication of 'do you want a coffee?'

I don't want to let Gav down by not listening when he needs to vent, but there's only so much of 'those fucking wankers', 'fuckers blame everything on the recession', and 'fucking hell, I'm fucked' that I can listen to while Amisha is giving me the 'get off the phone, now!' look.

I feel bad as I mumble an excuse to Gav, but really, I've got to go.

'You watch your step down there, Craig. Fuckers probably want to have a laugh by dragging you down there to tell you your job's gone.'

I arrange to meet him for a drink when I get back to Brum tonight and briefly summarise the situation for Amisha. 'Did you know it was going to happen?' I ask.

'Yeah,' she says, with a grimace. 'It's been on the cards a while I'm afraid. When they gave me this job there was a lot of talk about how I needed to make an impression, and fast. Which is why you and I are here now. Marketing's being consolidated into one team in this office, with most activity outsourced. We need to position ourselves to make sure we're indispensable. You'd be interested in relocation, right?'

I mumble something that doesn't commit. She knew all this but didn't think to mention it? I'm glad I didn't get her job now, there's no way I could have fucked Gav over like that. OK, so he was never employee of the month material, but still, it's callous.

A few people are starting to gather for the meeting and Amisha's networking: shaking hands, smiling, swishing that hair. The men are smiling right back at her. Course they are. Not me though, no I'll just stand here and stir my coffee.

'Ready, Craig?' she asks, appearing by my shoulder again. 'Time to give this our best shot.'

'Yes, boss,' I say. 'Our best is all we can do.'

CHAPTER NINETEEN

CRAIG

My life just makes me die. I've turned up for cricket feeling crap and yesterday couldn't have been any worse.

Amisha was great at the meeting. She ought to be in charge of the sodding firm. Damn, I'd hire her myself, twice. So she was on a high on the train coming home, not in the mood for me to be challenging her about the Gav situation. I really should learn when to keep my mouth shut.

'You could have warned him to sharpen up if you saw it coming,' I said.

'Face facts, Craig: someone had to go. Would you rather it had been you? No, you'd rather it had been me, right? You've never got over the fact I got this job.'

'"Free from guile" that's what you said you were. Do you think Gav would agree with that right now?'

'Life isn't easy, you know. It isn't straight forward. But I intend to keep my job and go somewhere with it. If you're not interested in surviving, fine. We did a great job in that meeting. We make a good team. There's definitely potential for us to hang on here. You want to throw it away because you're feeling loyal to Gav? Go right ahead.'

I pretended I hadn't seen her dabbing at her eyes, ignored the tell tale jangle of bracelets as she lifted her hand to her face. I hadn't wanted to make her cry but frankly, I was the one who was about to have to pick up the pieces of Gav. I was the one who deserved some sympathy. She barged past me when we got off the train at New Street and slipped through the crowd to head up the stairs. I loitered at the back, waiting behind the fuckwits with huge bags who don't realise there's an escalator if you go round the other side. It's not like I was in a hurry to meet Gav.

He was already drunk when I joined him in the pub. He was slumped on the bar with his collection of executive desk toys in a Tesco's bag by his feet.

'Craig man!' he yelled and drew too much attention to us. The pub was already busy with Friday after-work drinkers and I decided to get him out of there, fast. 'Yeah,' he agreed, 'a pub crawl! Let's go to Broad Street.'

Broad Street is not what it was. I hadn't been there in months, since Davo left I guess, but it's changed. Doesn't feel like party central any more. All feels a bit sad, especially when you're in the company of a newly redundant, drunken mate. The bouncers were not kind to us, several suggested 'Leave it for tonight, lads.'

I was tired; I'd had four queasy pints on an empty stomach, I'd more or less persuaded Gav that we should get some chips then find our buses home when a bad day got worse. I'd managed to get him in the chip shop without too much fuss. Then, with the honesty of the drink inside him, he apologised to a girl he'd jostled in the queue. 'I'm really, really sorry,' he slurred. 'I wouldn't have bumped into you, it's just, you see, it's just that you're really fat.'

We managed to get out of there without a fight, but also minus chips, and if I had every moment in the whole year to choose from, that one was the worst possible moment for me to bump into Trev. So of couse that's what fucking happened.

We looked at each other for a few seconds, me holding Gav like he was a bull terrier on a leash, Trev holding hands with a blonde in high heels and no skirt or top that I could see. I'd swear she had nothing but underwear on. There was no other way that situation could end except with some fucker getting hurt.

Gav took the worst of the physical pain, but I'll claim the emotional scars. I was paralysed, I couldn't move or say anything – which didn't matter, because Gav took control of the situation effortlessly.

'Are you telling me this wanker's Trev?' he said, and turned to aim a punch at Trev's face.

Blondie yelped and moved away as fast as she could hobble on her stupid shoes. Trev ducked the punch easily and put a restraining hand out to Gav, who went down like he was in the penalty box. A group of girls tottered past, giving us a wide berth while the windows of a passing pimped up Peugeot were wound down to allow the boys inside a better view of proceedings. I was determined that there was nothing to see though, even once they'd added the thumping bass soundtrack.

'Let's leave it, OK?' I said to Trev as I helped Gav up. He wasn't bleeding or broken, just looking confused as if unsure how it was him on the floor rather than Trev. 'You carry on with your nice night out. I'll keep busy with my fucked up life.'

'Is he all right? I barely touched him.'

'Orl roight?' Gav managed to slur, the beer having added several more vowels to his Black Country accent. 'Don't talk to me about all right!'

'Really, let's leave it.' I was keen to get moving. The bouncers at the pub next door were adjusting their flourescent arm-bands and getting ready to dive in and I didn't fancy a personal introduction between their fists, my head and the pavement.

'I'd like to talk some time though, Craig. Set the record straight, you know.'

Yeah, I know. He wanted to make himself feel better, make it all my fault that he's a wanker. 'Whatever,' I said, 'but not fucking now.'

I managed to get Gav away without anyone hitting him which was some kind of fucking miracle. He did spew his guts out at the bus stop though. Cue screaming from yet more hordes of dippy girls. There were nights when I'd have been interested in them, now all I get is Wolfie, or Mum or fuckers like Gav to look after.

And now, today, when I'm feeling like seven shades of shit, I have to strap on my pads and walk out to the wicket. Where I will be facing the spin bowling of Dasbal who has already started with the taunts: 'Hear you know my sister, man. She's your boss, innit?'

My number's coming up in the batting order. It won't be long before he's dispatched Stevo and I'm next man in. Yep, there's the applause from the outfield. Time to leave the safety of the pavilion. Time to be fucking crucified.

~

SUSAN

I'm not sure I'll be able to sleep here. I may only have been away a few weeks, but I've become used to not having to share the bed. Now I'm back lying tense beside the bulk of Pete, counting the gaps in between his snores, and finding I even miss the noise from the Moseley Road: the late night mini cabs, the drumming stereos, the police sirens.

That doesn't happen in Alcester; not in our road anyway. This is a respectable area where everyone abides by certain rules, such as not saying what they're thinking.

I wondered briefly about sleeping in the guest bedroom, but Pete clearly expected me to return to his side and it seemed to be the right thing to do – to come in here with him. We're using the sheets from the guest room though; I don't know when Pete had last washed the easy care set I bought for our bed. It'll take me a while to get the house straight again. Lying next to my husband on high thread count bed linen, I'm not sure I've ever been more uncomfortable. The thought that I'll have to iron these sheets isn't helping.

It is the right thing to do though. To show that I'm committed to my marriage and that, if I can do this, then I expect Pete to stand by his promises too. I expect more consideration, more attention, for my opinions to be listened to. I've come back here with more confidence than I've ever had. This is a turning point for us.

Not that it started well. I suppose I was still emotional from leaving Tall Trees on the busiest I've known there. From the moment Andy unlocked the doors there was a constant turnaround of customers in for breakfasts, coffees, lunches, and teas.

We wedged the sticky door open and let warm air from outdoors fill the room, bringing customers with it. As soon as a table was free, the chairs were taken again almost before I'd had time to finish wiping things down.

The new waitress, Tina, started work as well. She seems OK. She's prepared to work hard at least. Perhaps she's too loud though: brash and breezy with the customers, cheeky with Mark and bossy with Andy.

It felt a lot less like a family business with her there. She wouldn't have been my first choice, but I have to remember, it's not my business – in many ways.

Mark let her leave a few minutes early, while I finished sweeping the floor. 'It was nice to meet you, Susie,' she said, Mark's version of my name sounding all wrong in her mouth. 'You take care now, bab.'

I felt like saying that she must be the one to take care – of Tall Trees, of Mark and Andy – but my throat was already tight and dry and I mumbled 'Enjoy the job,' with a tremor in my voice.

'You've enjoyed it, haven't you?' Mark asked as Tina slammed the door shut behind her. He placed a tentative hand on my arm and spoke quietly, his usual easy manner gone. 'I mean, we've really loved having you here – you've been brilliant.'

'Of course I've enjoyed it, how could I not?' I sniffed and blinked away the tears which had rushed to my eyes. 'And you're to carry on being the best chef in south Birmingham, you know. I might come back to check up on you sometime.'

He laughed. 'Promise you'll do that,' he said, voice back to its normal strength. 'And wear this when you come, so we can be sure it's really you.'

Andy had joined us and Mark took a small parcel from him to hand to me. It was wrapped in black tissue, fastened with a sticker bearing the name of the jewellery shop next door.

'Just a little something to say thank you,' Andy said. 'We weren't sure what you'd like.'

I turned the package over in my hands, unable to speak for fear of crying. I hadn't expected a gift. I hadn't expected them to be so kind, although I've no idea why – they're both so thoughtful.

'Well open it then!' Mark said, giving me a nudge.

I slid my thumbnail around the edge of the sticker to loosen it and peeled it back from one end of the folded tissue paper before smoothing that out to get access to the contents.

Mark sighed dramatically. 'Get on with it, Susie, before we die waiting.'

I looked from him to Andy and said 'Thank you' as I tipped the parcel to slide the contents into the palm of my other hand. It was a necklace. A short, light, silver chain from which a pendant made of some kind of plastic or resin hung, a pendant in the shape of a leaf coloured a deep shade of reddish purple.

'From a tall tree,' Andy said, 'so you'll never forget us.'

'It's beautiful.' I was unable to stop tears falling and my voice shaking. 'Thank you so much.'

'Oh, come here.' Mark put his arms around me and held me tight for a moment, before releasing me and swiping a hand over his own damp eyes. 'Let's see how it looks.' He took the necklace from me and undid the catch. I lifted my hair away from my neck so he could fasten it in place, the leaf cool as it fell against my skin. 'Beautiful,' he said. 'Now you take good care of yourself, Susie. And remember that promise to come back and see us.'

He squeezed my hands and went into the kitchen, leaving Andy and me alone.

'It suits you,' Andy said and stepped forward to touch the leaf, lifting it from my skin. I was aware of the knuckle of his thumb as it brushed against my collarbone and realised I was holding my breath. 'It's always been a dream of mine to see the trees change colour in New England – you know, the oranges and reds spreading across the mountains in autumn. Some of the leaves turn purple, just like this.' He let the leaf go and I took a breath. 'I'm going to add it to my wishlist that I'll get to see you again one day too,' he said.

I looked up to meet his eyes and he lifted his hand again to stroke the path of the tears down my face. Andy had never been tactile with me as Mark had, and the intimacy of his skin against mine then – while our emotions were fraught with pain of saying goodbye – was making me faint. The scents of Tall Trees in the afternoon – of coffee and baking – had infused the fabric of his shirt and wafts of those aromas filled my nose as he stepped even closer and held me. His arms enclosed me, his cheek rested against the side of my head and I breathed it all in. The strength and the friendship I'd found in that room would always be there. But anything else I may have felt for Andy, or he for me, would have to remain uninvestigated.

I stepped out of his arms and said goodbye to Tall Trees.

~

James came to pick me up from the flat and brought me back here, to my home, to my family, to Pete, who gave me a clumsy hug with his unhurt arm and told James to put on the kettle. I came upstairs to unpack, opened the mother of pearl inlaid lid of my jewellery box, and placed the leaf pendant inside. The purple leaf seemed to glow against the padded cream silk which lines the top tray. I stroked the leaf, closed the lid and went downstairs for that cup of tea.

My first funeral – 1985

Grandad died last week. He'd been in hospital for weeks, so it was only a matter of time. That's what they kept saying, 'only a matter of time'. Like that would make it easier to bear when it happened. He'd even talked with Mum and Dad about what hymns he wanted for the funeral, who to invite, all that stuff. I can't imagine ever having to think about it. I couldn't plan for it.

I'm going to miss him so much. He was always kind to me, he stood up for me when Mum was trying to make me do stuff I didn't want to, like get a job in the shop where she works. She told me off at the funeral, said I should control myself when I cried during the burial. She said I shouldn't show my emotions like that, I should be restrained, not draw attention to myself. Grandad would have understood. He always told me I should just be myself.

CHAPTER TWENTY

CRAIG

There was a time when Sunday night was homework night. A rush to catch up with whatever it was I should have done days ago because it had to be handed in Monday morning. I was always one to leave things just a bit too fucking late. More recently, Sunday night was film night. Julia liked to see a film to round off the weekend. After late nights Friday and Saturday, it was all I could do not to fall asleep in the cinema. Wouldn't have happened if we'd gone to see my choice of film of course.

This Sunday night is 'catch up with Trev' night. Fuck me, things have gone downhill.

I walk into the Wetherspoons in town to find him already at the bar. At least there's no girls in their undies with him tonight. 'Trev,' I say.

'Craig. Pint, is it?'

He gestures to get the barman's attention. I don't know what to say, so I stare at the silent screen scrolling the Sky Sports headlines until I've got the glass in my hand, when I say, 'Cheers.' Why the fuck did I agree to this? I don't want to hear what he's got to say, I don't want to have to sit here and be nice to him. I'd quite like to take Gav's approach and ram my fist into the wanker's face. Remembering the football incident though, and looking at the number of burly blokes surrounding me now, I don't. I just sip my lager and wait for him to break the ice.

'How's Wolfie? Have you seen him?'

That was not what I expected and I take another sip of beer to drown the smile that the mention of Wolfie brought to my lips. The fact I've had a fantastic afternoon watching Wolfie go mad in a soft play area with Adam from cricket's son is none of Trev's business.

'Yeah, he's good.'

'I was sorry, you know, to find out he wasn't my boy. That's my biggest regret about everything. Me and Julia were arguing so much about money and stuff, and she gave away that she wasn't certain he was mine. So I couldn't rest til I'd found out. Fucking regretted that didn't I?'

Wolfie is not perfect. I'm not so blind I can't see that. There was the ice cream related tantrum this afternoon, which triggered a red-faced screaming for his mum. Gutted is the best way to describe what I felt then. But if I found out now that he wasn't mine, that I wasn't going to see him any more, well that would be worse. Fucking gutting, in fact.

'You could have stayed with them,' I pointed out to Trev. 'You didn't have to give him up.'

'Couldn't do that to you, could I? I'd trashed our friendship, taken your girlfriend, but I couldn't live with the thought of keeping Wolfie from you.'

'Right,' I said. This was complicated. 'How's your Dad?'

213

I only intended the question to buy me thinking time, after all, mention of Wolfie had brought the other Wolfgang of our acquaintance to mind.

'Not so good. Lung cancer.'

'Fucking hell.' That really wasn't so good. 'Sorry to hear that.'

'How about your mum, how's she?'

'Oh, you know, up and down.' With the scale of Trev's news, I realised maybe I'd been getting Mum's problems out of proportion. 'She asks after you.'

'What do you tell her?' Trev manages a smile over the lip of his rapidly emptying glass.

'That you're a fucking bastard.' I smile back. He knows I'm joking.

'Does Wolfie ever say anything about me?'

I can't lie to him, but, hell, Wolfie's two years old. What does Trev expect? Logical analysis and a forty page report complete with pie charts? I shake my head.

'Good,' Trev says, putting his empty glass down with a slam. 'He's young enough to only remember you then. That's how it should be.'

I catch the barman's eye and order another couple of pints. Foam slops over the rims of the glasses as he puts them down and both Trev and I lift our drinks carefully, supping at the liquid to bring it to a safe level for normal drinking.

'So, how's work?' he asks.

'Crap. Redundancies, shit bosses, same old. And you?'

'Same old. Got any good news?'

I had to think; it wouldn't have been tactful to share any of the Wolfie stories I had after all. 'Oh yeah, I've been playing a bit of cricket.'

'Cricket? You're shit at cricket.'

'Well, that is where you are wrong.' I nearly added 'my friend', but cut it off in time. The banter had almost tricked me into thinking things were normal between us. But they're not. Not yet. 'Yesterday I played a blinding shot off some supposed shit hot spin bowler. Massive six. You should have seen his face.'

Trev smiles. 'It was a fluke, right? You're a flukey bastard sometimes.'

Yeah, maybe sometimes I am. But as long as those times are when it counts, well, I'll take that, thank you very much.

~

SUSAN

Pete and I have been alone for most of yesterday and today. James has gone to visit some college friends and usually on Sundays, Pete would have gone to play golf, or to the driving range for a couple of hours at least. It'll be a while before he can take that up again.

We walked into town so I could get some food at the small supermarket. I can't think that Pete and I have regularly walked anywhere together – he'd take the car for the shortest journey, saying he preferred to do his walking on the golf course. Even on holiday he'd always hire us a car because he hated to feel tied down.

Yesterday though, we had to walk. I did suggest he didn't need to come, but 'No, we should do more things as a couple,' he said. I was extremely uncomfortable walking with him. He felt the need to comment on the state of the neighbours' front gardens, in a voice which I'm certain carried in through their open windows. When not imagining himself as a judge at the Chelsea Flower Show, he began a rant about how appalling the council are at maintaining the roads and pavements. I couldn't help thinking back to those walks I'd taken with Andy – silent and contemplative until we sat and conversed quietly. I'm not sure comtemplate or converse are words Pete's familiar with.

'How about a swift half?' he said as we got into town.

I wasn't keen, I was thinking more about getting home to carry on with the housework. But he pushed the oak door of The Lion open with his unbandaged arm before I'd even had time to speak. Inside, clustered at the dark wooden bar was a line up of people I hadn't expected to encounter again. Most of them, to be honest, I hadn't wanted to see again.

I glanced around while Pete greeted them, engaging in banter and accepting the offer of a pint. So much for the 'swift half'. It was too early for the Sunday lunches to be served, but a few of the heavily varnished tables were laid with faded placemats, cutlery rolled in white paper napkins and sachets of condiments. The scent of roasting meat hung in the air. An elderly couple sat at one table, both on the same side so they faced into the room, he reading the Mail on Sunday, she looking glazed.

'What can I get for you, Susan?' Dominic asked. He leant around Pete's shoulder to catch my eye. Pete had done his usual trick of joining the ranks of the group without leaving space to include me.

'Hi, Dominic. I'll have an orange juice, please.'

'I'm sure you need something stronger.'

I shook my head and looked away, wondering how much of the discussion I'd had with Adrienne she'd shared with her husband. I was trying to recall exactly what I had said, when Adrienne herself appeared from the ladies' loo.

She was dabbing at her hands with a tissue and frowned as she had to squeeze past a pair of young men leaning on a quiz machine as she crossed the lounge. A space in the group opened to admit her the instant she reached us and, a second later, she noticed that Pete and I were there too. 'Susan! What are you doing here?'

I blushed, not keen to discuss my marriage in front of Pete's friends and hoping she wouldn't say anything to embarrass me further. 'She's seen sense and come back to Alcester,' Pete said, and actually turned to usher me into the circle.

Adrienne reached out to take my left hand, giving it a squeeze as she said, 'Welcome back,' at the same time as delivering a pinch to the finger on which my wedding ring was reinstated. 'Perhaps we can get together for coffee? Tomorrow.'

I was back to being bossed around then. Except by Adrienne this time; unless Jo heard I was back and sent her instructions as well.

It was an uncomfortable hour. Adrienne and Dominic left soon after we arrived, at her insistence. Which left me, Pete and three men he knew from golf, or school, or some other club and their less than fascinating conversation. They all found plenty to laugh about. My attention wandered and I was trying to think of ways in which I could get Pete to leave without making me sound like a whining child when he drained his glass and said, 'Come on then, let's get you to this shop.' I felt like a child without having even opened my mouth.

The rest of the day was quiet. I made us dinner. We watched TV. Pete sat in his armchair. I sat on my own.

~

This morning I went to Adrienne's for coffee. I left Pete in front of the TV again. She must have seen me walking up the road and was at her front door before I'd had time to ring the bell.

'What are you doing?' she asked. Her accent gave extra emphasis to how scandalised she sounded.

'Um, you invited me for coffee...' I said, at once certain I must have misunderstood something.

'No, no, no. Not here! Yes, here. What are you doing back with that man?'

She'd taken my arm and dragged me into her house, down the hallway and into her pristine kitchen.

'He needs me,' I mumbled. If I'd been expecting the stiff formality of coffee mornings with Jo, I was mistaken. We were straight into the nitty gritty.

'Do you need him?'

I didn't reply.

'No! You don't. So why are you here?'

'Well, Pete really can't cope and James was having to do everything.' My reasoning sounded rather thin against the passion of her alternative viewpoint.

'James!' It was clear she didn't have a high opinion of James either. I was considering taking offence, he is my son after all, but couldn't quite summon the energy.

I perched on the edge of a leather topped stool and leant on her granite breakfast bar as she measured coffee into a cafetiere. She poured the water carefully as if surveying the exact amount required and left it to brew as she turned to me.

'I thought you were brave,' she said. 'I was impressed that you left him, that you went to Birmingham by yourself, without telling anyone what you were up to. Jo couldn't believe it – she was convinced you couldn't have done it. But I was just impressed.'

'Thank you.'

She lifted both hands in a gesture of frustration. 'But now, to find you back here! This I will not sit quietly about. "Don't get involved," Dominic tells me. Well, no. I will not allow you to do this. Did you really have such a bad time in Birmingham that coming back here was better?'

My time in Birmingham I did have the energy to defend. 'No, it was wonderful,' I said.

'Tell me.' She turned to pour the coffee and I told her. I told her about the flat, about my friendship with Craig, about finding a job – and enjoying it. And I told her about Andy. Not everything; but enough to make her raise her eyebrows.

'What did this Andy say about you leaving?'

'He didn't want me to. But he didn't try to stop me. He understood that I'm a married woman – I have responibilities.'

'You have a husband who is an idiot and a son who is an adult. You have responsibilities to yourself too.'

I'm not sure Adrienne and I are still friends. No matter how impressed she'd been by my leaving Pete, she can't accept my decision to come back. She was frosty for the remaining time I spent with her. So much for my hopes for a new found friend. I wonder what inquisition Jo will put me through.

CHAPTER TWENTY ONE

CRAIG

Joy upon fucking joy. After two days of Amisha being short with me like she's still brooding over the argument on Friday, and having to make all my own drinks because Gav's no longer here, now I get summoned to the director's office. Amisha's in there when I arrive, so I perch on the edge of Frank's PA's desk. They never stay long in that job and I can't remember this one's name. Blonde number four, Gav called her.

Not that I get long to chat, because the door opens, Amisha comes out and makes direct eye contact with me. Very direct. Telling me something, although what I don't know because, guess what? I don't speak Mad Cow.

'Come on in, Craig.'

I smile at Amisha, hop off the desk and give Frank a firm handshake. No messing. It's just us men now, so let's see what he's got to say.

'I've got bad news I'm afraid.'

Shit. No messing at all. I tune my face to an appropriate level of concern.

'I'm sure you'll have heard that the firm's not doing too well. At the end of the day, our last quarter's results didn't feed through to the targets we were set and the board have decided to go forward with a reduction in the workforce. Unfortunately for us in Birmingham, we've had significantly more challenges than some of the other branches.'

He can waffle on with the management bullshit, can Frank. I'd prefer to get to the point. 'They're axing us?'

'Not entirely. Some of our departments, some of our staff have been mentioned in dispatches. Mostly notably you and Amisha. Well, I won't lie to you, Craig, mostly her.'

No, Frank, that's fine, I won't take any water with it. 'Which means?'

'I've just been on a bird table telecon with her and Phil, the Director in London. He's asked her to go down there to lead the marketing team and she says she'd like to take you with her.'

She would? 'That's extremely flattering, Frank. But I assume that job would be in London.'

'London, yes. This office will be wound down. There aren't the manufacturing firms in the West Midlands to generate enough profit opportunities for us any more.'

'And if I don't go to London?'

'Then I'll ask HR to draw up your redundancy package same as everyone else. Bad times for all of us. If I were you lad, I'd go. One hundred and ten per cent.'

Yeah, Frank, but you're not me are you? You're in your sixties, with your Jag, and your mortgage-free detached house in Solihull, and your kids off your hands, and your wife off her head on gin. You haven't got to think about my Mum, or Wolfie and who's going to look after them if I'm not around. Or the negative equity on my flat. Or the fact that this sounds like the best opportunity I might get this decade and I'm going to have to say no.

'Can I think about it overnight, please?'

'Of course, but you already know there's only one right answer.'

I keep my head down as I pass Amisha's office and head for the kitchen. While the kettle's boiling I lean against the counter and rub my eyes. Why can't life be simple? Why can't things happen in the right fucking order? Why can't annoying women leave me be? Here she comes, tip tapping along the corridor.

'What do you think then, Craig? Coming to London with me?'

I turn away and make busy with the tea bags. 'I don't know yet, I've got a lot to think about. Thanks for thinking of me though.' No need to be ungrateful after all.

'I didn't do it as a favour. You and me can sort that team out.' She puts a hand on my arm and squeezes. 'And it'd be an adventure.'

An adventure. She can't know how tempting that sounds. She can't know that she's just echoed something Trev said on Sunday about how he's going travelling for a year: to have an adventure. There's no way she can even imagine how fucking jealous I am right now.

~

SUSAN

Time drags here. I'd found two days off a week hard to fill in Birmingham, but here – where in theory I have housework and cooking to occupy me and companionship to distract me – time passes more slowly I'm sure. I feel the same torpor as I did during visits to Dad's parents when I was little – the measured tick tock of the mantlepiece clock, the drift of dust motes tracked by beams of sunlight, the snag of my bitten fingernails as they picked at the lace on an antimacassar. The visits were interminable, dreaded for days beforehand and shuddered over afterwards.

Sitting with Pete in the afternoon is as bad.

This morning we had the distraction of a visit to the surgery for his dressings to be changed. I can only assume the nurse gave him a telling off while she was at it.

'Stupid bitch,' was his response to my enquiry about how it had gone. 'Some people don't know when to shut up and do their job.'

I know better than to express an opinion. It would only trigger a rant during which one, if not several, of his hobby-horse theories would be given a trot around the paddock. Passing facts and unrelated incidents would be drafted in to prove that, beyond any doubt whatsoever, Peter Clarke should be in charge of the country.

I have debated with him, in the past. But my contributions were barely given consideration before the steamroller of his conviction shoved me aside.

So I didn't ask what the nurse had said, just nodded and bleeped the button to unlock the car. We've borrowed it from Dominic, who's getting Adrienne to drive him to work each morning until we buy a new one. That won't happen until Pete gets some kind of feedback from the insurance company.

At least he's not losing his temper with them yet.

I drove us back to the yellow brick prison with its fake lead bars at the window and counted how many seconds before the TV was turned on. Twenty. Only so slow because he stopped to take off his shoes. That was for my benefit. An exaggerated concession to my complaint about how dirty the pale carpets had become in my short absence. I'm sure he only bothered because they're slip ons. He'd have to have bent down otherwise and that would have been too much effort.

Beige and cream carpets were Pete's choice. I would never have selected something so impractical for a hallway. Not with two men in the house and one of them a teenager. James got back from visiting his friends this morning and went straight to bed. I'm not sure which I prefer: Pete talking too much or James not showing his face at all.

I went to the kitchen and closed the door. In there I can't hear the sports commentary from the TV, there's no thump of music from James's room. I can sit at the kitchen table in almost silence. The road is a cul de sac so traffic noise is infrequent and most of the neighbours work or their kids are at school, so they make no sound. A cat from down the road prowls the gardens, meaning birds steer clear. It feels sterile.

The road is too clean. The garden's too pruned and trimmed and primped into submission. The interior lacks personality. It's not that I miss my grubby flat, or the police sirens through the night. I don't long to hear odd thumps in the night from upstairs, or to work until my feet ache. But here in this house I feel dead.

The conversation with Adrienne played through my head as I sat at the kitchen table, spinning a place mat. 'What are you doing here?' she'd asked. 'What?'

What indeed? I had no answer for her then and I'm still uncertain now. As I sat there I knew the only thing I'd achieved was to allow Pete and James to do as they pleased. Not anything to do with what pleased me.

No matter what Pete had promised, so far nothing had changed. I'd willingly put my hands back into the shackles. To save my son? From what? What would be the worst that could happen?

Would he give up everything – all his desires? Would he be buried alive as I was? No. He and his dad would struggle, but they'd survive. So, if I'm going to stay, I have to survive too. There has to be something here for me.

My first day at college – 1986

It felt so good not to put my school uniform on this morning. For college we can wear what we want, it's what we do that's important. That's what the tutor said. I still dressed smartly though. It's a secretarial course after all. I'm going to learn typing, shorthand, some basic accounting and a refresher on grammar. Not what Mum and Dad wanted me to do at all. Dad thought I should try nursing, Mum thought maybe I'd be better suited to shop work. Like her.

I knew what I wanted though, and I stood my ground. And college is going to be all I hoped for. The other girls seem really nice. We all want to go and work in big offices, in Birmingham or maybe even London. I'm so glad I insisted and that my teachers at school backed me up. I'm going to be brilliant at this, I just know I am.

~

CRAIG

Faking a phone call is a pathetic stunt. But I was not ready to speak to Amisha, so yanked the phone to my ear when my sonar sensed her approaching and kept up the fake chat until I heard her office door close.

Despite a sleepless night, I have not decided what to do. Having no fucker to talk about it with didn't help.

I mean, I couldn't run it by Mum, but I know what she'd say anyway: do it. And I could hardly ask Wolfie. But I don't need to ask either of them, they're the reasons I'm hesitating after all.

I always wished I had a brother. A big brother. One who'd have played games with me when we were growing up. The Butch to my Sundance. The mate who'd have looked out for me in the playground. The friend who'd have told me all the stuff I needed to know and the star who'd be here for me now. Someone who could actually help with all this crap.

I know who I'd really like to have talked to, Suze. Wonder what she's up to today. I can imagine her as some kind of domestic goddess, she really didn't fit in at the flats. All that nonsense about terrorists upstairs. I've seen that bloke, couldn't blow up a fucking balloon.

Point is, I've got to decide what to tell Frankie boy. And soon.

My finger was on the button to keep the phone disconnected when the bugger actually rang. Scared the shit out of me buzzing in my ear like that. Completely lost my cool and mumbled, 'Err, hello?' as I lifted my finger to connect the line.

'Craig, love. Is that you?'

'Mum? Are you OK, what's wrong?'

226

'I know I shouldn't ring you at work, but I needed to ask you if you'll come to the hospital appointment with me?'

Hadn't we been through this? 'Of course, Mum. I'll be there, I told you.'

'Yes, but I just had a call from them. They want me to go in tomorrow if possible. They had a cancellation.'

Tomorrow? That's a bit fucking quick. I wonder if that's something else to worry about or if the cancellation's true. I establish the time, confirm I'll be there to take her, make myself available by deleting a conference call from my electronic diary – the words 'There was a meeting? I'm so sorry, I have no record of that' already forming on my tongue – and get her off the phone as quick as I can.

'Sorry, love. I really wouldn't have called you at work, but I know you think this hospital stuff's important.'

Yeah, mum, and I've said I'll be there, so can you stop talking now? My brain's about to explode with all the stuff I'm not saying, all the lies I'm preparing and the decisions I know I have to make.

'I'll call you tonight OK, Mum? Bye.' It's the easiest of the lines I'll have to speak today.

Almost as if she was watching for me to hang up, Amisha's at my desk the moment I do. 'Well, Craig, what do you think?'

Fuck knows. I swivel the chair to face her, stand, and say, 'Let's get a coffee, shall we?'

The thing is, I don't only want this job for me. I don't want to let her down either. Look at her. Those melting chocolate eyes, the bitten bottom lip betraying the nerves she usually keeps under cover,

227

the tight-fitting top. OK, don't look at the tight top. I cannot be bought.

She takes a seat in one of the break out areas outside the kitchen while I get the drinks. I never was sure quite what those seats were meant for – breaking out in spots, breaking into song, breaking into a fucking sweat is what I'm doing now. Last time I sat there with her it was the day Julia told me about Wolfie and I feel about as messed up now.

Though then there were opportunities arising because, despite the shock of him, it was obvious that Wolfie was great. Now I'm about to close a big bastard of a door. I'm about to kiss my career goodbye.

'Don't drag it out, Craig. I've got things I need to be doing.'

So much for letting her down gently. 'I wish I could say yes, I really do. And if this had come up a few months ago then I would have said yes. Without hesitation.'

'But now you can't. Because of Wolfie?'

'Yeah. And Mum. I suddenly have all these responsibilities, you know?'

She squeezes my hand, 'I know. But you do understand there won't be a job for you here?'

Yeah. I fully comprehend the ramifications of turning down this marvellous opportunity. My grasp of all the implications is complete. The information has been digested, summarised and learnt by heart. Not to put too fine a point on it: I'm screwed. All the responsibilities, no cash.

'I do want to thank you for thinking of me though, Amisha. I know you'll do well down there and I'm gutted I won't be coming with you.'

Doubly gutted, because I won't get to see her any more either. And it surprises me how much that bothers me. She hasn't let go of my hand and I like it.

'Let's go for that drink, Craig,' she says.

I head to Frank's office while I'm on my feet. No point delaying. I pop into the Gents on the way which is a bad move because Frank's there. Sometimes life seems as though it can't get any worse. And then it does. What am I supposed to do? Step up to the urinal next to him, unzip and tell him what he doesn't want to hear over the sound of piss hitting porcelain? I even think about turning straight round and running before he sees me, but the second's hesitation I use to think that makes it too late. He's seen me.

I guess my face gave me away. 'You've made the wrong decision, haven't you?' he says.

'I really appreciate the opportunity, Frank,' I say, keeping my eyes bolted to his because looking down would be bad, very bad, 'but I have my son to think about and my mum's not well. I've got to put them first, hope you can understand that.'

He shakes his dick, zips up and turns to me. 'Course I understand, lad. But it's a shame, a real shame. Listen, you'll get a fantastic reference from us and, tell you what, I'll ring round some contacts, see if I can't find an opening for you.'

That would be great, so I smile at him in a manner I hope contains the adequately professional level of relief. But please wash your hands, Frank. Don't, no really don't, offer me one to shake. Oh shit, you're going to aren't you? I believe this is what they call the pits.

CHAPTER TWENTY TWO

SUSAN

James didn't get up until after lunchtime; just as I'd cleared the food away, loaded the dishwasher and wiped down the surfaces. He opened the fridge door and asked, 'Isn't there anything to eat?'

As I saw it, there were three potential answers to this: the lie: 'No', stooping to his level of sarcasm: 'Do you need your eyes testing?', or the good mother: 'I could make you an omelette.' I didn't need to answer. He assumed.

'Bacon sandwich would be nice.'

He slumped into a chair as I peeled the cellophane from the packet and lifted out three rashers. His bloodshot eyes betrayed his hangover. A huge yawn suggested he'd stayed up even later than the early hour at which I'd been woken when the front door slammed as he returned from the pub.

'Did you have a good evening?'

'Yeah, cool.'

I was determined to get more conversation than that from him. Bacon sandwiches don't grow on trees after all. 'Was it friends from your course you went to see at the weekend?'

'Yeah. What's with the third degree? You don't have to know where I am all the time. I am an adult you know.'

'Well that makes three of us then,' I said, and shoved the grill pan under the heat with a clang. 'Look, Jamie, I'm back here because I want you to be able to enjoy your life. I don't want you to have to take too much responsibility. But I need both you and your Dad to treat me with a little more courtesy. At least have a conversation with me. Please.'

I hated to sound as if I was begging. But I can't fall back into the same old routine. Things need to change around here if I'm to stay. I love James, I would do anything for him – I am doing – but I need him to understand that.

He sighed, and said, 'Sorry, Mum. Yeah, Jim and Mac are on my course; we're renting a house together next term. Me and Jim are talking about going backpacking this summer too. He went round South East Asia in his gap year and wants to try Europe next. I'm gonna ask Dad if he'll lend me some cash so I can go.'

I slid the grill pan out and turned the bacon over. He doesn't like it too crisp. The trouble of course with getting James to tell me about his life, is that it will make me jealous. I wanted to suggest that he should perhaps be getting a job, not relying on handouts from his Dad. I wanted to say that he can't always expect the world to be arranged for his convenience.

But I didn't want to nag, I didn't want to fall into acting out any stereotypes he'd expect. And I have learnt the most important lesson about being a

231

parent: it's not about me. So I said, 'How wonderful,' and asked where they might go.

'Oh you know, Amsterdam, Berlin, Budapest. Places where things happen.'

I buttered the bread and thought I'd like to be somewhere where things happened myself. One lesson I've learnt about being an adult is that occasionally you have to take action.

'Sounds great,' I said. 'I know you'll enjoy it. Wash up the grill pan when you've finished eating, won't you?'

His frown told me how the reference to domestic chores went down but his reaction was the least of my concerns. It was Pete whose behaviour I really needed to address.

I lifted the remote control from the arm of his chair and turned off the TV.

'Oi,' he said, but decided not to say more. A wise choice, and not the only one he's made recently. There's been no attempt at intimacy since my return. We may be sharing a bed, but he hasn't tried to touch me. It's as if he's aware that he could easily push me too far.

The bruises from the crash still decorate his face but I've shown no sympathy, just done what needed to be done. As I looked at him sitting there, I could see he was no different from his bratty, teenage son in the next room. And who'd allowed him to stay in that state of suspended teenage? Me. I'd put myself aside for both of them and would do so no longer.

'I want to go on holiday,' I said. 'A city break. How about New York? Will you take me?'

He didn't speak for a moment, but his eyes moved – casting about in panic for an excuse, a decision, anything. 'Isn't New York a bit…?'

'A bit what, Pete? Expensive? Too far? Tell me what your objection is.' I've never spoken to him like that before, I don't even know where I was finding the courage. All I knew was that if James was going to get a holiday, then so was I.

'Just not very us,' was all he could come up with.

'Define 'us'. You've never asked me where I'd like to go, you arranged every holiday we ever took around where you could play golf. I would like to go to New York.'

That wasn't entirely true. New York was just the first place which came to mind. Of course I'd like to see its sights, walk its avenues, browse its shops. Really though, I was picking a fight.

It was out of character and Pete didn't know how to react. I'd seen no evidence of the impact my leaving had on him, apart from the crash of course. But, towards me, he'd been arrogant, combative and confident throughout. That was what I wanted to challenge.

'We could get some brochures I suppose…'

'I'll pick them up tomorrow.'

I went back into the kitchen where James, on seeing me, leapt up from the table to take the grill pan to the sink. 'Just doing it, Mum.'

I was on a high from having kept the upper hand with Pete, so I gave Jamie a surprise as well. 'I don't think you should ask your Dad for the money for your travels. I think you should get a job and earn some money of your own. You'll be amazed how liberating that can be.'

~

CRAIG

An evening of Thomas the Tank Engine with Wolfie was just what I needed. Totally chilled me out. We built his model train track all the way down the hallway, linked the carriages together and trundled off across the carpet on hands and knees. Which is easier when you're his size.

I let him drive, no point encouraging a screaming fit, while I followed along to pick up the cargo his erratic acceleration left behind. I spun out the game, and bath time. I knew Julia would be waiting to talk to me and, when all I have to give her is the bad news that I won't be employed for much longer, it was a conversation I was keen to avoid.

If only that was what she wanted to talk about. What she actually said was 'I hear you and Trev are mates again.' So where the fuck did she get that juicy bit of gossip?

'I wouldn't describe us as mates.' Well, I wouldn't. Nothing's forgiven, nothing's forgotten. I've just got more pressing concerns right now. Fucking depressing, some of them.

'I mean, it's all right for you, getting to go off to pubs and hang out with your mates, while I'm stuck here where my parents are driving me nuts, living in the bedroom I had when I was a kid. And you get to go off to your office, then sleep through the night in your own flat without a toddler disturbing you.'

Fuck knows what had got into her, but after the day I've had, she wasn't going to get off lightly.

'So what are you saying, do you want Wolfie to come and live with me? Is that it? Can't handle being his mum anymore cos he's interfering with your social life? That's about right, always looking out for what would be best for you.'

I could see tears in her eyes but hell, she deserves to suffer. I mean, I suffered didn't I? Don't I go on suffering on an hourly fucking basis at the moment? But I'll take that, because I'm doing it for Mum and for Wolfie and they need me. Julia does not, and will not drag me into whatever her warped mind is up to now.

'Of course I want to be with Wolfie! I just find it all so hard,' she snuffles and collapses onto a chair at her mum's kitchen table. 'I texted Trev's sister to see if she wanted to come over for a chat but she texted straight back to say you and him are pals again so she won't get involved. And Mum and Dad are going off on holiday next week so I'll be here all alone.'

Oh crap. I am actually feeling sorry for her. The sight of the tears is doing it. And I know she and Wolfie adore each other, I've seen them gazing into each other's eyes in a whole love fest thing. And don't I know what it's like to love your mum?

'Being a parent is much harder than I thought it'd be,' she says.

Yeah, well being a son isn't all it's cracked up to be either. 'I know, but he's worth it, right?'

She smiles and nods. 'I just need to get on my feet, get out of here, take control of my life again.'

Well that, Julia, is the type of thing I am currently totally, fuckingly, unable to advise you on. So I keep my mouth shut.

She can't meet my eye as she carries on talking, 'You know, moving to Manchester really would be a good thing for me. And Wolfie; he'd get to see his cousins all the time…'

I can't listen any more. I can't lose anything else.

Except my temper. 'No. Just fucking no, Julia.'

~

SUSAN

Cooking is what I've always been good at, so I decided that cooking is what I would do to give me some purpose in life. Specifically the baking of cakes. My business plan stretched as far as to think, 'Who doesn't like cake?' I suppose there was a slightly crazy daydream in which my products would supply the stores and tea shops of West Warwickshire, but I know that's mad. There are probably all kinds of monopolies already in place.

I decided to start small and bake a single cake, a chocolate cake to make up for the fact I wasn't here to make one for Pete's birthday last month. It would prove I still could. I waited until after lunch when he was about to doze off for his afternoon nap on the sofa before I announced my intention to go to the supermarket. I admit it, I'm already craving time alone.

He couldn't be bothered to stir himself, so I grabbed my handbag and collection of hessian shopping bags and almost ran to Dominic's car. I am angry with myself for allowing Pete to fall straight back into his lazy and presumptuous ways, especially when he'd promised me more consideration. It's not as if I like it; it is however the easiest way to be. The path of least resistance. If I can find myself some kind of outlet, something that is only about me, perhaps he's right, perhaps we can make it work.

Driving to the supermarket along quiet roads, past attractive houses and with glimpses of open countryside made me feel at home again. I'm no fan of our 1980s new build house, but away from that

Alcester is a beautiful town. Looking out across fields to the vestiges of the Forest of Arden, I couldn't help thinking of Andy and how he'd probably be able to tell me the history of the woodland, the types of trees. His enthusiasm would make it fascinating. If I mentioned the woods to Pete he'd probably just comment that they got in the way of the golf course.

My cake baking business daydream had been founded in a passing thought that Tall Trees could do with a better supply of cakes than those Mark turned out in between concentrating on the savoury dishes that were his real passion. I'd vaguely thought of offering to help but been afraid not only of his professional kitchen, but also of him laughing at what I thought of as my talent. Not that he'd ever have laughed in a cruel way, just not thought I was quite polished enough to compete next to his output perhaps.

The menu at Tall Trees was not my concern today though; my mission was purely to have a little outing to the supermarket to entertain myself and to bake my husband a birthday cake to make amends.

There weren't many other cars in the car park, so I parked near the entrance and selected a medium sized trolley from the complex array of choices. Whatever your family dynamic, it seems they've designed the perfect trolley/child seat combination. If you don't need the child seat, perhaps you'd prefer the one designed to load cases of beer or wine? If you buy nothing but bouquets and baguettes, they've thought of that too.

Laughing to myself about the lengths retailers go to, I was smiling as I passed though the sliding doors and inhaled the bakery aroma. A visit to the supermarket is something I'd missed. Of course there were supermarkets in Kings Heath and Moseley, but without a car I felt unable to do a big shop and had no real need to anyway. Cooking for myself was no fun, and unnecessary when I could eat leftovers at the café. And my provisioning when entertaining Craig had all been done in the small shops across the road. I'd missed the temple to food effect of a decent supermarket, and this one has so much more: clothes, electrical items, a café. I could almost move in.

I don't know if it was the sight of me, or the sight of me with a smile on my face which shocked Jo most. She certainly hadn't heard that I'd returned to Alcester because she greeted me with, 'What are you doing here?'

Amused that I'd ruffled her composure, I answered with a breezy confidence that wasn't really me, 'Shopping, Jo. Aren't you?'

She is not accustomed to being cheeked by me and it didn't go down well. She glared in fact. 'You left,' she said. 'Pete said you left him.'

'Yes, I did. But he can't live without me, so, I'm back.' My voice belonged to someone far more assured than me but one thing I had certainly not missed about my life in Alcester was Jo. We've known each other since school. She was two years above me, part of a clique who laughed at shy, quiet types like me. It was only being away from her influence that's allowed me to see she's continued to treat me that way into our adult years. As someone to be pitied if not openly mocked. Well, that's one role to which I don't intend to return.

'Minxy's still eating well then,' I said, glancing at her trolley piled with dog food.

She didn't respond. I could almost see her brain processing the information about my return, sending conflicting signals to her mouth. Finally she managed to speak, grudgingly suggesting that I should come over soon, for coffee.

'I'll have to see if I can squeeze it in,' I replied and wheeled off to immerse myself in the array of choice on the laden shelves. I've never seen Jo flummoxed like that. I imagine that me leaving was hard enough for her to understand. Catching me back and in a good mood was obviously far too much for her to take in. She didn't even finish her shopping, just abandoned the loaded trolley and almost ran to the car park.

CHAPTER TWENTY THREE

CRAIG

What is it with hospitals that they are determined to piss you off? From the moment you walk in the door it's all Blue Zone this, White Zone that, this lift for in patients only, that door only opens from the other side.

With the speed Mum walks at it's some kind of miracle that we were in the right department at the right fucking time at all. I guess her suggestion that we set out an hour before the appointment was a good plan after all.

Now we wait. No matter that the appointment was for ten o'clock. No matter that my work phone is showing three missed calls already. No matter that it's now quarter to fucking twelve. We'll just wait here on the ripped plastic seats while nurses wander about with cups of tea and medical students pretend like they run the place.

'They know we're here, love,' Mum says. 'They'll be with us soon.'

Well I'm glad she's confident. I'm more and more convinced that she only got this appointment because some poor bastard died before they got to him. It's one way of clearing the waiting lists.

We've already been called into a consulting room where some student was dressed up in a tie and a white coat tying to look like an expert. All he did was go through Mum's paperwork before giving her a form and sending us to get an X-ray. Unbelievable. Surely they knew they'd want an X-ray of her knees, surely they could have sent us there first. I mean, it's not as if walking about is easy for her for fuck's sake.

Now we're waiting again, who knows what for. I'm sliding lower and lower down in the seat and wondering if they might be not only leaving us here until Mum's died, but until I have too, when they finally call her name. We go into a different consulting room to see a bloke who at least looks as if he's had his medical degree for a few years. He looks at her lumpy knees, looks at the X-ray pics and pronounces 'Osteoarthritis. Very common.'

Is the fact that all Mum's medical troubles are common supposed to make us feel better? Whoever's advising these docs on their bedside manner needs to stop and reconsider. Everyone wants to think they're special after all.

He goes on to quiz Mum about the drugs she's been taking – no, they don't really help with her mobility, and her range of movement – it's the stairs that are the biggest problem, before scrawling some notes. Finally he comes to his conclusion.

'You have two options. We can perform knee replacement surgery on both knees, one at a time, probably with a gap of about a year between them. The operation is usually very successful – with some physiotherapy you'd get a lot more strength and movement back in the joint. You're at a good age for the operation, you'd get a lot of wear out of the new joint and your general health is good. Yes, I'd recommend that's what we should do.'

'Or?' I ask. The butcher takes his eyes off Mum's knees and glances at me. 'The second option?' I prompt.

'Oh, yes, well you could up the dose of the anti-inflammatories and try some physio, but I think the effect would only be a minimal improvement, if any.'

He's not going to be happy unless he gets to chop into Mum's knees and stick bits of bionic woman in there, I can tell. But she's looking queasy and I need details so I press him for some.

'Patients are usually in hospital for around a week and the first six weeks will be difficult. You'll need help at home although you will be able to start walking with crutches.'

He doesn't want to talk to me, but I'm the one with all the questions. 'And there's a waiting list, I assume?'

'Two to three months.'

'I think I should go for it,' Mum pipes up.

Fine.

~

We're riding back to hers in a taxi and I'm trying to reassure her. 'Of course it's the right decision. You'll be able to get about a lot more easily. You're not ready for your grave yet, are you?'

'But what about when I come out of hospital? He said I'll need to have someone with me.'

'Yeah, and I'll be there. I'll move back in while you need me. We'll work it out.' I haven't mentioned to her that I might not have a job by that point, that I might actually need to move back in for good and will have plenty of time on my hands. But of course I'd be there for her when she needed me. How the hell could I not?

'But if I can't get to the loo, or into the shower...' She doesn't want to say that, generous though my offer is, it's a bit fucking useless.

'Mum. We'll work it out.'

I pay the driver and help her out of the car and into the house. She has to lean heavily on my arm to get up the front step. Why hadn't I noticed how bad things had got? If she hadn't had that infection and dizzy spell, it might have been months before she'd have seen the GP and been sent down the hospital. She wouldn't have suggested it.

'I've got to get to work, Mum.'

'Wait, I'll make you a sandwich.'

'No time. I call you later, OK?' I bend to kiss her before hareing off to the bus stop. Guilty because I've been out longer than I told Amisha I would be. Guilty because I haven't done enough for my mum. Fucking guilty because while I know it's what I've got to do, I don't want to. I don't want to look after her. I don't want to look after Wolfie. I want to go to London with Amisha and be a big shot. Wanker.

~

SUSAN

I started to make Pete's birthday cake when I got in from the shop: chocolate sponge with coffee buttercream filling and 'Happy Birthday' piped on top beside the plastic figure of a golfer in plus fours that has crowned every birthday cake I've ever made him. The radio burbled while I was baking, the talk about small businesses which were surviving the recession.

243

Small businesses selling affordable treats or feel good services. Things like cafés perhaps. Or cakes? So I was daydreaming as I filled the piping bag, imagining names for my cake making company: Teatime Treats, or Susan's Sponges.

Twee names. Gently amusing. Let the cakes be the things to attract attention. It was only a daydream.

The smell enticed James into the room. 'Put the kettle on, Jamie, then go tell your Dad it's his birthday.' I smiled, this cake was guaranteed to ensure that they both appreciated having me back. I wasn't sure I had the courage to mention my business idea to Pete. It was too precious a dream to have him destroy it with a snort of laughter. I allowed myself one imagined vision of how the cake would look in the glass fronted cabinet at the entrance to the café, with 'Tall Trees' piped across its top and the golfer consigned to the bin. I wished I could serve large slices to Andy and Mark, to show them how far my talents extended. They'd understand. They'd understand my dreams as well.

I was placing the cake on the table when the doorbell rang. James was slouching over the kettle monitoring its progress towards boiling. 'Get your dad,' I said. 'I'll get the door.'

It was Jo. Her presence on the doorstep surprised me. When she had something to say she usually summoned me. She didn't come over. It was strange that she hadn't rung first. 'Jo, come in. We're just about to have a drink.'

The other thing which was odd was how she looked. Not groomed and well dressed in her usual style. Her hair was unbrushed, her outfit dishevelled and her make up smudged. She pushed past me and went straight into the living room. I was thinking 'At least I have fresh cake to offer her' as I followed. I'll always remember that. At least there was cake. I mean, cake is a symbolic food; the physical manifestation of ritual: birthday cakes, wedding cakes, christening cakes, cakes for Christmas, for parties, for funerals. No event is complete without a cake.

Finding the living room empty, she continued through to the kitchen. I suppose I had registered that this was odd, that it was somewhat out of the norm for someone as versed in etiquette as Jo to barge through someone else's house without invitation. I didn't try to stop her though. Meek little Susan just followed on behind.

Pete was in the kitchen, bent to examine the cake. Jo marched up to him, lifted her right arm with her hand screwed into a fist and thumped it down on his back.

'Hey,' he said, and reached to rub where she'd hit him. As he turned, he saw who it was and the scowl on his face dropped into wide-eyed panic. That was the point at which I stopped following behind and realised exactly what I was witnessing. His expression told me everything I needed to know because behind that panic was guilt.

Jo took a deep breath as if about to speak, but I got in before her. 'Put the cake knife down, Pete. And James, you'd better pour us all some of that coffee; I think we need it. Jo, perhaps you'd like to take a seat.'

Jo might be the one to take charge in her own house, and I might have let her push me around before, but right there, right then, was my event. I'd let her eat some of my cake if she wanted it, but she wasn't running the show. I was.

'I take it you two are rather more familiar with each other than you were,' I said, crossing my arms and standing between Pete and the chair Jo had dropped on to.

'You said she'd left,' Jo snapped at Pete. 'You said she'd gone for good.'

'I thought she had,' Pete mumbled.

'I have a name,' I interrupted. 'And I had left for good. So perhaps someone could tell me why exactly I'm back if there's something else going on?'

'It's you I need, Susan. Not her.' Pete had decided which card to play very quickly. But Jo was unable to accept being the scorned woman. No wonder she'd been thrown by seeing me in the supermarket.

'That is not what you said. You said you were glad to see the back of her!'

I was aware of James clattering the lid onto the cafetiere before letting the kitchen door slam behind him. And running away was obviously the option Pete would have preferred to take at that point too. But it wasn't my style. Not this time.

'Susan, it was a mistake. I was an idiot.'

As Pete looked at me I could see the foolish boy he still was pleading through the sagging eyes of a middle aged man. It gave me the strength I needed. It wasn't that they'd handed me the excuse I needed to get out, after all, I wasn't totally convinced that Pete had always been faithful to me anyway. What I knew at that moment though, was that Pete needed to grow up, that James would survive without me, and that Jo was no kind of friend.

Most importantly I knew that I was too good to be stuck in that kitchen baking birthday cakes.

I shook off the grip Pete had on my arm and

began pouring the coffee, impressed by how steady my hands were. 'Please, Susan,' he went on, 'It was one night, one mistake…'

'One night in which you made me all kinds of promises,' Jo interrupted. 'You said you were glad to be finally rid of her, that as soon as you got things organised then you could be with the kind of woman you'd always wanted. A woman like me.'

'Calm down, Jo,' I said and placed her drink in front of her. 'I take it from your reaction that you actually believed Pete and thought you might be about to leave your husband and move in with mine?'

'As if I'd move in here! I was visiting my sister last weekend, persuading her that mum should go and live with them so I could get the house to myself. Then he texted to say he wasn't well and couldn't I come and visit, only to text again the following day to say 'don't worry, I'll be fine.' Little did I know that it was because you were back on the scene.'

It went on for a while: Pete trying to blame Jo for manipulating him when all he wanted was for me to come home, Jo sniping and moaning that he'd made her promises and didn't we all know that she was unhappy too and he'd misled her while I'd destroyed her. I cut myself a large slice of cake and took a big bite, savouring the flavour while they played out their drama.

Eventually it became boring, like the script of a daytime soap opera. I'd always known Jo was manipulative and only considered what was best for her, but I'd been an idiot to think that my responsibilities as a wife and mother meant I should come back to be a bit part player in Pete's life. I dusted the cake crumbs from my fingers onto the

247

plate.

'Well,' I said, 'it really does seem as if I'm not needed here any more. So I'll pop up and pack my bags then be off to Birmingham. You'll find James is going travelling in a couple of weeks, Pete, so you might want to pull yourself together before then. I can't imagine you'll listen to any advice from me, Jo, so I'll only say good luck.'

I don't know how they'll work things out, or even if they can. All I know is that the only people I do have a responsibility towards are my son and myself. James drove me back to the flat and helped me carry my bags upstairs.

'Are you sure you're OK here, Mum?'

'For now,' I said, because I do have a plan.

CHAPTER TWENTY FOUR

CRAIG

I'm walking towards the boardroom for the meeting we've all been summoned to when I see Stevo ahead of me and hurry to catch up with him. 'This is the bit where they break the bad news to everyone, right?'

He nods, and leans towards me to whisper, 'I've got an interview next week. How about you, anything in the pipeline?'

I don't have time to answer before we're in the door and finding seats. The big table's gone and plastic chairs have been lined up as if it's school assembly or some shit. There's a murmur of nervous whispering among the staff and I see Amisha talking to Frank at the front of the room, her head bent towards him, a loop of glossy hair sliding from her shoulder to cover her face. She straightens up, leaves the room and Frank stands to address the troops.

To be honest, I can't even listen to the man. Every word that comes out of his smarmy mouth is management bullshit. It's all phrases like 'current climate', 'corporate downsizing' and 'reduced portfolios'. There's jargon about 'redeployment', 'transitional arrangements' and 'bottom lines'. I'll tell you the bottom line, folks. We're doomed. He announces that the office will be closing in four weeks time and I glance round at the faces. Some of the idiots are shocked, clearly hadn't noticed there was something going on. Others are shooting evils at Frank, holding him personally responsible. A few look frightened. I guess they're deepest in debt.

I loiter once we're dismissed, I've no desire to go through the debrief with the rest of the team. I notice the lad from the post room start to stack the chairs, so I pick up a few from my row and begin to build piles. Frank comes over. 'No surprises for you there, but I do have some good news. A bloke I know at Cresswells is about to advertise a job you might be interested in. Shall I put in a word for you?'

Cresswells are a shitty firm, but they're local and a job's a job after all. 'Thanks, Frank,' I say and return to the chair mountain I'm building.

'I can't take stacks of more than seven,' the post lad says, coming over to inspect my work. Course he can't. More than his job's worth even now he doesn't have a job.

He's a bit slow, and stutters over the word beginning with M. I suddenly wonder if he'll find any other opportunities. 'What's your name, mate?'

'Micky.' Fucking heart breakingly ironic that. He spits it out eventually.

'OK, Micky, I'll do it by the book,' I say and give him a smile. I've spent too long ignoring people and concentrating on the job. But right now, my people need me. Not Micky, clearly; he's got the whole chair stacking routine sussed and I'm just in his way. But Mum needs me, and Wolfie needs me and I'm going to be there for them. Fucking Number One Son and Best Dad in the World – that's me. If Julia thinks she can bugger off to Manchester and take Wolfie away from me, she can think again.

~

I take the bus straight to Mum's from work, I've got to tell her the truth about the job. With any luck, she'll cook me my tea while I'm there. There's always a silver lining. Like this job at Cresswells – it might be OK. I might be able to turn that place around. And it'll be nowhere near as pressured as my current job, so I'll have more time for Mum and Wolfie. It's all good.

'Hello, love,' she says as I wander into the living room, unravelling my tie from my collar and bending to kiss her cheek. 'I was going to call you.'

'I must be psychic,' I reply, in a teasing impersonation of the TV programmes she likes. 'I could feel the vibrations, I knew you had a message for me.'

'As it turns out, I do. You're off the hook. Your Auntie Jean is going to come and look after me when I get out of hospital. She's going to sell her place down in Weston and move back to Brum. We always said we'd live together again when we were old ladies.'

I don't know what to say. Talk about wind dropping out of fucking sails. I'm supposed to be the hero here, not Auntie Jean. It's like work all over again – I'm up for a job, dead cert to get it, then some fucking woman comes in and nabs it from under my nose. 'Oh,' I say, 'well, that'll be nice.'

'Won't it? She's been lonely since your Uncle Alan died, and it was him that wanted to go to Weston really, not her. She can't wait to come back.' Mum drivelled on like that for a good few minutes while I rolled my tie into a ball and stuffed it in a pocket. I 'mmm'd and nodded at intervals to imply I was listening to the tale of how Mum was going to go there for a few weeks to help Jean pack and have a little holiday before they'd both come here. They could spend the money from Jean's house being sold on doing some work on this one and oh, wasn't everything just working out perfectly. 'You'll have to clear your room out though, love. Jean'll need it.'

'Course, Mum,' I mumble. She's looking brighter, enthusiastic about the idea. Happy to have her sister coming to stay. I am not what she needs right now.

I slump onto the sofa and let her fuss round me. I'm no hero. I'm a useless son and maybe Wolfie would be better off in Manchester. What can I give him here? Duff careers advice and a crap football team to follow. The lad should aim for the stars, not the fucking gutter.

~

SUSAN

With James to help me move into the flat this time, there was no need for a stranger to snigger over my things and leave me feeling nervous. Being back felt good. I'd left with far more conviction this time and that gave me confidence. Not that I'd intended to go back when I left Pete the first time; but I'd been scared. Whereas now I feel exhilarated.

I don't for a moment think Pete and Jo have a future together, no matter what ideas she was brewing. And it wasn't as if I needed the confirmation of Pete's capacity to deceive. The thing that's different this time is my attitude. I don't feel guilty for leaving and James doesn't blame me any more.

I'll have to start over and find another job. This time though I'm not intimidated. I'll get a good reference from Tall Trees and I already know Andy, Mark and Craig so I don't feel completely alone. Ideally I'd go back to the café of course but, even though it's only been a week or so, they'll have moved on. I know I have.

Craig has too. I couldn't wait for him to get in from work so I could tell him I was back. He grinned as he opened his door to my knock. 'Knew you couldn't stay away, Suze.'

'Come over for a cuppa,' I said as he released me from his welcome back hug, 'and tell me how your mum's getting on.'

He was pleased to have someone to offload his latest troubles with as much as anything else. He's matured over the past few days – a good contrast to how I'm regressing.

'I'm not looking forward to packing up all the stuff from when I was a kid,' he said. 'My football sticker albums, all my gadgets. My Bart Simpson collection. All that shit, it's like part of who I am. I don't need it. It's useless junk. I just like having it there; in my old room.'

Of course he does, when everything else has changed around him he wants to retain that link to the boy he was in a happier time. Just as my 'Book' holds my memories, that room holds his.

'Sometimes you have to let go though,' I said. 'Time to move on.'

The noise from upstairs started while we were talking. Thump. Then a dragging sound. A pause; then repeated. I looked at the ceiling and sighed. I'd forgotten how bad it was.

'Is that what it's always like?' Craig asked. 'I'm going to have a word with him then.'

'No, really, it's fine.' I tried to stop him. I didn't really believe I had a terrorist living upstairs, but I didn't want to spark a dispute with a neighbour either. Craig was ready to pick a fight with someone though and there was nothing I could do to stop him stomping up the stairs and banging on the door. I followed a few steps behind, fearful that actual violence might erupt.

His protective nature had been awakened and then rejected by his mum, so he was deploying it on my behalf. The local headlines ran through my head; stories about stabbings, petty arguments getting out of control and revenge being taken.

The door opened slightly and the bearded man frowned at us. I have to admit that I'd have been alarmed to have heard a knock like Craig's at my door too.

'We're from the flats downstairs,' Craig said, 'I was in Suze's place and can't hear myself think for the noise you're making, mate. She says it happens all the time so I'm here to tell you it's not on. What are you up to anyway?'

'I'm not doing anything,' the man said. He had a polite voice, with a trace of an Asian accent mixed with the Brummie. 'I was only playing on the Wii.'

'Oh.' Craig dropped the agression from his voice. 'Is that all?'

'Yeah, mate, Wii Cricket.' He opened the door fully and leaned to look at me round Craig's shoulders. 'Sorry about the noise, I didn't realise you could hear.'

The words 'that's OK' jumped automatically to my

tongue, but I swallowed them down. It wasn't OK; I did want him to stop, but felt so guilty about having ignorantly branded him a terrorist when he was clearly a perfectly ordinary man minding his own business in his own flat that I couldn't quite say so.

Fortunately Craig was there to help. 'Yeah, it's pretty loud downstairs. Are you bowling?' His interest in the game was overcoming his need to act as my protector.

'In the Ashes Test at Edgbaston.'

'Maybe you could stand on a rug or something?' Now Craig was the one craning his neck, trying to see into the man's flat. 'I could help you move things…'

I left them to it and went back downstairs where I made myself another cup of tea. For a while there was the sound of furniture being moved above me, then the dampened thudding sound of Craig getting to try the game out. Men are lucky they often find common ground in sport and strike up friendships so easily. I'm left with my problem of no job and no female friends to turn to.

At my age it's not easy to find new friends. Most women didn't have their children as young as I had James, so they're still busy with little ones now. The school gate is the best place to meet new people and strike up friendships with women in the same situation. No one's in my situation; I'm doing everything in the wrong order. It's not as if I could find myself invited in by a neighbour to play a computer game either. I need to put myself out there.

~

CRAIG
This bloke, Jas, is totally sport obsessed. It's like the rest of the world doesn't exist for him.

'Yeah, I train in the nets as often as I can,' he says when I mention that I've seen him coming in with a cricket kit bag. I figure it's best not to mention that Suze thought he had bomb making gear in it.

'I play a bit of cricket. Used to prefer footie, but...' Well, maybe best not to get into why I'm not playing football at the moment. I can't get the hang of this Wii game, not much like holding a cricket bat so I give it up and decide to be nosy instead. 'So, what do you do?'

'Sports teacher. Living the dream.'

'Really? The kids aren't just fucking annoying then?'

'No, man. Not in PE. Not unless it's raining. I love it, I coach footie at the weekends too.'

Makes my weekends of boozing and lie ins sound a bit pathetic. Oh well, we can't all be heroes and I'm well out of the running for that job.

'Right, well, I'll see you around then.' No point asking him if he wants to go for a neighbourly beer. I'm not in the mood for any 'my body is a temple' shit, or actual temple shit if he's that way inclined.

'Maybe we could go for a beer sometime?' he says. Friendly bastard.

'Great, yeah. It's not against your religion or anything then?' Well, I had to ask.

'Nah, I'm a non-practising Sikh. Means I can do what I like. At least, I can now I live here. Living with the parents meant endless questions about when I was going to stop playing games and settle down with a nice girl. You know how it is.'

Yeah, I know how it is. Except that settling down with a nice girl has its attractions. 'Sikh? That's the temple up the road, yeah? Blokes in turbans?'

256

'That's my dad. It's not the lifestyle for me though. I'll leave it to Monty Panesar to be the Sikh role model and stick to the cricket.'

'Fair enough. I'll just go make sure Suze is OK. See you around.'

'Tell her sorry for me again, and we'll go for that beer sometime?'

I nod and leave him to it. Really can't believe I haven't made the effort to speak to him before. Guess Davo and I weren't exactly welcoming to anyone else when we were being lairy downstairs. Bit of a bad attitude I suppose.

I knock on Suze's door to ask, 'Any better?' She's almost as embarrased about thinking he was a terrorist as he was about disturbing her. Right pair.

As I sit down on my own sofa, the words 'role model' come back to me. What kind of a fucking role model am I for Wolfie? Redundant, bad tempered, waste of space. Nothing for the lad to aspire to. But what's stopping me doing something about it? I could. Just need to decide what.

Certainly not this. Sitting around feeling sorry for myself cos my career's gone arse up and my mum's doing fine without me.

And not letting Julia manipulate me either, or cut me out of Wolfie's life. I need to sort that fucking situation out so it's best for the boy. There's no way that involves me and his mum getting back together though. She's deluded if she still thinks there's any hope of that.

So, what can I do? What will impress them all, while at the same time allowing me to meet beautiful women and drink beer? Now who's the deluded fucker?

I get a beer out the fridge. It might be good to go for a drink with that Jas. Actually, he probably knows the best curry place to go too, now there's a thought. Wonder if he'll go on about cricket for the entire evening though. The bloke's got the boring kind of one track mind. I mean, I don't mind the game. Obviously when I'm scoring sixes off arrogant shits then I don't like cricket, I love it. Footie's my sport though. I need to get into a team again.

I flick on the TV and watch the sports news for a while. Athletics and Grand Prix. Why are there so many utter tossers involved in sport? It's just not fucking cricket. Maybe it'd be good if Wolfie wasn't into sport at all. Maybe he could be a concert pianist or something. I'm guessing the symphony crowd wouldn't laugh at his name either. Poor kid.

On the other hand though, the sporty kids need to be taught better. And maybe I'm the man to do it. What was that Jas was saying about coaching footie? I could do that, I could teach kids how to kick a ball and not behave like wankers. I'd be fucking good at it too.

I fire up the laptop and search for 'football coaching'. Turns out you need a qualification, but hell, I'm bright, right? And I've spent enough time listening to coaches who haven't got a fucking clue to know what not to do. As well as enough time experiencing bad management to know what does inspire a team.

I don't have to play with the big boys when the little boys will be more inclined to do what I tell them. Fewer opportunities for going for a beer with them admittedly, but there might be the odd sexy single mum. And when Wolfie's a bit bigger, he can come along too, though I'll have to watch out for favouritism. Won't be a problem cos he'll have inherited his Dad's ball skills and be a cert for the team.

This is a fucking brilliant idea. I jump up from my seat to go tell Suze about it, but realise it's after eleven and she might consider that antisocial. Can't wait to hear what she thinks though.

I might have to get myself some dead end day job at Cresswells, but I can see my boys team winning their league. Now that's what I'm fucking talking about.

CHAPTER TWENTY FIVE

CRAIG

Julia is not taking the news well that I'll only be in paid employment for another couple of weeks. Selfish bitch, does she think I'm pleased about it? I've had a great Sunday afternoon with Wolfie and, after the week I've just been through, an argument is not the way I wanted it to end.

'There's no way I'll be able to afford a place of my own if you aren't paying maintenance for Wolfie,' she moans.

'I'll always find the money for Wolfie, but you can think again if you're aiming to rent some fancy pad cos that's what you'd prefer.'

'It's not about what I'd prefer. It's about what's best for Wolfie.'

'And that is not fucking Manchester. Don't even think that taking him where I can't see him is what he wants. I love that boy, and he loves spending time with me. You know he does.'

She was never good at arguing. Never wanted to confront an issue. Which I guess is why she went behind my back and started seeing Trev. Managed to make the whole thing about me and him instead of me and her. Now I'm making this about me and Wolfie and she's turning on the waterworks.

'I know he adores you.' She sniffs and looks up at me through her eyelashes. Huh, she can flatter and flirt all she likes, I'm standing my ground.

'So let's sit down and work out the money, work out what benefits you should be getting and what you could afford to spend on rent so you can get out of this dump,' I gesture around her parent's kitchen as if it didn't look like something out of a homes magazine, 'and into somewhere for you. Somewhere that can be Wolfie's home. And I'll get my place sorted so he can stay with me a few nights a week. Then you can have time out too. OK?'

She nods. I have to get this job at Cresswells. Or any job. Soon. The redundancy money won't go far to sort this problem out. But I'm loving the thought of having Wolfie come to stay with me.

Fact is, once Julia is out and about it won't be long before she's got some bloke in tow. Fair enough I suppose. But that bloke will not be taking my place in Wolfie's life. No way. The boy might get two homes, an odd assortment of relatives and a mum who has her psycho moments, but he's only got one dad: me.

~

SUSAN

After two days back in Birmingham sorting out the flat, I was restless. I needed a proper plan and knew I should be brave and at least find out where I stood with the job at Tall Trees. I didn't dare hope that I'd be able to go straight back to them, but Mark and Andy would at least advise me. Anyway, I couldn't deny that I wanted to see them again, especially Andy.

Even the thought of seeing him made me smile, though I wasn't letting myself dwell on the things he'd said to me.

So at just before the Tall Trees five o'clock closing time, I loitered on the other side of the road hoping not to be noticed while assessing what was happening inside. I could see Andy, his blue checked shirt coming untucked at the back as he stretched to straighten bags of coffee beans on the shelf behind the counter. I could see Tina, the new waitress, not quite sweeping right into the corners of the floors. The day's customers had left and the slowness of Andy's movements suggested it had been a busy day at the café. I fiddled with the purple leaf pendant hanging round my neck remembering how I'd described him as 'perfect' to his face. My cheeks flushed and my stomach churned.

Tina finished, took off her apron and I turned to study the window display of the flooring shop I stood outside as she came to the Tall Trees door. She called out 'Bye' to the now empty room and headed off down the street. I crossed quickly, before I lost my confidence, and pushed the door open. It stuck against the floor board it always scraped, alerting Andy to the fact someone had entered.

'Sorry, we're closed…' he called out as he came back through from the kitchen. A smile spread across his face when he saw me, a grin I couldn't help returning.

'Even for your regulars?'

'I think we could make an exception.' He came towards me, hesitant about the greeting. With all the tension I'd been through in the last few days I really needed a hug, so initiated it myself. As always, the coffee aroma had woven itself into the soft fabric of his shirt and it brought that scene in my kitchen sharply back to mind. The cafetiere, the chocolate cake, Pete and Jo. I hadn't let myself think about it too much. I'd been too busy coping, deciding, acting.

With that whiff of coffee though, the scent memory made me shudder and I couldn't hold back the tears. As I sobbed into Andy's chest I was vaguely aware of Mark coming in and a whispered conversation between him and Andy taking place. I heard Mark's footsteps leave, to return a few minutes later accompanied by the familiar clink of teapot and cups on a tray and then the back door closing. Andy just kept squeezing me tight.

I pulled back, looked up at him and apologised.

'Your usual?' he asked, with a hint of a smile.

I wiped my eyes and nodded, letting him lead me to the table where Mark had left the tea tray. I'd only been gone a week, but things seemed unfamiliar already, as if it was my first visit again. I remembered how nervous I'd been then and realised I had much less to be afraid of now.

Andy stirred the pot and poured us both a cup. I noticed the tremor in his hand as he did so, the stream of liquid faltered and splashed into my saucer. His nerves were as bad as ever.

He put the teapot down firmly and took a deep breath. 'Can I ask you something which probably shouldn't be my first question? I mean, something other than 'how are you?' or 'what have you been up to?''

He glanced up from the pot and I nodded.

'Are you back for good, Susan, or just a visit?'

I had no desire to torment him. 'For good.'

263

'Ah, um,' he mumbled, clearly trying to hide a smile. 'So, er, how are you?'

'Well, as I'm sure you guessed from that display of tears, things didn't quite work out as I expected back home. But I'm fine now. I think.'

'The tears didn't suggest 'fine' to me…'

'No, I think I'll be OK though. With a little help from my friends.'

'You've come to the right place for that,' he said, and reached out to touch my hand. 'It's good to see you, we really didn't think you'd be back.'

It was lovely to sit there with him. There was no pressure, no challenge. We sat and talked and drank tea. I told him what had happened back in Alcester and he complimented me on how I'd handled it. Eventually, I found the courage to say, 'I remembered how much I loved to bake.'

'Bake?'

'As in cakes. I used to make huge creations for James' birthday parties: rockets, trains, football boots – you know the sort of thing. Ones for grown ups too. It made me think that, of all the things I could possibly do with my life, maybe I could make some kind of business out of cakes somehow.'

He smiled at me. 'Starting a business isn't easy, you know.'

'I know. It's only a dream I suppose and I'll have to find a real job.'

'For those with contacts in the catering industry though, opportunities may arise…'

I raised an eyebrow. 'They may?' We were flirting and I knew it wasn't necessarily sensible. But I felt so light hearted after everything that had happened in the last few weeks that I didn't want to stop having fun.

'I'll have to talk to Mark obviously, but if we could find an opening for you, maybe something in the waiting and baking line, would you be interested in coming back?'

The huge smile curved my lips again. Of course I was interested and I had no words to express how grateful I felt.

~

CRAIG

Makes a nice fucking change to be having fun. Watching cartoons on TV with Wolfie before reading him a story was exactly the relaxation I needed. No hassle from Julia or any of her family. Just in, see the boy, and out. And what could be nicer way to round off the evening than having a civilised drink or two to give a valued colleague a send off.

Course it helps that the leaving do is for the gorgeous Amisha who's getting giggly on spritzers and leaning more on me than against the bar. Well, who'd complain? I'm glad she's enjoying herself. Not much of a turn out for her, but with redundancy hanging over the rest of us, I don't fucking blame the others for making excuses. Those who have turned up are mostly ignoring Amisha, huddling in small groups and bitching about the firm.

Stevo's here, draining his pint and looking glum. I step slightly back from Amisha to talk to him; leaving a hand on her waist, obviously. 'So, how'd the interview go?'

'Not great. Not good at all, actually.'

Bummer. Best to be encouraging though, he's a miserable drunk. 'You're a good accountant, got loads of experience. There'll be more opportunities. You don't have to panic you know.'

'Yeah,' he says. 'Think I'll head home.'

And that's the general mood. They all came straight from work and are now ready to call it a night. While I had the Wolfie interlude, taxi dash back here, and Amisha giving me slow burn smiles. I'm fucking happy to see the crowd disperse, if slightly guilty about not giving Stevo more support.

We're in a city centre bar which always gets a lot of after work trade, but now it's quieter. The corner of the room our group had taken over feels almost private now they're gone.

'So,' I say, once we're left alone, 'how's tricks?'

'Tricky,' she replies. 'Ve-ry tricky.' She places a finger tip on my chest and draws a circle. 'You see, I'm still your boss; but for one night only. From tomorrow evening well, I'll be out of here. But tonight; tonight I can still tell you what to do.'

Well, well. Things are certainly looking up. As it were. 'Yes, ma'am,' I say, and give her a salute with the hand which hasn't slipped further around her waist.

She's no seductress though. The giggles return so I settle for wrapping her in a cuddle. I squeeze her and wonder if there's any potential that I might get her back to mine. I do a quick stock check: yes, I did tidy up recently, yes, there is milk in the fridge which hasn't turned to yoghurt, yes, the sheets have been washed within the last fortnight, and yes, I do have condoms in the bedside drawer. I'm cleared for take-off.

Of course it helps that, unlike Stevo, I actually got some promising job-related news today. The bloke from Cresswells called me up and asked me in for an interview on Monday. I guess Frankie-boy made good on the promise to see me right if he could. My ego needed a bit of polish and a beautiful woman practically throwing herself at me isn't going to hurt.

But this is no ordinary beautiful woman. Amisha's got to me more than I'd ever tell her. I really am sorry she's leaving Brum. She's not my usual type at all – way too serious most of the time. But hell, I've fucking changed. Who'd have thought I'd be making a two year old my top priority? Don't know when I last had the games console on I've been so busy with Wolfie and Mum and work and cricket. And Amisha is squeezable in all the right places as well as interesting to talk to. Very decorative too. She's changed out of her work gear into skin tight shiny black trousers and a low cut top. The power dressing stilettos are still firmly in place, bringing her almost up to my height.

She's going to live in London though. How much of a pisser is that? The thought makes me cuddle her tighter, my nose nestled into her hair where I can still catch the fruity scent from her shampoo. She turns and eases slightly out of my grip. Her face is right by mine now, her mouth so close I can feel her breath on my chin. The silky fabric of her top rucks up under my hands and there's no way I'm going to be able to resist kissing her.

All I can hear is my blood pumping, drowning out the dance beats from the bar's sound system. All I can feel is her hot skin as my hand slips up her back, under her top. And all I want is to be alone with her.

Thank fuck she wants the same thing.

We stumble out the door and into a handily positioned cab. I mumble my address at the driver and resume activities, slightly restrained by her going shy now we're under brighter lights. The journey seems to take forever. The streetlights move from practically daylight in the city centre to pulses of light as we pass into the suburbs so I see my hand lit, then in darkness as I slide it along her thigh. I take advantage of a dark pulse to slide a little higher, which triggers a yelping giggle from her.

Finally we get to the flats and I tip the guy and get her indoors as quick as I can. Great though it is to chat to Suze or Jas, right now they're the last people I want to see. I've got to get Amisha inside because I can't control myself much longer.

'Coffee?' I offer as I close the door behind us.

'Not right now,' she replies. 'but I would like the guided tour. Especially of the bedroom.'

I take her hand and lead her into the corridor. 'Rest of the flat,' I say with a gesture in the general direction, 'and bedroom.'

~

SUSAN

At the library this morning I used the computers to research business ideas. I'm surprised Andy wasn't more discouraging about my vague plans to make money baking cakes. After all, he knows how hard it is to run your own business, and all the websites I read seemed to be giving the advice: 'Don't do it!' Apparently I'd need working capital, a business plan, to research my customers' needs, a marketing strategy, equipment, insurance and book keeping skills. None of which I had.

We'd agreed that I'd pop in again today after Andy had spoken to Mark. He confirmed they'd continued to be busy on the back of the Food Snoop review which was brilliant – but exhausting for them. I could only hope that they'd work out there might be room for another employee on the Tall Trees team. Even if the job was straightforward waitressing, I knew I'd take it to give myself some time to consider what to do next.

I left the library and bought the ingredients for a Madeira cake at the supermarket. 'Someone's about to do some baking,' the woman who bleeped my items through her check out said. The smile on her face at the thought reminded me why I wanted to do this and I went back to the flat feeling a little more positive.

I'd brought my electric whisk and some baking tins from Alcester this time and I set to work. I weighed out flour, butter and sugar. Then I beat the butter and sugar together, until the colour became light. The texture changed from creamy to a more gloopy liquid as I added whisked eggs before folding in sifted flour. A splash of milk kept things moist enough and the zest I'd scraped from the lemon scented the bowl.

I lifted the mixture gently with my spatula, transferred it to a lined tin and smoothed the top. While I hadn't baked using the oven in the flat before, its interior had a brand-new gleam which suggested no-one else had either. Given what Craig had told me about his friend who'd been the previous occupant, home cooking was not something he'd been familiar with. Anyway, the oven was newer than my one back in Alcester, so I trusted it to do its job.

I set the timer for thirty minutes and cleared up. All the time I'd been cooking I'd hummed to myself, feeling the contentment of exercising a skill in which I was confident. In addition to searching on how to go about starting a business, I'd also looked up local cake makers on the internet. One was well presented: her website was modern, professional and fresh looking, her cakes had been featured in wedding magazines. Her prices made my eyebrows rise. Another was rather basic – turning out character cakes for children's parties with no finesse. Surely there was scope for something in the middle?

At the very least, if I could go back to Tall Trees, I wanted to persuade Mark to let me try to extend the range of scones, flapjacks and Victoria sponge that he produced for the afternoon teas there. He could concentrate on the lunches while I whipped up some sweet treats.

The shrill ring of the buzzer made me jump. I grabbed the oven gloves, lifted the cake out and transferred it to a cooling rack. It smelt fantastic, biscuity with a tang of the citrus sharpness. I dabbed my finger to pick up the few crumbs which had fallen onto the work surface and tasted them. Perfect. I made myself a cup of tea while it cooled.

At five pm I was back outside Tall Trees with my cake in a bag, waiting for them to close. The final customers paid and Andy saw me as he looked up from the till. He tilted his head to beckon me in.

'We're clo…,' Tina began to say, before she recognised me.

'Just visiting,' I said. 'How are you getting on?'

'Fine, yes, fine,' she said with a frown. She was obviously calculating what my return might mean for her.

'Susie!' Mark burst out of the kitchen and embraced me, smacking a kiss on my cheek. 'It is so good to see you. Now, shall I make us a brew or are we going to the pub?'

'Tea I think,' Andy said. 'We'll just have a quiet chat here. You can head off if you're done, Tina. See you tomorrow.'

She untied her apron and left it draped over a chair. My appearance had worried her and Andy's businesslike dismissal clearly stung. The door slammed behind her as she left.

'I brought you something,' I said and handed the bag to Andy. He took out the foil wrapped cake and peeled it open, lifting it close to his face to inhale the aroma.

'Mmm, smells good.'

'So why did you never mention that you were a domestic goddess?' Mark asked as he took the cake from Andy, removed the wrapping and examined it.

I was pleased it still looked good – perfectly browned and crisp on top. I kept my fingers crossed under the table that when Mark cut it, it would stand up to his scrutiny. He went to fetch a knife and some plates.

'I wanted to make you something, for being so kind. This is rather a basic recipe, but it's the kind of thing I used to do as a base for celebration cakes and I wanted your advice about whether I'm just dreaming about the cake business thing.' I gave Andy a tight smile and twisted my hands in my lap, nervous now my idea was exposed to their criticism.

'Any new business is a risk,' Andy said.

Mark placed a board under the cake and cut it. He lay the slice down and looked at it closely, before picking it up, sniffing and finally taking a bite. At that point I really understood how nervous he'd been when Food Snoop was in the room. I couldn't breathe. My heart was racing and I heard buzzing in my ears.

'Well, well, Susie,' he said, his voice muffled by crumbs, 'that is lovely. Moist, tasty, light – but with a satisfyingly dense texture.'

'Give me a piece then,' Andy said and took the knife from his brother to cut himself a thick slice from which he took a large bite. 'Oh yes, that is very good.'

'Sorry, Susie, did you want some?' Mark took the knife back to cut me a slice and handed me it on a plate while Andy poured the tea. This was so close to my dream come true – my cake on a Tall Trees plate and being shared with friends – that tears filled my eyes.

I swallowed my sobs. 'So, what have I missed?' I hadn't been away long, but so much had happened to me, I felt things ought to have changed here too.

'Well,' Andy said, 'Tina's settled in OK.'

'We've been busy,' Mark added.

'But really, um, nothing.'

'Oh,' I said. It was only me who'd been having a dramatic time then.

'The cake really is great,' Andy said. 'But the thing is, we're not sure we can afford to employ an additional member of staff and take you back. I mean, we haven't made Tina permanent yet, but it would feel wrong to just throw her out.'

'We could use something like this on the menu though.' Mark interrupted Andy's apology. 'Maybe Susie could come in part time, help with the breakfast rush and then join me in the kitchen and bake up some elevenses or tea time snacks?'

I held my breath again. Mark's idea sounded wonderful. But it was down to Andy, who couldn't meet my eye and seemed to be struggling to stick to his analytical approach.

'It's not that I don't want you back with us, Susan, please believe that. I just really am worried about the money...'

I'd been thinking all afternoon while I waited for the cake to cool. I'd been planning strategies, developing ideas. I wasn't silly enough to believe that my cake baking empire would spring into life without a struggle; and I hadn't presumed that I could walk back in to Tall Trees and pick up where I left off either. 'I'd only take a part time salary if you'd let me order ingredients through your wholesalers and advertise in the window. I could do the hours Mark suggested, bake for the café, and fill in on Tina's day off. I'd really like to try this and I'd love to be back here too.' I hadn't counted on Mark's support, I'd thought it was him who'd need persuading rather than Andy, but my proposal was sound enough for either of them.

Andy smiled. 'Oh, OK. Let's give it a try. Perhaps you can start next week? It'll give me a chance to explain things to Tina tomorrow.'

I could have hugged him. Instead I just raised my cup to him in a toast. 'To Tall Trees,' I said.

'And the cakes they bake there,' Mark added as he clinked his cup against mine.

~

Once we'd finished, Andy walked with me towards the bus stop. For all the approaches to intimacy there'd been between us, I was still aware that he was, once again, my boss and that his business was always going to come first. All the pain I'd been suppressing about what had happened in Alcester made me nervous too. Tears were too close to the surface for me to want to talk about anything which involved my emotions.

As we reached the bus shelter I said, 'I'll see you Monday morning then.'

'Actually, um, I was wondering.' Andy blushed and rubbed at his neck with one hand. 'Are you busy on Sunday? I was going to Cannon Hill park because there's a band playing outside the arts centre in the afternoon. A friend's in the band. Um, they're good — the band, that is.'

The logical business man was gone, he was behaving like a schoolboy trying to find courage to ask out the girl he fancied. Tempted, I encouraged him, 'That sounds interesting.'

'Oh. Great. So, um, would you like to come with me? I could pick you up, organise us a picnic or something…'

'Lovely,' I said. 'Can't wait.'

CHAPTER TWENTY SIX

CRAIG

Wolfie's hammering on the table as if he's deranged. From the looks the people across the aisle are sending me, they're not brimming over with calm sanity either. But what can I do? I've got him, the buggy and our bags on the train, which is some kind of fucking miracle. Now they want me to make him behave too? Yeah, good luck with that.

He's drumming with the flat of his sticky palms on the plastic and he's doing my head in as well. 'Hey, Wolfie, look,' I say in an attempt to distract him. But there's nothing to look at out the window yet, we're less than ten minutes out of New Street and all there is to see is the back gardens of Kings Norton. Nothing that would be more exciting to a boy than how loud it is when he slaps his hands on the table.

I delve in the bag Julia handed me to find something to distract him with. Julia was actually really cool about this mad idea of mine to take off this weekend on an adventure with my son. With a redundancy cheque winging its way towards my bank account, I thought I'd splash some cash on taking me and the Wolf-man to Weston to visit Mum and Aunty Jean for the weekend.

I want to take him to eat ice cream on the pier. I want to put him on a donkey and see if he screams like I did. I want to let him dig up the entire beach to burn off this energy he's got. 'Come on, mate. Let's have a bit of quiet. How about you try this drink while I see what else your mum's given you.'

Thank fuck the drink distracts him. Just like his Dad when offered a pint. Could do with one now quite frankly. I'm not sure what I've committed myself to – bringing him away overnight on my own. Course mum and Jean will want to take over once we're with them. I'll be glad of the break, a quick snooze in front of the telly should see me right. But I was surprised Julia agreed so quickly when it was a snap decision.

I only thought of it last night. After another rough day at work, but for different reasons this time: Amisha's last day with us. She'd left mine during the early hours – not that I'd wanted her to go. But she showed up bright and fresh at the office at 9am, all polished and professional looking. Guess she couldn't have pulled that off if she'd stayed at mine. We wouldn't have got any sleep, for one thing.

I'm sad to see her go, and not only because she's the only lucky one who's still got a job. But what she said was promising.

'I'll be back in Birmingham all the time – to see family and stuff. We could always go for a drink, catch up, you know…'

It's the 'you know' bit that's tempting me.

Another Friday night home alone wasn't going to make the wait more bearable so I called Julia up and asked if I could pop over to see Wolfie again. Me and him were playing trains while she watched something on TV about holidays. They showed a shot of a man and his boy building a sandcastle and I needed to be that man. I had to have the dream and it couldn't come soon enough. Even having to wait until this morning was a pisser. A call to suggest it to mum later and Julia was sold. Probably because she can go out on the lash tonight with Wolfie off her hands.

So here I am, in sole charge of a toddler and a two hour journey ahead of me. The drink has lost its appeal, but fortunately now there is something to look at outside. 'Hey, look, cows!' I say, and he stands on his seat to get a better view.

Its an automatic reaction – I immediately place a hand on his back to steady him, I'm ready to catch him if he falls and save him smashing his head open on the table edge. After sneering at every email I was sent about it at work, who knew I was health and safety trained after all? I guess it's the kind of skill that'll come in handy for the football coaching if I get that off the ground. Can't wait for the season to start; Jas says he'll let me tag along with him to see how it works. I'll need the excitement if I do end up working at Cresswell's. Ideally, by the time Wolfie's old enough to play, I'll have the certificates and he can join my little team. Not that we don't already make the best team.

'So, Wolfie,' I say and give him a cuddle, 'how much are we looking forward to our weekend away?' Obviously he doesn't have a clue what's going on. He just knows he likes the train, he likes the table and he likes the cows. 'We'll build the biggest sandcastle and eat the biggest ice creams and then we'll let two lovely old ladies spoil us rotten. How does that sound for a plan?'

~

SUSAN

The thought of Andy taking me out on what could actually be described as 'a date' put me in a state of excited anticipation I hadn't felt since I was a teenager. It was terrifying, thrilling and brought a smile to my face every time it came to mind, which was almost constantly.

The newness of the sensation delighted me. It was all I could do not to sneak down to Kings Heath and do a little snooping of my own on the Tall Trees team. I couldn't wait to be back with them; specifically with Andy. I knew I was letting myself get carried away. I ought to be sensible. I should beware, protect myself, think practically. But all I could think of was how good it felt to be around him.

I wanted to make him feel good too. To ease some of those nerves that troubled him and be an asset to his business, not a risk – strategically or emotionally. So, I went shopping.

My first stop was a large bookshop in the city centre where I flicked through a few of the latest cook books they were promoting and let the pictures from the baking sections influence my thinking. It was clearly a long time since a Micky Mouse-shaped cake would be enough to impress at a children's birthday party. But the glossy images didn't worry me. I knew my abilities were up to producing creations just as professional looking, and possibly tastier. I didn't need my own TV series to prove it.

I glanced at the other people browsing the books. If cooking was in fashion, would any of them be potential customers for my cakes or would they all be able to make their own? I doubted it. The young, thin woman to my left was scanning a book detailing the importance of organically grown food; the man to my right was more likely to be choosing a present for his wife. Surely either of them would buy a cake for a special occasion.

Once my mind was reeling with ideas, I purchased one book because it included specialist recipes for those on gluten-free diets. It had never been an issue when Jamie was little, but watching TV and the odd comment from Mark, had informed me that food allergies were common these days and I ought to understand and be able to cater for them. That section of the bookshop's shelves did seem to be well stocked with varied titles.

Business planning having taken one step forward, I turned to more frivolous concerns: an outfit for my date. I blushed even to think of it and steered well clear of the lingerie departments. The forecast was for a warm, sunny day though, and a summer dress didn't seem a terrible extravagance. If it was flattering and pretty too, well, where was the harm?

In the department store, I took a few frocks into a changing room, drew the heavy curtain and slipped one over my head. It hung beautifully, the length to just below my knee and the close fit of the top half drew attention to my small waist. From the other cubicles I could hear pairs or groups of women chatting, admiring each others' choices or giving advice.

I was jealous of their friendships and wished I had a friend to share this moment with. Perhaps Tina would warm to me one day? Even if we were still friends, Adrienne would never be seen in a chain store changing room, that was certain.

I drew the curtain and took a step back into the gangway to view my reflection from a greater distance.

'Oh, you look lovely in that!' The woman who'd spoken was holding a tiny red satin cocktail dress on a hanger, while a girl who must have been her daugher twisted to get a better view of the short, tight, black one she already wore. The girl had a good figure but there was no escaping that the dress was tarty and cheap looking.

It took a moment to realise the woman was talking to me. 'It fits you so well, and the colour's lovely on you too.'

The girl glanced away from her mirror and didn't even bother to try to hide her dismissive expression. She grabbed the red dress from her mother and swung the curtain to her cubicle shut with a rattle of brass rings against the pole.

I smiled at her mother as I turned to get a side-on view of the lilac dress. 'Thank you. It's a long time since I bought anything like this.'

'Well, that one would definitely be a good choice. Is it for a special occasion?'

I was too shy to tell her and just nodded.

'We're choosing something for her eighteenth birthday party.' The woman raised plucked eyebrows as she tilted her head towards her daughter's cubicle. 'It has to be sexy, apparently.'

The girl reappeared, parts of her now sheathed in the red satin. It was certainly sexy. 'You look great in that,' I told her. I was hardly in a position to criticise anyone for wanting to look attractive to a man after all.

~

Half an hour before Andy was due to pick me up, I was getting changed into the dress when my mobile rang. 'Hi, Mum,' Jamie said. 'Just wanted to see if you were OK.'

'I'm fine, darling.' I could hardly keep the joy out of my voice to have him call me about something so thoughtful, so charming. 'I think everything's working out all right. How about you though? Where are you now?'

'Back in Bristol. Couldn't stay home with Dad. He's a nightmare, and that Jo's worse. Don't know why you were ever friends with her.'

'Well, I wasn't. Not really. I didn't have anyone else. But I have now.' I was dying to tell him about Andy, but held back. Perhaps the upheaval of his Dad's romantic entanglements was enough for him to deal with for now. Especially when he surely had his own friends and lovers to worry about. 'So what are you up to this weekend?'

'Not much. Not many people around. But Shona from next door showed up today and I might go down the pub with her later.'

I smiled. Friends and lovers, as predicted. 'Well, you have a good time, love. Come and see me soon, won't you?'

'Sure, Mum. Bye then.'

I slipped the phone into my handbag and took a final look at myself in the mirror. Perhaps slightly overdressed for an afternoon in the park, but it boosted my confidence to see that I did look good in the dress. It made me seem bright, younger. And happy.

The buzzer sounded and my heart stopped. I rushed to let Andy in downstairs, then flew about tidying up the odds and ends I'd strewn around while preparing for his arrival before opening the door as he was about to knock.

'Hi,' I said, grinning as he slowly lowered the knuckles he'd raised to rap with.

'Hi. Um, you look, er, beautiful. I mean, um…'

I interrupted to allow him to recover from the fit of nerves and embarrasment. 'Thank you. So, shall we go?'

He relaxed as he drove us to Cannon Hill, telling me a little about the friend whose band we were going to see, how they'd known each other at school and met again recently in a pub in Kings Heath. The music was just a hobby for Colin, an antidote to the boredom he endured in his career in insurance.

'Doesn't stop him dreaming he might make a career of it though, especially when they get a gig as big as this one. OK, so it's a free concert outdoors on a Sunday afternoon, but there'll be a lot of people around.'

'Nothing wrong with having a dream,' I replied.

'No. Nothing wrong with that at all.'

We strolled around the lake, Andy carrying our picnic in a rucksack slung on his shoulder, me swinging my handbag while I looked around in interest and enjoyed the pleasant sensation of the sun warming my back. Water spouted from a fountain and fell back to the lake with a sound like a ripple of applause. The playpark was crowded with children climbing, swinging and shouting while their parents lounged against the railings or sat on nearby benches.

Couples promenaded the paths and a few fishermen dangled rods into the lake, although I couldn't imagine what they hoped to catch. The water looked stagnant around the edges where a thin scum crusted the surface. Mallards and Canada geese were the only live wildlife I could see, although an urban safari of giraffe print pram blankets and leopard spotted T-shirts adorned some of the passers by. The ducks and geese mobbed anyone who loitered near the edge, especially those holding long plastic bread bags containing stale ends to throw them.

We didn't talk much as we walked, but the silence wasn't uncomfortable. We both walked and looked, gazing upwards at the trees, or out across the open lawns where family groups played impromptu cricket or football matches. A small girl careered towards us on her bicycle, pink streamers flowing from the handlebars as her legs pumped too fast to compensate for being in the wrong gear.

'It's lovely here,' I said as we stepped aside, 'so lively.'

'What I like about parks like this, is they're one of the few places in the city where you see Birmingham's diverse population all in one space. Everyone's in the shopping centres, but other than there, it can feel a bit segregated sometimes and I hate that.'

I looked around. He was right. All races were represented. All of the families were out enjoying the park in the same way – they wanted some space, some air, some greenery around them. In such a landlocked city, it made sense that everyone congregated here.

'What about you?' I said. 'Do you feel at home here? I mean, there's plenty of trees to keep you happy.'

I nudged his arm gently with my elbow so he'd be sure I was teasing him.

'Yeah, they're not too bad,' he replied. 'How about we stop for our lunch?'

He led the way off the path and up the wide expanse of lawn until he found space under the shade of a sycamore tree to spread out the rug he pulled from his rucksack. I felt like a princess in a fairytale as he unpacked boxes and plates and laid out everything we needed for lunch.

'Wow, you're good at this!'

'Ah. Well. I have to admit that Mark might have lent a hand with the food…'

'When you have a brother who's a top chef, that's nothing to be ashamed of.' I helped him loosen some of the lids and took the opportunity to peek inside at the spread which had been laid on for me. There were servings of some of my favourites from the café – a cous cous salad and some slices of chicken cooked in a herby marinade – as well as crusty bread and olives: the things I would have chosen from the Tall Trees menu, if I'd been there for lunch. As an employee I'd rarely been able to indulge in them; the day's supply usually sold out.

'You remembered what I liked!' After years of cooking other people's favourite dishes, I was flattered someone had bothered to provide mine.

Andy blushed and handed me a paper plate and a napkin.

After we'd eaten and tidied away the packaging, he stretched out on the picnic rug seeming far more relaxed. Our conversation had been unforced, he'd been less hesitant and more forthcoming in his answers to my questions.

Now he rested back on his elbows and stretched out his legs as if utterly comfortable in my company. What he hadn't done however, was give me any indication that he thought of me as anything more than a friend, whether the speech he'd delivered a few weeks ago still represented how he felt.

Without the clutter of the picnic between us, I became aware of how close we were on the rug. His long legs stretched past me, blue socks peeking out below the frayed hem of his faded jeans. His elbow was close to my hip, his face near my arm. My heart was beating fast and the wind breathed a thrumming sound through the leaves and seed propellers on the branches stretched above us.

Silent minutes passed, interrupted only by shouts and calls from people playing with their children and by the snuffles of an inquisitive dog who took an interest in Andy's rucksack until its owner called it away.

Desperate to clear what had begun to feel like a difficult atmosphere, I turned to him as he pushed himself up from his reclined position. Our faces were close and he lifted one hand to stroke my cheek as he said, 'I feel so comfortable here with you. But I guess we should head over if we want to hear the band.'

Only I was nervous then, only I felt uncomfortable. He stood up and offered a hand to help me up from the rug. He folded the fabric, stowed it in his rucksack and asked 'Ready?'

'Not quite,' I replied.

Before the frown even had time to form on his face I reached out and took hold of his hand again. Not because I needed it for balance. Not because he was being courteous, or because I was upset. I did it purely because it felt good to have his fingers laced through mine as we walked.

THE END

AUTHOR'S NOTE

Many thanks to everyone who helped with input to and feedback on Park Life, and to you for reading. Particular thanks to Jane Dixon-Smith at jdsmith-design.co.uk and Jenn Ashworth at thewritingsmithy.co.uk.

The people and places in this story have been imagined. The actual suburbs of south Birmingham are similar to those featured in the story but, sadly, Tall Trees café doesn't exist. I wish it did; I'd love to go there for a cup of tea. There are lots of brilliant, independently-run cafés around Moseley and Kings Heath and my visits to them inspired Tall Trees. The parks are all real – you should take a walk in one some time.

~

To find out more, including bonus material based on this story and information about other books by this author, please visit www.katharinedsouza.co.uk

47791943R00180

Made in the USA
San Bernardino, CA
08 April 2017